His Forbidden Fiancée
by Christie Ridgway

ଚ ☙✱❧ ଡ

How *Not* To Marry A Millionaire:

1. Drive to his lodge in the middle of the night to break off your engagement.

2. Find yourself stranded at his place with nothing but the wet clothes on your back.

3. Resolve to tell him you're through right then and there.

4. Lose your nerve.

5. Kiss him.

6. Ask him to make love to you.

7. Hate him for acting like a gentleman.

8. Break off your engagement.

9. Kiss him again.

10. Thank him for forgetting how to be a gentleman…

The Royal Wedding Night
by Day Leclaire

꙳ ꙳ ꙳

"You're here because I can't let you go – "

Brandt's words held a raspy edge. "I won't."

"And I won't be your consolation prize." Miri marched across the room and snatched up her purse. "You don't have the right to keep me here. I want to go home."

Surging to his feet, Brandt came for her. "There's only one place you're going." Before she had time to react, he scooped her up in his arms and carried her towards the door.

"What do you think you're doing?"

"Taking you to bed. Maybe once I have you there again you'll remember why you stayed the last time."

**Available in April 2008
from Mills & Boon® Desire™**

His Forbidden Fiancée
by Christie Ridgway
&
The Royal Wedding Night
by Day Leclaire

১০৮৮৩

The Amalfi Bride
by Ann Major
&
Blackmailed into Bed
by Heidi Betts

১০৮৮৩

Bound by Marriage
by Nalini Singh
&
The Durango Affair
by Brenda Jackson

His Forbidden Fiancée
CHRISTIE RIDGWAY

The Royal Wedding Night
DAY LECLAIRE

™ MILLS & BOON®

Pure reading pleasure

*First published in Great Britain 2008
by Harlequin Mills & Boon Limited,
Eton House, 18-24 Paradise Road, Richmond, Surrey TW9 1SR*

The publisher acknowledges the copyright holders of the
individual works as follows:

His Forbidden Fiancée © Christie Ridgway 2007
The Royal Wedding Night © Day Totton Smith 2007

ISBN: 978 0 263 85897 6

51-0408

*Printed and bound in Spain
by Litografía Rosés S.A., Barcelona*

HIS FORBIDDEN FIANCÉE

by
Christie Ridgway

Dear Reader,

The romance-writing community is a small one. After a time you count many authors as friends or friends of friends. Not many degrees separate each one of us.

It's a fabulous perk of the job, and I'm always thrilled to meet and get to know other authors because so often I already know their work. (Writers are the most voracious of readers, or at least this one is!) So when a friend mentioned coming up with a series for the Desire™ line, it didn't take long for us to gather together other friends. No surprise that we ended up writing about friends, too!

OK, yes, they're male friends, and rich, and sexy...but, boy, did our group have fun dreaming up their group. I hope you'll have fun with them, too. My hero, Luke Barton, is like all the other Samurai. Rich and sexy. But he's also ruthless and driven, and hurting for reasons that seem to come together when a blonde shows up on the doorstep in the rain...

I hope you enjoy watching a hard man find the tenderness inside him. It's been a pleasure to tell his story.

Best,

Christie Ridgway

CHRISTIE RIDGWAY

is a *USA TODAY* bestselling author who has been writing contemporary romance for over a decade. Her love of romances began when she spent all her babysitting money on novels, and she's still happiest when reading a story with a guaranteed happy-ever-after.

A native Californian, she has a busy family life (husband, two sons, yellow labrador, two turtles, a tortoise, four parakeets, two crawdads, two bearded dragon lizards and assorted fish) and lives in the "corner house," which is a natural gathering place for the neighbourhood kids (all boys). She loves the chaos – that is, until the feeder-crickets escape captivity. Then her office is her retreat, and her stories are her escape.

For Elizabeth Bevarly, Maureen Child,
Susan Crosby, Anna DePalo and Susan Mallery.
Thanks for making this project so much fun!

One

The only thing the first-class-all-the-way log house lacked was a sexy female in the master bedroom's quilt-covered sleigh bed. Make that a naked sexy female. Blond. Curvy.

Make that lots of curves.

Coat hangers with legs didn't interest Luke Barton. He liked his women built for pleasure. His pleasure.

"Did you say something, Mr. Barton?"

He started, then tore his gaze from the decadent bed to frown at the caretaker who was showing him through the home that was his for the next month. Had he been talking out loud? Luke shoved his hands in his pockets and tried out a noncommittal smile before trailing the woman toward the adjoining bathroom.

She was attractive enough, he supposed, and somewhere in her twenties as well as sort of blondish, but it wasn't her who had sparked his imagination. It was that luxurious bed, he decided, glancing back at it over his shoulder. That quilt-covered bed with a mattress wide enough to rival the sizable slice of Lake Tahoe that he could see through the room's tall windows.

There was a stone fireplace near the bed's carved footboard with wood neatly laid inside and Luke could imagine the logs burning brightly, licking golden color along the naked, fair flesh of his fantasy woman. He'd follow suit with his tongue, tasting her warm—

"Mr. Barton?"

His attention jolted to the caretaker again and he realized he was standing, frozen, in the middle of the room. "Call me Luke," he said.

"What?" The caretaker frowned. "We were expecting Matthias Barton this month."

Perplexed, Luke stared at her for a moment. Matthias?

Oh. *Matthias*. Matt. That luxurious decadent bed was making him forget everything. It wasn't often that Luke Barton forgot his bastard of a twin brother, Matt. And it was never that he did his bastard of a brother a favor.

Except for now.

Damn Matt.

When his assistant had called Luke's assistant he'd wished like hell he could have turned the cheating, thieving SOB down flat. *"Your brother has to take care of some unexpected business and he wants to know if you'll switch months with him,"* Elaine had imparted, as if it wasn't damn strange that identical siblings refused to speak to each other.

But for once, Luke had been unable to refuse his brother's request.

"I'm sorry. I meant to mention it right away," Luke told the caretaker. Apparently she hadn't noticed the cryptic note Nathan left behind had been addressed to him. "Something came up and my brother and I had to trade months." The ol' twin switcheroo.

"Oh, I suppose that's all right," the woman replied, then gestured him forward. "So, as I was saying, Luke, you must spend the next month in the lodge in order to fulfill the requirements of Hunter's will. Your friend Nathan was here last month and your brother Matthias will then take your place in the fifth month."

Luke knew all that. A while back, letters had been received by each of the remaining "Seven Samurai" as they'd called themselves in college. The six had lost touch after the death of Hunter Palmer and graduation, but with the arrival of those letters they'd been reminded of the promise they'd once made to one another as they closed in on getting their diplomas. Though they were from families of distinction and wealth, they'd been determined to each make their own mark on the world. In ten years, they'd vowed.

Over a table filled with empty beer bottles they'd pledged to build a lodge on the shores of Lake Tahoe and in ten years, each of them would take the place for a month. At the end of the seventh month, the plan had been that they'd all come together for a celebration of their friendship and the successes they'd achieved.

But after Hunter's illness and subsequent death, that dream had died with him.

Though apparently not for Hunter. Even aware he wouldn't be there to share it with them, he'd made arrangements for a lodge to be built at the lake. The letters he'd written to each of the friends said that he expected them to honor the vow they'd taken all those years ago.

The caretaker stepped aside as they reached another arched doorway. "And here's the master bathroom."

As Luke stepped inside, the fantasy blond popped back into his thoughts. The light of a fire was tracing her skin again, all that pretty, pretty skin, as she lowered herself into the deep porcelain tub that was surrounded by slate and butted up against yet another fireplace. The ends of her hair darkened as they swished against her wet shoulders. Bubbles played peekaboo with her rosy nipples.

"Do you think you'll be comfortable here?"

Sidetracked again by his enticing little vision, Luke was jolted once more by the sound of the caretaker's voice.

Damn! What was the matter with him? he wondered, firmly banishing the distracting beauty splashing in his suddenly sex-obsessed brain.

"I'll be just fine here, thank you." Even though he was going to be "just fine" three months early, all for the sake of his brother.

He must have been scowling at the thought, because the woman's eyebrows rose. "Is something wrong?"

"No. Not at all." There was no reason to expose the family laundry to a stranger. "I guess I'm just thinking of…of Hunter."

The woman's gaze dropped. "I'm sorry." The toe of

her sensible black shoe appeared to fascinate her. "I think…I think he intended this as a nice gesture."

"Hunter Palmer was a very nice man." The best of the seven of them. The very best. Luke let himself remember Hunter's wide grin, his infectious laugh, the way he could rally their group to do anything from nailing all the furniture in the freshman-dorm rec room to the ceiling to organizing a charity three-man basketball tournament senior year.

Hunter had been part of Luke's squad. They'd won the whole shebang, too. What a team they'd made, Hunter and Luke…and Matt.

In those days, like never before and never since, Luke and Matt had played on the same side.

But it was Hunter who Luke had been thinking of when he'd agreed to take his brother's place for the next month. Their dead friend's last request had been for the six other men to spend time at the lodge he'd built. If they fulfilled his request, then twenty million dollars and the lodge itself would be turned over to the town of Hunter's Landing, here on the shores of Lake Tahoe.

Luke wasn't going to be the reason that didn't happen, no matter how he felt about his brother.

So he followed the caretaker through the rest of the rooms, keeping his mind off the fantasy blond by thinking of the twin switcheroo and how he was replacing Matt Barton, #1 bastard. He spent little time looking on the framed Samurai photos mounted in the second-floor hallway. If he were really playing the part of Matt, Luke thought, it would mean keeping his tie knotted tight, his smiles as cold as Sierra snow, and his mind open to how he could take advantage of any situation without regard to kith, kin or even common decency.

That was how his brother operated.

Finally the caretaker gave him the ornate keychain that contained the house key and departed, leaving Luke alone inside the big house with only his grim thoughts for company. The place was quiet and absent of any signs of Nathan Barrister—who had been staying here the month before—unless you counted the hastily written note Luke had found from him. But Nathan hadn't gone far. He'd fallen for the mayor of Hunter's Landing, Keira Sanders, and now they were flitting between the Tahoe town and sun-filled Barbados, where his old friend was presumably mixing business with pleasure.

Jacket and tie discarded, Luke found a beer in the overstocked fridge and settled himself by the window of the great room. Through the trees was another spectacular view of the lake. It wasn't its famous clear-blue at the moment, not only because it was settling into evening, but also because gray clouds were gathering overhead.

Dark clouds that reflected Luke's mood.

What the hell was he going to do with himself for a month?

Nathan had done okay here, apparently. His note said it wasn't "exactly the black hole I thought" and he'd occupied himself by jumping into a full-on love affair. Luke didn't wish that potential quagmire on himself, though a visit from that blond sweetheart of his imagination might make the month pass just a little bit faster. It was too damn bad she couldn't stroll out of his fantasies and straight into this room.

Yes, that would make the thirty days more interesting.

Except it wasn't going to happen unless Matt had invited someone to join him here. And even if that were the case, blond sweethearts just weren't Matt's type. Being identical twins didn't mean they had identical taste when it came to women.

Luke hooked his heels around a nearby ottoman and dragged it closer as the first drops of what appeared to be a heavy spring rain started to hit the windows and roll down like tears. Yeah, he'd be crying, too, if the vision from his daydream showed up on his doorstep looking for Matt.

Though he shouldn't rule that out, come to think of it. His brother might set up just such a thing to shake Luke's cage. Matt ruined Luke's life any chance he got.

To be fair—unlike his brother—Luke had to admit that it was their father, Samuel Sullivan Barton, who had sowed the seeds of their ugly rivalry. He'd run their childhood like an endless season of *The Apprentice,* with himself playing Donald Trump, constantly orchestrating cutthroat competitions between his two sons.

Their enmity had abated in college. But after Hunter had died, so had their father, and he'd left behind one last contest that rekindled his sons' competitive fire. Whichever twin made a million dollars first would win the family holdings. Both of them had separately gone to work on developing wireless technology—Luke doing it hands-on, using his engineering degree, while Matt tapped into his undeniable business acumen to hire someone to work with him.

When it came to any kind of gadgetry, his brother

was all thumbs. But when it came to building a successful team, Matt was a master.

Of course, that time he'd ensured his mastery by bribing a supplier and knocking Luke right out of the running. Matt had made the first mil and won all the family assets, to boot.

Luke hadn't spoken to his brother since, though he'd gone on to do a damn fine job with his own company—a meaner and leaner version of what Matt continued to build upon with the Barton family wealth behind him. That was Luke in a nutshell these days: a leaner—okay, maybe by only a pound or two—but definitely meaner version of his brother Matt.

Working his ass off had a way of doing that to a man, Luke thought. And maybe bitterness, too. He couldn't deny it.

The rain was really coming down now, and the house took on a chill. He got up and lit the fire laid in the great room's massive fireplace—it took up one huge stone wall—and the flames set him thinking about his blond again.

When he got back to his own condo in the San Francisco Bay Area he was going to have to make a few phone calls, apparently. This fantasy woman was a new fixation for him. Work usually was his only obsession—work and finding some way to pay back his brother at some future date—so his sex life was more sporadic than people believed. It looked as if he needed to be paying more attention to his bodily needs, though.

Or maybe the blame rested on this house, he thought. Or the fireplaces. *That bed.*

The blond continued insinuating herself into his thoughts. He could practically smell her now. Her scent was like rain—clean, cool rain—and he'd sip the drops off her mouth, her neck, her collarbone.

Closing his eyes, he rested his head against the back of the chair. As his fantasy played on, his heart started to hammer.

Except that it wasn't his heart.

His eyes popped open. He stared out the windows, trying to determine if the pouring rain or the waving trees were causing the loud drumming.

He decided it was neither one.

Luke set his beer down and rose, following the noise to the front door. Who the hell would be here now and in this spring deluge?

He jerked open the door. As he took in the dark shadow of a figure on the porch, a chilly blast of wind and a spray of rain wafted over him. Suppressing a shiver, he fumbled for the light switches. Brightness blazed over the porch and in the foyer.

The shadowy figure became a woman.

Her white blouse was plastered to her body. Wet denim clung to her thighs.

She raised a hand to her hair and tried fluffing the drenched stuff. A few locks gamely sprung from straight strands into bedraggled curls that hinted at gold.

Luke looked back at her clothes again.

More accurately, he looked at the curves cupped by all that wet cloth.

Her nipples were hard buds topping spectacular breasts.

Even from the front he could surmise she had a round backside, too, just the way he liked it.

She was exactly how he liked it.

Bemused, he continued to stare at her as he tried figuring out what combination of beer, rain and rampant fantasy had brought such a sight to his front door.

Could she possibly be real? And if so, whom did he have to thank for such a surprising gift?

She frowned at him. Her lips were generously pillowed, too. "Matthias, aren't you going to invite your fiancée in?"

Fiancée? Matthias?

Luke spent a few more long moments staring at the wet blonde on his doorstep. When another cold blast of air and rain slapped him, he blinked and finally stepped back to let his brother's fiancée inside.

As she moved forward, questions circled in his mind. Was this some joke? That trick he hadn't put past his brother? Or could Matt really be engaged? If so, it was news to Luke. He'd thought his brother was the same kind of workaholic confirmed bachelor he was. And when had Matt's taste turned to blondes?

Inside, with the door shut behind her, the young woman wrapped her arms around herself and licked her bottom lip in what seemed a nervous gesture. "I, um, know you weren't expecting me. It was sort of an—an impulse."

"Oh?"

"Yes. I jumped in my car and before long I was almost here. Then it started pouring rain and now…" Her voice drifted off and she shrugged, her gaze going to her feet. "And now I'm dripping all over this beautiful carpet."

She was right. She was as wet as his bathtub fantasy, and probably cold, too. He gestured up the stairs toward the great room and its crackling fire. "Let's get you warmed up and dried off."

He tried to be a gentleman and keep his gaze above her neck as she preceded him into the other room but, hell, he knew he was no gentleman. So he confirmed what he'd already suspected by running his gaze from her nape to her heels. She was just his type.

Except she was his brother's fiancée. Or was she? It could still be a trick…

Stopping in front of the roaring fire, she faced him again. Another rush of words spilled out, giving him the idea that she chattered when she was anxious. "My mother would kill me if she knew I came up here. 'Lauren,' she'd say in that disapproving tone of hers, 'is this another one of your Bad Ideas?' That's just how she says it, with capitals. Capital *B*, Bad. Capital *I*, Ideas. 'Another one of Lauren's Bad Ideas.'" A nervous laugh escaped before her hands came up to try to suppress it.

Lauren. Her name was Lauren. It didn't ring any bells, but Luke didn't keep tabs on Matt's social life. Maybe he should, if his brother was really going around snatching up just the sort of women that Luke liked. For God's sake, Matt shouldn't be allowed to have everything Luke wanted.

She shivered and he spotted a wool throw draped over a nearby chair. He grabbed for it then brought it to her. As she took it from his hand, she looked up at him, all big, blue eyes. Her pink tongue darted out to wet that pouty lower lip.

"You've got to be wondering why I'm here, Matthias."

"I'm not—" Matthias. But something made him hold that last word back. He ran his hand through his hair, buying himself some time. "I guess I am a little surprised to see you."

She gave another small laugh and then turned toward the fire. "This whole engagement thing has been a little surprising, don't you agree?"

"Yeah." He could be honest about that, anyway. "I suppose so."

She continued to study the fire. "I mean, we don't know each other that well, right? You've worked with my father and Conover Industries for years, of course…"

Hell, Luke thought. She was Conover's kid. Ralph Conover's daughter. Ralph Conover, who'd been the first to cozy up to Matt after he'd cheated Luke out of his fair chance to win the Barton family holdings.

"…but there's the fact that we haven't talked that much or ever really been…um, alone together."

What? Luke stared at the back of her head and the gold curls that were starting to spring up there. His brother was engaged to marry a woman he'd never been alone with? Luke had a guess to what that was code for and, if he was right, it meant Matt *hadn't* suddenly developed a yen for cute curvy blondes.

Instead, it meant Matt had developed a yen to more tightly cement his relationship with Conover Industries. Luke's mind raced ahead as he imagined all the implications this could have for Eagle Wireless, his own smaller company. With Conover Industries and Barton Limited "married," Eagle could find its own perch in the wireless world very precarious.

God. Damn. It.

Lauren turned toward him again, clutching the throw at her chest. "You haven't said what you think about that, Matthias."

Because Luke hadn't had enough time to think it through completely. He cleared his throat. "I suppose some people would find it a bit odd that we haven't…" Since he didn't know precisely what Matt and Lauren had or hadn't, he let the sentence hang.

"Touched?" she conveniently supplied. "Even kissed, really?" Then color reddened her cheeks. "And we certainly haven't made love."

Staring into her big, blue eyes, suddenly Luke could picture—in vivid detail—doing just that very thing with her. He saw it on his mind's high-def big screen, the two of them making love in that big bathtub upstairs, Lauren's soft, wet thighs wrapped around his hips. Or on that quilt-covered bed, her blond curls spread out against the pillowcase.

Her eyes darkened and he heard a tiny gasp as her breath suddenly caught. Was she reading his thoughts?

Or did she feel that same sharp tug of attraction that he did?

Could she possibly share the images dealing out like X-rated playing cards in his mind?

Blond, curvy Lauren, and Luke, the mean twin.

The cheated twin.

He lifted his hand and trailed one knuckle along the

downy softness of her cheek, wondering if she would taste as sweet as she looked. His fingertip touched the center of her bottom lip and he saw her eyes widen.

Oh, yeah, the message in them made it clear that she felt the attraction, too. And the bit of confusion he could read as well told him she hadn't felt it for Matt.

Luke ran his thumb over her bottom lip this time, moving inside just a little so that he grazed the damp inner surface. She stood frozen before him, trapped between the fire and his touch. In the sudden heavy silence of the room he could hear the light, fast pants of her breath. Color ran high on her cheeks.

God, she was beautiful.

And we certainly haven't made love.

She'd said that, and that's where Luke's brother had slipped up. If she were Luke's, he wouldn't have wasted any time before taking their engagement—even one motivated by business reasons—to a more serious level.

Okay, be honest. He wouldn't have been able to stop himself.

The pulse along her throat was racing, begging him to touch it with his mouth. And now that her hair was starting to dry, he could smell her shampoo, something flowery, but not cloying. It was a fresh smell and he wanted to rub himself against it. He wanted to smell her on his own skin.

Really, it came down to one very simple thing. He wanted his brother's bride-to-be.

"M-Matthias?" she whispered.

Luke didn't flinch at the wrong name. Instead, he tucked a damp curl behind her ear. At the sight of the goose bumps that raced down her neck in response, he smiled, careful to keep the wolfishness out of it.

But he felt wolfish.

Smug, satisfied and ready to eat Goldilocks up in one big bite.

And then he'd want to do it again, this time taking his time to savor every taste.

His hand lingered near her shell of an ear. He'd mixed up his fairy tales, hadn't he? The wolf was Little Red Ridinghood's nemesis, wasn't he? But no matter. Lauren was most certainly Goldilocks and Luke hadn't felt this predatory in a long, long while.

Catching her gaze with his, he grazed his thumb along her velvety cheek.

She released her grip on the wool throw. It fell at her feet as she circled his wrist to pull his hand away from her face. "What do you think you're doing?"

Goldilocks wasn't quite so ready to test out feather mattresses as he'd thought. But that was okay. He needed some time to process all this himself. "Nothing you don't want," he reassured her, stepping back and trying on another smile.

She shivered again.

Frowning, he ran his gaze over her, noting that her wet clothes still clung. He shoved his hands in his pockets to disguise the effect her curves had on him and cleared his throat. "Why don't you take a hot shower? Warm up."

So he could cool down. Think things through. Decide what to do with all the sexual dynamite in the room, especially when they were standing so close to the fire.

Especially when the woman who had walked out of his fantasies was his brother's bride-to-be.

"Take a shower *here?*" She was already shaking her head. "No, no, no. I only came to talk and then—"

"What?" Luke interrupted. "Go back out in that?" He gestured toward the windows and the full-on storm and wilderness-level darkness beyond them. "Now *that* would definitely be a Bad Idea, Lauren."

She made a face. "Oh, thanks for reminding me."

He allowed himself a little grin. "Fair warning, kid. Never show me your weakness. I'll use it against you."

"Kid." She made the face again, though he could see the appellation relaxed her. "I'm twenty-six years old."

"Be a grown-up then. Go upstairs and take a hot shower. Then we'll put your clothes in the dryer, I'll rustle us up some dinner and after that we'll reassess."

Her eyes narrowed. "Reassess what?"

She was a suspicious little thing, but God knows that was sensible of her. He shrugged. "We'll reassess whatever occurs to us." Like whether he should let her know who he really was. Like whether he could let her drive away from him tonight.

After another swift glance at the scene outside the windows, she appeared to make up her mind. "All right." She bent to retrieve the throw.

As she handed it to him on her way toward the stairs, he used it to reel her closer.

"What?" she said, startled. Round blue eyes. Quivering curls.

"We haven't had our hello kiss," he murmured.

Then, curious as to what it might be like, he placed his mouth on top of hers.

At contact, his heart kicked hard inside his chest. Heat flashed across his flesh, burning from scalp to groin.

Lauren had the softest, most pillowy lips he'd ever encountered in thirty-one years of living. Eighteen years of kissing. His biceps were tight as he lifted his hands to cradle her face.

He took a breath in preparation, then touched the tip of his tongue to hers.

Pow.

They both leaped away from the sweet, hot explosion.

She regained her breath first. "I'll…I'll just take that shower," she said, her gaze glued to his face as if she were afraid to turn her back on him.

"Sure, fine, go on up," he managed to get out, when he should have said, *"Run, Goldilocks. Run as far and as fast as you can."*

As if he wouldn't run right after her if she tried.

Two

Lauren Conover stared at her bedraggled reflection in the bathroom mirror, looking for any evidence of the backbone she'd thought she'd found this morning before driving to Lake Tahoe. Instead, all she saw was a wet woman with reddened lips and a confused expression in her eyes.

"You were supposed to walk in and break it off with him immediately," she whispered fiercely to that dazed-looking creature staring back at her. "Nowhere in the plan were you supposed to find him attractive."

But she had! That was the crazy, spine-melting trouble. When the door to the magnificent log house had opened, there stood Matthias Barton, looking as he always had on those few occasions they'd been together. Dark hair, dark eyes, a lean face that she couldn't deny was handsome—and yet, never before had it drawn her.

Then he'd invited her inside and when she'd been looking up at him with the fire at her back she'd felt fire at her front, too. A man-woman kind of fire that made her skin prickle and her heart beat fast.

The kind of fire that a woman might be persuaded to marry for.

And she'd come all this way to tell him it wasn't going to happen.

And it wasn't!

When her mother had plopped a stack of bridal magazines onto the breakfast table that morning, Lauren had looked at them and then at her thirteen-year-old sister's face. Her tough-as-nails tomboy sister who had been giving Lauren grief since the engagement had been announced two weeks before.

"You'd better do something quick," Kaitlyn had said, backing away from the glossy magazines as if they were a tangle of hissing snakes. "Or the next thing you know, Mom will have me in some horrid junior bridesmaid's dress that I'll never, ever forgive you for."

Lauren had known Kaitlyn was right. Her mother's steamroller qualities were exactly why she'd found herself engaged to a man she barely knew in the first place. That is, her mother's steamroller qualities combined with her father's heavy-handed hints about this marriage being good for the family business he always claimed was faltering. As well as Lauren's own embarrassment over her three previous attempts to make it down the aisle.

She'd picked those men herself and the engagements had each ended in disaster.

So it had been hard to disagree with her mother and father that their choice couldn't be any worse, despite Kaitlyn's teenage disgust.

But the sight of those pages and pages of bridal gowns had woken Lauren from the stupor that she'd been suffering since returning home from Paris six months before. Hanging a third now-never-to-be-worn wedding dress in the back of her family's cedar-lined luggage closet had sent her to a colorless, emotionless place where she'd slept too much, watched TV too much and responded almost robot-like to her parents' commands.

Until glimpsing that tulled and tiara-ed bride on the front cover of *Matrimonial*, that is. The sight had hit her like a wake-up slap to the face. What was she thinking? She couldn't marry Matthias Barton. She couldn't marry a man for the same cold, cutthroat reasons her father picked a new business partner.

So she'd grabbed her keys and gathered her self-confidence and driven straight to where Matthias had mentioned he'd be staying for the next month, determined to get him out of her life.

Now she couldn't get him out of her mind.

Sighing, she turned away from the mirror and adjusted the spray in the shower. She'd found the master bedroom right off—my God, that luxurious bed had almost made her swoon!—but spun a quick about-face and entered a smaller guest bed and bath instead.

The hot water felt heavenly and some of her uneasiness went down the drain with it. All she had to do was walk back out there and tell that gorgeous hunk of a man that she wasn't marrying him. He'd probably be as relieved as she was. After that she'd drive home, face the certain-to-be-discordant music chez Conover and get on with the rest of her life.

The rest of her life that wouldn't include any more engagements to wrong men.

A few minutes later, wrapped in an oversized terry robe she'd found hanging on the bathroom door and carrying her damp clothes in hand, Lauren made her way to the staircase. Some framed photos lined the walls but she didn't give them but a cursory glance as she was more concerned with getting away from the house than anything. She could tell it was still raining and even from the second-floor landing the downstairs fire looked cozy and inviting, but she straightened her shoulders and mentally fused her vertebrae together.

Break it off, Lauren, she ordered herself as she descended the steps. *At once. Then get in your car and drive home.* Who cared about not waiting to dry the wet clothes? The robe covered her up just fine.

She could see Matthias standing by the fireplace now. He looked up…and somehow made her feel as if she wasn't wearing anything at all.

A flush heated all the skin under the suddenly scratchy terry cloth. Lauren's nipples hardened— though she wasn't the least bit cold, oh no sir—and she knew they were poking at the thick fabric. Would he notice? Could he tell?

Would he care?

Trying to pretend nothing was the least amiss, she made herself continue downward. But, man-oh-man, was he something to look at. He'd rolled up the sleeves of his dress shirt and unfastened a second button at the throat. The vee of undershirt she could see was blinding white and contrasted with the dark, past-five-o'clock stubble on his chin and around his mouth.

His mouth made her think of his kiss again. It was just a regular man's mouth, she supposed, but she liked the wideness of it and the deep etch of his upper lip. She really liked how it had felt on hers and, then, when his tongue had touched—

"Don't look at me like that," he suddenly said.

She was two steps from the bottom and the rasp in his voice made her grab for the railing. "I'm sorry," she said, unable to move, hardly able to speak. "What?"

"You look at me like that and I forget all about my intentions."

Her mouth went dry. "What intentions?" Maybe they were bad intentions…yet why did the idea of that sound so very good?

Matthias glanced over his shoulder. "My intention to feed you before anything else. Didn't I promise to rustle up dinner?"

Behind him she could see he'd set two places on the coffee table pulled up before a wide, soft-cushioned couch. Something was steaming—she could smell it, beef bourguignonne?—on two plates and ruby-colored liquid filled two wineglasses. Candles flickered in low votives.

Had she mentioned she was a sucker for candle-light?

She took another whiff of that delicious-smelling food. "Are you a good cook?"

He smiled and she liked that, too. His teeth were as white as his undershirt and they sent another wave of hot prickles across her flesh. "Maybe. Probably. But I've never tried."

She had to laugh at that. "Are you usually so confident? Even if you haven't attempted something you just expect you'll excel at it?"

"Of course. 'Assume success, deny failure.' My father taught us that."

"Yikes." And Lauren thought *her* cold-blooded *père* knew how to apply the screws. "That's a little harsh."

"You think so?" Matthias walked over to take her wet clothes in one hand and her free hand in the other.

He insinuated his long fingers between hers and the heat of his palm against hers shot toward her shoulder. "I think…I think…" Lauren couldn't remember what she was about to say. "Never mind."

He was smiling at her again, as if he understood her distraction. He led her toward the couch. "Let me put your clothes in the dryer, then we'll eat."

She stared after his retreating form for a moment, then started back to awareness. She was supposed to take the wet clothes home! Right after she told him the engagement was over! Right before walking out the door without dinner, without anything but her car keys and the comforting thought that she'd done the right thing.

But now he was coming toward her again, that small smile on his face and that appreciative light in his eyes. He brought that attraction between them back into the room, too—all that twitching, pulsing heat that drew her heart to her throat and her blood to several lower locations.

Tell him it's over! Her good sense shouted.

Tell him later, her sexuality purred, with a languid little stretch.

"Sit down," Matthias said, reaching out to touch her cheek.

Her knees gave way.

Merely postponing the inevitable. Lauren assured herself that she'd take care of what she came for and leave. Soon.

Except, an excellent dinner later, she was feeling a bit fuzzy from more merlot than she was used to. As well as a lot charmed by the man who had taken their dishes into the kitchen and was now sitting back on the cushions beside her, dangling the stem of his wineglass between his fingers.

Over the meal he'd entertained her with stories that all revolved around his adventures in take-out dining. If she needed any further evidence that he was a business-obsessed workaholic like her father—and why else would Papa Conover have pushed so hard for her to marry Matthias?—now she had it. The man couldn't remember the last time he'd eaten food prepared in a home.

"Even this doesn't qualify, I'm afraid," he said, gesturing to where their plates had been. "The cartons were printed with the name of some gourmet catering place in town."

"Hunter's Landing, right?" Lauren asked. "Though it's not named after your friend from college? The one who built this house?"

Matthias shook his head. "No. Just a little joke on his part, I guess. He had a wild sense of humor."

The suddenly hoarse note in his voice made her throat tighten. He missed his friend, that was certain. Swallowing a sigh, she closed her eyes. This wasn't the way it was supposed to be. This wasn't the way *he* was supposed to be. She didn't want her parent-picked fiancé to be sexy or charming or vulnerable and, for God's sake, certainly not all three. It only made it that much harder to break it off with him.

She was always such a nitwit when it came to men. There was a reason she'd been engaged three times before now. There was a reason she'd picked the wrong men and then stuck with them until the humiliating end—until they walked out on her.

"So," Matthias said, breaking into her morose thoughts. "Enough about me. Tell me all about Lauren."

All about Lauren? Her eyes popped open and her spirits picked up. Was this the answer? If she told Mr. Assume-Success-Deny-Failure Barton all about Lauren, he might break it off between them himself! Because the truth was, when it came to romance, she was all about failure. And obviously more accustomed to getting dumped than the other way around.

Drawing her legs onto the couch, she turned on her side to face him.

Except his face was directed at her legs, bared by the edges of the terry robe that had opened with her movement. Heat rushing over her face, she yanked the fabric over her pale skin. She wasn't trying to come on to him. She was trying to get him to see that a marriage between the two of them would never work.

When she cleared her throat, he looked up, without a hint of shame on his face. "Great legs."

The compliment only served to discombobulate her further. The heat found its way to the back of her neck and she blurted out, "You know, you're fiancé number four."

He stared. "Number four?"

Ha. That had him. Now he'd turn off the charm and dam up that oozing sex appeal. She nodded. "I've been engaged before. Three other times."

He gave a small smile. "Optimistic little thing, aren't you?"

She frowned, bothered that he seemed more amused than appalled by her confession. Maybe he didn't believe her. Maybe he thought she was joking. Holding up her hand, she ticked them off. "Trevor, Joe and Jean-Paul."

"All right." He drained the remainder of his wine and set the glass on the table, as if ready for business. "Give me the down and dirty."

He still seemed amused. And charming. And sexy.

Blast him.

Lauren took a breath. "I almost married Trevor when we were nineteen. It was going to be a sunset ceremony on the beach, followed by a honeymoon—one that I'd planned and paid for—that would hit all the best surfing spots in Costa Rica. On my wedding day, I was supposed to wear a white bandeau top, a grass skirt I found in a secondhand shop in Santa Cruz, and a crown of plumeria blossoms straight from Hawaii."

"Sounds fetching," he said, "though I don't see you as a surfer."

"That's probably the biggest reason Trevor ran off without me. He cashed in our first class tickets for coach ones and took his best surfing buddy to Central America instead. I haven't heard from him since."

Lauren experienced a little pang thinking of the bleached-blond she would always consider her first love. He'd driven her parents nuts, she recalled with a reminiscent smile. He'd been the perfect anti-Conover.

"Okay. That's number one. But why aren't you now Mrs. Joe…?"

"Rutkowski. His name is Joe Rutkowski."

Matthias bit his lip. "You're kidding."

"No. Joe Rutkowski was—well, *is*—my father's mechanic. If you find a good car-man, you don't break up with him—even if he breaks up with your daughter. That's what my father says, anyway."

"So what gave good ol' Joe second thoughts?"

"His pregnant other girlfriend."

"Oh."

"Little Jolene was born on my birthday, which also happened to be our proposed wedding date."

"Tell me you sent a baby gift. Little coveralls? A tiny timing light?"

Lauren narrowed her eyes at him. He didn't seem to be getting her point. "My heart was broken. My mother sent a certificate for a month of diaper service and signed my name." It still annoyed her that she'd lost the opportunity to watch her hoity-toity parents introduce the town's best Mercedes mechanic as their new son-in-law.

"But your broken heart recovered enough to find yourself in the arms of—what did you say his name was?—Jacques Cousteau?"

"Very funny. Jean-Paul Gagnon." Her father hated

Frenchmen. "I met him in Paris. We were going to get married on top of the Eiffel Tower. I had a tailored white linen suit with a long skirt that went to my ankles and was so tight that I couldn't run after the nasty little urchin who stole my purse on the way to the ceremony."

"I hope you're going to tell me that Jean-Paul took after the urchin himself."

"He did. But when he came back with my purse he told me that it had given him time to think about what he was doing. And marrying me was not what he wanted to do, after all." She gazed off into the distance, remembering her disappointment at not being able to shock her parents with the groom she brought home from Europe. "I really *liked* Jean-Paul."

"In the morning, I'll find some place that will feed you crepes."

In the morning? Lauren jerked her head toward him. "Have you been listening to a thing I said?"

"Of course I have." He moved closer and wrapped his hands around her wrists. "I just haven't figured out what the hell it has to do with you and me."

Lauren swallowed. Here was the opening she'd been waiting for. Now was the time to say, "There is no you and me, Matthias. There never really was."

Except the words wouldn't come out. They were stuck in her tight throat—and all it could handle was breathing, a task that seemed to be so much more complex when he was touching her.

"This is a lot harder than I thought," she whispered.

A ghost of a smile quirked one corner of his handsome mouth as he slid his fingers between hers. "You're telling me."

Despite her breathlessness, she found she could still laugh. "Are you being bad?"

"Not yet. But the night's still young."

Night? Good Lord, she'd completely lost track of time. It had been early evening just a minute ago. She checked her watch. "I've got to leave." Scooting back, she tried yanking her hands from his.

He merely held her tighter. "Not now, honey."

"But Matthias was…"

Something flickered in his eyes, but he didn't let go. "I may be an SOB, but I'm not completely black-hearted. It's too late, too dark, too stormy for me to let you leave tonight. It wouldn't be safe."

She looked out the windows and could tell he was right. The rain hadn't let up in the hours she'd been at the house and it was still coming down in torrents. Oh, great. She was stuck with the man she couldn't bring herself to break up with and her heart was thrumming so fast and he was so gorgeous she worried that if she didn't get away from him soon she'd… "I'm not so sure it's safe here, either."

"Will anyone be worrying about you? Do you need to make a call?"

Registering that he hadn't addressed the safety issue, she shook her head. "I had planned to stay with a friend in San Francisco for a few days on my way back. She said she'd expect me when she saw me."

"So here we are." He dropped her right hand so he could toy with one of her curls instead. "All alone on a dark and stormy night."

"So here we are," she echoed. "All alone." Oh, but her mother definitely could have called this one.

Coming up here was truly another of Lauren's Bad Ideas.

"How do you propose we entertain ourselves?" Matthias asked, twining a lock of her hair around his forefinger.

Lauren pretended not to notice. "Swap ghost stories? That sounds appropriate."

"But then we might be too scared to sleep."

Oh God. Her heart jumped and her gaze locked on his face. He was wearing that little smile again, as if he knew that mentioning the words *we* and *sleep* in the same sentence had her thinking of the two of them together, in a bed, doing everything *but* sleeping.

What the heck was going on? In the last few months, she'd chitchatted with Matthias at parties, danced with him a couple of times at charity events, pretended to be interested during family dinners while he talked shop with her father. Not once had she felt the slightest shiver of sexual attraction and now it was all she could do not to squirm in her seat.

Or squirm all over him.

"How come you weren't like this before?" she demanded.

His teeth flashed white. "I suppose I'll take that as a compliment."

"Seriously. Matthias—"

He put his hand over her mouth. "Shh. Don't talk."

She reached up to pull his fingers away. "If I don't talk I'm afraid I'll—"

And then he stopped that sentence, too, by swooping forward to kiss her for a second time. "Sorry," he said against her mouth. "I just can't help myself."

But *she* was helping him already by spearing her fingers through the crisp hair at the back of his head. He angled one way, she angled another and then they were *really* kissing, lips opening, tongues touching, tasting, their breaths and the sweet tang of merlot mingling.

Goose bumps rolled in a wave from the top of her scalp to the tickly skin behind her knees. She scooted closer to him, bumping the outside of his legs. Without breaking the connection of their mouths, he gathered her and the voluminous terry cloth onto his lap. In the move, the robe's hem rode up and she found herself settling onto him with nothing between her bare behind and his hard slacks-covered thighs.

Yanking her mouth from his, she glanced down, relieved to see that her front was covered decently enough and that the robe was draping her legs modestly, too. Still… "We shouldn't be doing this," she said, taking her hands from his hair.

"What?" His voice was hoarse.

Where to start? The engagement? The kiss? The lap? Or the bare skin which only felt barer because it was against the soft fabric that was clothing all those male muscles? "You know exactly what I'm talking about."

His eyelashes were spiky and dark, as masculine as the rest of him. "So you're holding out for the wedding night?"

The edge in his voice didn't surprise her. She felt edgy, too, torn between what her head was advising and what her body was demanding.

"We hardly know each other," she said. "So all this… this…"

"Hankering for hanky-panky?"

She narrowed her eyes at him. "…is a product of the rain, the wine, the—"

"The stone cold truth that we turn each other on hard and fast, Goldilocks, no explanations, no apologies. And to be honest, I'm as floored by it as you are."

"You are?" Not that she figured he considered her an ogre or anything, but the idea that this kind of "hankering for hanky-panky" wasn't standard for him, either, was a fascinating notion.

He laughed. "You look awfully pleased with yourself about it."

"Hey, in the past few years, I've been rejected on a regular basis, so forgive my dented ego for giving a little cheer." The merlot had seriously loosened her tongue.

"Fiancés one through four were idiots."

"*You're* number four," she reminded him.

"I'm trying to forget that." At the frown on her face, he shook his head and pinched her chin. "Goldilocks, I'm suggesting we try to forget everything but the fact that it's a dark and stormy night and we're alone together with our hankering. What do you say? Why not see where it takes us?"

She stared at him. "That's male reasoning."

He raised a dark eyebrow. "Cogent? To the point?"

"Shortsighted and all about sex."

"And your point is?"

Oh, he was making her laugh again. And *that* made her wiggle against his lap. And that made him groan and she was so…well, captivated by the powerful feeling the sound gave her that she leaned in to buss him on the mouth.

Which he turned into a real kiss.

Next thing she knew their tongues were twining and her hands were buried in his hair again. Heat was pouring off of him and his skin tasted a tiny bit salty as she kissed the corner of his mouth. "I want to bottle up this feeling," she told him, awed by its strength. Sexual chemistry, who knew? "We could market it and make a kabillion dollars."

"A kabillion is a lot," he murmured, then turned his attention to her left ear.

Goose bumps sprinted across every inch of her skin as his tongue feathered over the rim to tickle the lobe. "A kabillion-ten," she corrected herself. "In the first year."

He traveled back to her mouth, then took his time there, leisurely playing with all the surfaces. Her breath backed up in her lungs when he sucked her bottom lip into his mouth. Her fingers tightened on his scalp when he slid the tip of his tongue along the damp skin inside her upper lip. She moaned when he thrust inside her mouth, filling her with his purpose and male demand.

And all the while she was excruciatingly aware of her nakedness under the robe. Of her bareness resting against his pant legs. The soft wool scratched at her skin now, sensitized as it was by the kisses that never let up and the hands that never wandered beyond her hair and her face.

She was fast losing all the reasons why she should be happy about that. In the face of this "hankering" as he called it, she'd been unable to stand up against the kissing. It wasn't such a bad thing, though, was it? For goodness sake, she *was* engaged to the man.

Still.

A little voice somewhere in the dim recesses of her mind reminded her she was here to put an end to that engagement, but she shushed the crabby killjoy. Because this man could *kiss*, and there was no reason to deny herself the pleasure.

Except that kissing was quickly becoming not quite enough.

To ease the growing ache, she squeezed her thighs together and wiggled her naked behind. Matthias tore his lips from hers to gaze at her with serious eyes. "You're making me crazy." His mouth was wet.

She dried it with the edge of her thumb. "What'd you say?" She stroked her thumb the other way and he caught it between his teeth. Nipped.

Lauren shivered once and then again when his tongue swiped over her fingertip. The inside of his mouth was hot and wet and she leaned forward to taste it again.

He caught her shoulders, keeping her a breath away. "Lauren, maybe you were right…"

"Just one more." She pushed at his hands and, as they fell, they took the robe with them. It dropped to her waist.

Leaving her naked from her belly button up.

And frozen between caution and desire.

His gaze stayed on her face, but when she made no move to cover herself, he let it wander southward. Slowly.

Like a caress, she felt it move across her features, from her nose, to her mouth, over her chin and then down the column of her neck.

It traced the edges of her collarbone and her breath caught, held, as he finally stared at her breasts. Under the weight of his gaze, her nipples went from tight to tighter. She glanced down, noticing how hard and darker they looked against the pale skin of her swollen breasts.

Without thinking, she moved her arms up to cover herself.

"Don't." He caught her wrists. "Don't keep them from me."

Hot chills tumbled down her naked spine. She didn't want to keep them from him. She didn't want to keep any part of herself from him.

In a blur of movement, he stood, lifting her in his arms. "Wh—?" she began.

"Shh," he said. "Don't talk." He strode for the staircase, rushing up the steps as if she weighed nothing.

She felt weightless, too, as if she were floating on a cloud of desire. And a cloud of impossible dreams. Good God, could her parents have been right? Had they picked the right man for her after all?

He didn't hesitate at the top of the stairs, but headed straight for the master bedroom. At the foot of the enormous sleigh bed, he hesitated.

Lauren rested her head against his chest, his heart beating hard and fast in her ear. There was nothing she wanted more than to get naked, completely naked, with him. She smiled up at his face, seductively, she thought. "Matthias? Aren't you going to make love to me?"

Three

Lauren stirred, stretched, came awake to the knowledge that she was in a strange bed in a strange room, wearing a near-stranger's T-shirt and nothing else. A trio of emotions washed through her. Relief. Embarrassment. Annoyance that her parent-picked fiancé proved to be more cautious and in control of his libido than she was of hers.

Last night, when she'd said, "Matthias? Aren't you going to make love to me?" he'd gone still and silent. Further prodding, "Matthias? Matthias?" had caused him to close his eyes as if in pain. Then he'd taken a long deep breath and replied, "No."

In less than forty-five seconds he'd left her in the guest bedroom with one of his shirts and a kiss on the nose.

You had to hate that kind of self-control in a man.

But now it was morning and from the quiet sound of it, the rain had stopped, so she was free to take herself and her humiliation out of his house. She'd give herself a pass on breaking off the engagement in person. When she got a safe one-hundred miles or so away, she'd give him a call. Better yet, she'd send an e-mail from an anonymous account. Or perhaps a note by slow-flying carrier pigeon.

She wasn't going to face him again, even if it meant driving home in a knee-length T-shirt and nothing else.

A woman who wasn't yet thirty and yet who'd been rejected at both the altar and in the bedroom didn't need to eat any more humble pie, thank you very much.

However, she wasn't destined for near-naked driving that day. When she inched open the bedroom door, she found a neat pile of her dried clothing. Once she'd pulled it on, she crossed to the door again, listened to the quiet for a moment, then tiptoed along the hall and down the stairs on the first leg of her furtive escape.

Only to find her host was watching her take those exaggerated silent footsteps over the rim of a coffee cup.

"Oh, uh, hi." She tried tacking on a casual expression to convince him that strutting like a soundless rooster was one of her normal morning activities. "I didn't, um, see you there."

Seeing him was the problem! Seeing him reminded her of what he'd looked like last night, smiling at her, touching her hair, her face, coming close-up for kisses that were burned into her mind. Crossing her arms over her chest, she tried banishing the memories of his dark gaze on her naked breasts.

How *much* she'd wanted him to touch her.

In an abrupt move, he half turned away, the liquid in his cup sloshing dangerously close to the edge. "Are you ready for that breakfast I promised?"

"Breakfast?" She sounded stupid, but she felt stupid that even *sans* merlot, cozy firelight and distant drumming of the rain, her attraction to him was alive and quite, quite well.

Her attraction to the man who'd been able to deny everything she'd offered him last night.

"I said I'd feed you." He turned back. "And if I don't get some decent caffeine I might start gnawing on table legs. I freely admit to being a coffee snob and this stuff isn't up to my usual standards. This stuff is instant. There isn't anything else in the house."

"Oh. Well. Then." She would have liked nothing better than to grab her keys and get out of there, but she was suddenly rediscovering that spine of hers. And her pride. Instead of running off like a cowardly ninny, she'd spend another hour with him.

Then she'd hide off someplace where she could rent a pigeon.

An hour without making a further fool of herself. That shouldn't be so hard, should it?

She chalked up the silence of the car ride into the tiny town of Hunter's Landing to his need for quality caffeine. For herself, she managed to clamp down on her usual nervous babble by digging her fingernails into her palms whenever she felt compelled to volley a conversational gambit.

She was afraid a neutral comment intended to sound like "Beautiful morning, isn't it?" might come out as a plaintive "Why didn't you go to bed with me last night?"

So she created some half-moon marks in her hands and applied herself to observing the view outside his SUV's windows. It *was* a beautiful morning. The road was narrow and windy, taking them through heavy woods with pine boughs that still held raindrops winking like crystals in the sunlight. Every once in a while she'd catch a glimpse of the lake, its deep blue a match of the spring sky overhead.

As they neared the town, there was a slow-moving parade of "traffic"—actually a short line of cars in both directions that were pulling into or out of parking lots of small stores and cafés. Matthias glanced over at her. "Have you been to the lake before?"

She nodded. "But only during ski season."

"You downhill? Cross-country? Snowboard?"

"Truth? I'm best at hot chocolate and stoking the fire."

He grinned. "A woman after my own heart."

Ha. After last night, they both knew that wasn't true. "What, you don't like snow activities that much either?"

"No, I like all sorts of snow activities. But when I'm done playing, I like a warm beverage, a warm fire and a warm woman waiting."

She curled her lip at him. "That's an incredibly sexist thing to say."

He steered the car into a parking space outside a restaurant called Clearwater's. "Hey, I didn't say I expected it to be that way, only that I liked it. Since you do, too, I don't see the problem."

What did he mean by that? Did he mean he didn't see the problem that she had with his comment or that, given their natural proclivities, he didn't think they'd have a problem with their marriage during ski season?

Except they weren't getting married. And she wasn't going to bother making that point in case he really was only referring to the comment and he'd think her assumption about thinking he was referring to their marriage incredibly presumptuous. Oh, God. Now she was babbling to herself.

Get out of the car, Lauren. Get out. Eat breakfast and don't make a fool of yourself for a single, simple hour.

They were shown to a table by the window, overlooking a spectacular view of the lake. Boats of all shapes and sizes were already on the water and Lauren shivered, thinking how chilly it must be out in the wind. Matthias had given her a sweater of his before they left the house and she was grateful for the soft warmth.

And the delicious smell of him that clung to it.

She shivered again.

Matthias looked over his open menu. "You all right?"

"Sure." She looked down at the offerings to avoid gazing at his face. Unlike last night, he was close-shaven now, and she itched to run her fingers along the smooth line of his jaw. *Don't do something dumb, Lauren.*

"Sorry about this, but I don't see crepes."

She glanced up. "Crepes?"

"Remember? I was going to get them for you as a way of making up for Gaston's absence in your life."

"*Gagnon*. Jean-Paul Gagnon. Gaston is from Disney's *Beauty and the Beast*. You know, the ego-inflated villain."

"See? I was right after all."

She found herself smiling at him.

He reached out and brushed her bottom lip. "I like that. You've been very serious this morning."

Her gaze dropped back to her menu while her lip throbbed in reaction to his light touch. "I need my caffeine, too."

"Amazing how compatible we are," he murmured.

She pretended not to hear him. Compatibility made her think of marriage again and made her wonder if *he* was thinking of marriage, and also made her wonder if he was really seriously considering putting a wedding band on her finger or if was he going to dump her like all her other fiancés had.

No, wait. See how confused he made her? She was going to be dumping *him*.

The waitress came by, served up the gourmet caffeine, then took their order. They sipped coffee until the food arrived—the whole nine yards for him, oatmeal and fruit for her—and she had a mouthful of the brown-sugary stuff when he spoke again.

"You know, I just realized I'm not completely clear on why you came to the house last night."

To give herself thinking time, she pointed to her full mouth and did the whole pantomime that translated to "just a second, let me chew and swallow." Once the spoonful was on its way to her stomach, however, the best she could come up with was misdirection.

"Well, you know, I'm not completely clear on why

you're at that beautiful house in the first place." She held her breath, hoping he'd fall for her ruse.

"I didn't mention it?"

"Nope. Not exactly why you're living there. My father was the one who gave me the address. I only know that it has something to do with your college friend Hunter."

He cleared his throat. "Hunter Palmer."

"I think my family knows some Palmers. Palm Springs? Bel-Air?"

Luke nodded. "That's his family. Pharmaceuticals and personal-care products. We met in college. There was a group of us, we called ourselves the Seven Samurai."

Lauren smiled. "And you males think *The Sisterhood of the Traveling Pants* sounds silly."

He sipped at his coffee. "Ours was a special friendship, I'll give you that."

"Tell me about them."

"We were all privileged sons of prestigious families. But what brought us together was that we weren't content to merely suck from straws stuck in family trust funds. We wanted to make our own ways, our own marks. And we did. We have."

The conviction in his voice made him only more interesting. "How does that relate to a Lake Tahoe log house?"

The quick flash of a grin. "Oh, well, that's a bit less noble. I think it was the beer talking. No, it was definitely the beer talking."

She laughed. "Thank you for showing the statues' feet of clay."

"I won't mention the aching heads the next morning."

"Oh, come on. Tell."

He pulled his coffee cup closer and stared into the black liquid as if it was a screen on the past. A small smile quirked the edges of his lips. "After a little too much partying one night, we made a pact that in ten years, we'd build a house on Lake Tahoe. Then we'd live there in successive months, meeting after the last one to celebrate all that we were certain we would have accomplished."

The smile deepened and he looked up to meet her gaze. "I'll say it for you. Arrogant brats."

She put her elbow on the table and rested her chin on her hand. "I don't know. You said that you arrogant brats had done what you set out to do."

"Guess so." He shrugged. "Besides me, there's Nathan Barrister, who continues making money hand-over-fist for his family's hotel chain; Ryan Matheson, who has his own pockets full of cable companies; Devlin Campbell, über-banker; and Jack Howington, our adventurer."

"That's only five," she pointed out.

"You know that Hunter died. Right before graduation." His gaze returned to his coffee. "I still miss him."

Lauren's heart squeezed, but she could still count. "That makes six."

His coffee appeared to fascinate him. "And then there's my brother."

She'd wondered if he'd be able to bring himself to mention his twin. Though she was aware of their estrangement, she didn't know the particulars. It seemed a shame—but then she'd never met Luke Barton. Maybe he really was enemy number one.

"Let's not talk about him," Matthias said.

The sudden strain in his voice and the tension in his expression made Lauren want to, though.

"Let's talk about you instead," he continued.

Lauren started. Uh-oh. Not her. Talk about her could lead to trouble. The kind where she ended up humiliated again.

"I already know about the fiancés in your past. But I don't know much about your work—"

"You know I'm a freelance translator." Okay. Work was a safe topic. She could talk about work. "It pays well, even though my father was sure my dual degrees in French and Spanish would never amount to anything."

"That's why you were in Paris?"

She nodded. "A long-term project. Unfortunately, I had to give up my apartment before I left the States, so now I'm back with Mom and Dad until—"

"The convenient merger of the Bartons and the Conovers," he inserted, a new, hard edge to his voice.

A shiver rippled down Lauren's back, not a sexy shiver, but a what's-going-on-here warning. Her expression must have betrayed her dismay, because he reached over for her hand.

"Sorry," he said, squeezing her fingers. "Don't mind me."

The fact that the marriage would be good for both family businesses had been hammered home to her by her father. Wrapped up in the cotton wool of what she had to acknowledge now was likely a depression, she'd barely felt a prick of worry over it. And she'd assumed Matthias was happy about that part of the deal. He didn't look happy now.

"Look…" she started.

"Shh." He lifted her hand and kissed her knuckles.

There was that other shiver. The one she was now familiar with when she was around him. It tickled up her arm and trailed down her back.

Without breaking her gaze, he ran his thumb across her knuckles. "I'm a bastard."

"I thought something similar myself last night," Lauren heard herself say—then wished it back with all her might. Dang it. Dang it! *Humiliation, here I come.*

Matthias's hand tightened on hers. "I—"

"Don't bother coming up with an excuse," she said hastily. "You were right. That was smart. We barely know each other and the bedroom isn't the best way to rectify that. Cooler heads prevailed. Give the man first prize."

"Lauren…"

She knew her face must be red because she felt heat from her neck on up. And she was babbling like she always did when she was uncomfortable, but it was too late to alter a lifetime's bad habit now. "I should thank you. I do. Thank you. Thank you very much. I appreciate your restraint and your…uh…uh…disinterest."

"Disinterest?" He was staring at her as if she'd grown another head. She wanted to take the single one she did have and bang it against the tabletop.

"Did you say *disinterest*?"

She tried to pull her hand from his. "Maybe. No. Yes. Whatever you think you heard I probably said."

"Hell!" He threw his napkin onto the table. "That's

it. We're done." He stood up, threw some bills on the table, then pulled her from her chair. Her napkin fell to the floor but he didn't give her time to pick it up. Instead, he hustled her out of the restaurant then started walking, dragging her along beside him.

There was a pretty footpath along the lake, but she didn't get much chance to appreciate the view because his long strides made her nearly run to keep up. When they reached a small covered lookout, he yanked her inside and then dropped onto the wooden bench. She was tugged down beside him.

"For the record, I was *not* disinterested last night," he said. "How could you even think that?"

"Uh, guest room? Long T-shirt? The way you practically ran away?"

"I was trying to be a good guy, you know that."

"Bet that's what my three previous fiancés told themselves, too."

He groaned. "Lauren."

Maybe she was being a tad unreasonable. Remember, she'd been grateful this morning that he'd showed restraint last night.

Oh, who was she kidding? She'd been mostly irritated that he'd been all dazzle but no follow-through. And she'd been hurt. And in serious doubt about her particular powers to ever really capture and keep the interest of a man.

"I've been going through a bad stretch, okay?" she said. "And there I was, practically begging, and you backed away. It's…"

Mortifying. And, oh, now even more so, as she felt the sting of tears at the corners of her eyes. She jerked her face away from his and toward the lake. "My, this wind is brisk, isn't it?"

He groaned again. "Lauren. Lauren, please." His fingers grasped her chin and he brought her face back to his. "Damn it. Last night, this morning, right now, I've been frustrated in four thousand different ways. My good intentions are running on empty, Goldilocks, and—oh, forget it."

Then he kissed her again.

Finally.

It tasted wonderful…and perhaps a touch angry.

"It's just so good," she whispered against his mouth.

He buried one hand in her hair as he deepened the kiss. The other hand slipped under his own oversized sweater to mold her breast. Her nipple contracted to a hard, desperate point. His thumb grazed over it.

As payback, Lauren ran her hand up his lean thigh to cup the hard bulge in his jeans. He jerked against her palm and his thumb moved over her nipple again. Harder.

She moaned. *It's just so good.*

So good that bells were ringing.

Matthias yanked his mouth from hers. "Hell." His hand left her, too, as he stood and dug in his front pocket.

The bells were still ringing. No, the *cell phone* was still ringing. Matthias's BlackBerry. He looked at the screen, muttered another curse, then pointed a finger at her. "Stay there," he barked, then ducked out of the little shelter.

Boneless, she fell back against the bench's seat. Now that she'd come clean about her feelings, she wasn't going anywhere. It hadn't been so humiliating after all. It had felt a lot more like heaven.

The call was from Luke's Eagle Wireless office. He ran his hand through his hair, trying to cool himself down before answering. Lauren had walked straight out of his fantasies to wreak havoc on his self-control and it didn't help that the sexual attraction ran so fast and hot both ways. Last night he'd come too close to letting sex take over his common sense.

He needed to get her out of the log house and away from him. She needed to go back to where she belonged. Back to her life.

Back to his brother.

That last thought took a vicious bite of him and he took it out on his assistant as he answered the call. "What do you want?"

"Good morning to you, too, Mary Sunshine."

He ignored her sarcastic rejoinder, then forgot it completely when she told him the reason she'd rung. She wanted to patch a call through from his brother.

"You know I don't talk to him." They hadn't spoken in seven years. Seven, like the Seven Samurai. Something about that stabbed like an ice pick to the chest, but he rubbed the useless feeling away. "Tell him to go to hell."

"He thought you'd say that. He told me to inform you he's in Germany, so you know he's already been there."

Luke almost laughed. Matt hated to travel overseas. Foreign flights, foreign food, foreign beds, they all put his brother off eating and sleeping. So why was his twin in Europe? Luke's mind raced through the possibilities, then locked on one that made the hair on the back of his neck rise. *Germany*. Anger burned like fire up his spine.

"Patch him through, Elaine."

And then there was Matt's voice. Tired, a little hoarse, but so damn familiar. "Yo, brother."

So damn familiar and so damn traitorous.

"Why are you in Germany?" Luke demanded.

"Is that any way to talk to the man who is calling to see how things are going at Hunter's house? I know you did this as a favor and—"

"I didn't do this as a favor to *you,* you bastard, and you know it. I agreed so that your 'last-minute business trip' wouldn't screw up Hunter's last wishes and now it looks as if you're screwing me over."

"I don't know what you're talking about."

"You're in Stuttgart, aren't you?" Stuttgart, the home base of a supplier Luke had been wooing for the last eight months. The deal he'd been nurturing would double his domestic profits. Triple the money he could make in China. He'd heard rumors that Conover Industries had been sniffing around, but Ralph Conover couldn't put together the kind of package that Luke could. Neither could Matt—not unless he got into bed with Conover.

Or Conover's daughter.

Damn them. Damn all of them.

"You're not going to cheat me this time, Matt," he ground out.

"I didn't cheat you *any* time, lunkhead."

Lunkhead. It was the name Matt had coined for him when they were kids. When they'd hated each other as much as they hated each other now. Only in college, those brief years when they'd really felt like brothers, had the nickname been said with affection.

"I don't have anything more to say to you." He flipped off the phone.

Shoving it in his pocket, he stared out at the lake, trying to get himself under control. That thieving bastard had tricked Luke into taking his place at Hunter's house so that he could head off to Germany undeterred and take over the deal that belonged to Eagle Wireless. Maybe Ernst would be loyal to what he'd already started with Luke. Maybe not.

Hell, probably not.

Loyalty wasn't something Luke had much faith in.

What he wouldn't give to screw over his brother as Matt had screwed over him! Just once, just once, Luke would like to take something that was his brother's. Then Matt would see what it was like to feel that sharp stab in the back from the one person who was supposed to be *watching* his back.

Luke turned to head back to his car and his gaze caught on the wooden lookout. Lauren. Hell, he'd nearly forgotten her.

Even as angry as he was, a little grin broke over his face. If he'd left her there she would have his liver for dinner. Sweet Lauren, who had thought he'd left her alone last night because he was disinterested! Sexy Lauren, who could be the model for the co-star in every hot dream he'd ever had.

He jogged over to the shelter and grabbed her hand to pull her up. "Let's go."

"Where?" She smiled.

Lauren smiled. Lauren who was engaged to his brother. Lauren who was Ralph Conover's daughter.

An idea, an oh-so-fitting idea, started creeping from a dark corner of his mind. And Luke let it. Then he pulled her against him and dropped a kiss on her bottom lip.

She looked up at him. Sweet. Sexy. Trusting.

"We never cleared up why you showed up at the house last night," Luke said.

Her eyes rounded. Her tongue darted out to wet her lower lip.

"No," she answered slowly.

Thinking back to all the things she'd said and the others she'd hinted at, Luke thought maybe she'd come to break the engagement. And if she *had* decided to give Matt the old heave-ho, then Luke would let her go. But after this month was up, if he still couldn't get her out of his head, he'd contact her and see if she felt the same way. He'd make it clear that Luke Barton was only after fun and games, but if she wanted to play, he was ready for a round or two.

However, if she was actually serious about this business-deal merger-marriage with Matt…

He had to find out for sure.

"So why'd you come, Lauren?"

"Ummm…"

He could hear the wheels turning in her head. "It's a simple question, Goldilocks." His fingers brushed back the hair from her forehead and a flush rose on her cheeks.

"I came to…umm…"

Her hair blew across her eyes and he caught it, then tucked it behind her ear. She shivered at his touch.

"Goldilocks?"

"I came to get to know you better," she blurted out. Her flush deepened. "We *are* barely acquainted and we *are* engaged, after all, and engaged people should know each other, don't you think? Because really…"

She continued chattering away, but he had stopped listening. He already had his answer. She hadn't come here to break it off with Matt.

Meaning Luke had in his hands right now, this minute, something that cheating, thieving Matt Barton wanted.

Oh, it was going to be sweet, sweet revenge when Matt discovered Luke had set out to seduce his brother's bride.

Luke wasn't going to feel bad about it.

Certainly not on Matt's behalf.

And not on Lauren's, either.

Because, after all, it was up to her whether or not he succeeded.

Four

Matthias pulled Lauren in the direction of the restaurant. "Let's go back to the house," he said.

She swallowed and tried hanging back. "Um. Uh. Right now?"

"You said you wanted to get to know me better."

Lauren's pulse quickened. Yes, yes, she'd said that, but there was a new, predatory gleam in her fiancé's eyes and maybe it was time to take a few deep breaths.

Back at the house there would be that decadent, quilt-covered bed, but would there be air?

"I was thinking it might be fun to explore the town," she said, slipping out of Matthias's hold. "You know. Look around." Which would give her time to consider her options and decide whether she should stay or whether she should go.

Matthias slid his hands in his pockets. "I don't know what there is to see," he said, sounding impatient.

"That's the whole point," Lauren replied. "Finding out what there is to see."

He paused a moment, then gave a little shrug followed by a small smile. She got the feeling he'd diagnosed her stall tactic and was indulging it…for the moment.

"Fine," he said, taking off at a pace so fast that his long legs ate up the path that would take them back toward the restaurant and, from there, to the rest of the little town of Hunter's Landing.

Lauren had to jog to catch up with him and her pace was still hurried as they traversed the streets of the small town, passing small shops, businesses and cafés. At the end of what Lauren supposed the residents called "downtown" sat the post office and Matthias paused beside the American flag that was flapping in the brisk breeze.

The wind fluttered his dark hair and tousled it over his forehead. The cool air or the sun or both had washed a tinge of ruddy color over the rise of his cheekbones and reddened his lips. Lauren stared at them, remembering the kisses from last night, how the burr of his evening beard had burned the tender edges of her mouth, rendering each caress hotter than the one before. She pressed the back of her hand over her own lips and shivered at the memory.

His eyes narrowed. "You're cold," he said. "And you've seen the whole of Hunter's Landing. Ready to go back now?"

Ready to go back? She shook her head. Not when

just the thought of kissing him continued to be so distracting. She needed more time.

"We've done the town," Matthias said, frowning. "What more do you want?"

That was easy. She wanted an un-befuddled head, one that wasn't affected by these inexplicable hormone rushes. She cleared her throat. "We haven't done the town, we rushed through it. Haven't you heard of strolling? Of enjoying the fresh air and the beautiful day?"

"To what end?"

She blinked. To what end? Must there always be an end? Obviously, the man needed to learn to relax. But he was already jiggling the change in his pocket, ready for action, so she gazed around her and hit upon inspiration.

"There. Coffee," she said, pointing across and down the street. A small shop called Java & More. "Didn't you say the house needs a fancier blend? I'll bet we can get some freshly ground at that store."

It worked. Sort of. Matthias set off in the direction she'd indicated, but first he slid his arm around her shoulders. And then, when she shivered in reaction, he drew her close against the side of his body.

"I'll keep you warm," he said, hugging her close as they crossed the street.

Too warm. Oh, much too warm.

Her hip bumped against him with each step. His fingers were five hot brands on the curve of her shoulder. He was near enough that she could feel the heat of his breath against her temple and the sensation made her skin jitter in reaction. His hand slid to the nape of her neck and gave a little squeeze. She glanced up.

Their eyes met and there it was again, an almost audible sexual snap, and it had her stumbling on the sidewalk. Matthias's hand tightened once more to keep her upright and she found herself leaning against him, her heart fluttering like that flag across the street, her nipples tightening as if they could feel the cold instead of all this delicious heat. With his free hand, he tilted her chin higher.

Tilting her mouth to his, he brushed his thumb across her bottom lip.

Heat tumbled from that point, rushing like a fall of water over her breasts and toward her womb. Lauren clutched his hard side as support for her rubbery knees.

His thumb feathered over her lip a second time. "Come back to the house," he whispered.

She watched his mouth descend.

"Come back to the house right now." He murmured it against her lips.

His kiss tasted like coffee and maple syrup and seduction.

It was a gentle press of mouth-to-mouth and she softened instantly, without thinking anything beyond how right it felt to be kissing this man. He angled his head to take it deeper and she opened her lips for him, but he did nothing more than breathe inside her mouth.

She wanted the thrust of his tongue!

He wasn't giving it up.

He was waiting for her.

Lauren felt heat again, flushing over all her skin. Matthias was waiting for *her* to make the next move. Waiting for her to make a decision. But before she could, a car honked.

The sudden noise caused her to jerk back. Matthias didn't move, though, instead remaining close and watching her with that same hungry light in his eyes she'd noticed after he'd returned from his phone call. It scared her.

Liar, it called to her.

Here was a man, not a boy-surfer, not a two-timing mechanic, not an intellectual yet indecisive cosmopolitan. Here was a one-hundred-percent red-blooded, single-minded American male animal who knew exactly what he wanted.

Her.

And she *did* want to get to know him better. She wanted to get to know *everything* about him. Her blood felt thick in her veins, and her heart beat harder inside her chest to move it through her body.

"Matthias." Her voice came out so hoarse that she had to clear her throat and start again. "Matthias. I'm ready to go back to the house."

He smiled. The fingers holding her chin slid down to caress the soft skin beneath and then to stroke along her neck. His thumb found the notch of her collarbone and rested there a moment. "A kabillion one hundred," he said.

The value of their bottled sexual chemistry had just gone up.

Taking her hand in his, Matthias turned them both back in the direction of the car and took off again at his brisk pace.

"We can still make a quick stop for the coffee," she said as they passed the shop.

He paused, and just then another couple exited the

door of Java & More. They weren't looking at them, they weren't looking at anything but each other, yet something about the two galvanized Matthias. Murmuring an indecipherable phrase beneath his breath, he quickly pushed her forward and then through the door of the neighboring business.

Lauren looked around the dim confines and found herself in teen paradise—a place stuffed with video-game and pinball machines, Skee-Ball ramps, an air-hockey table and a counter with a bored guy presumably able to provide change if only he'd look up from his magazine. Matthias shot a look out the streaky front window and guided Lauren farther inside.

"No pool table?" he murmured. "Hell, fine then." His fingers on the small of her back proceeded her toward an air-hockey table. He fished in his pocket for those coins that had been jangling earlier.

"You play?" he said, glancing out the front window once more. "Let's play. First to seven points wins."

Since her little sister Kaitlyn had walked all over her at a similar table not long before, Lauren released a sigh, but didn't try to talk him out of it. She might be an altar reject, but she wasn't completely clueless. For some reason Matthias wanted to avoid that other couple. They'd looked harmless enough to her—a man about Matthias's age and a woman about her own, in love, but she didn't have more time to ponder the situation because already Matthias was flinging that air-hockey puck in her direction.

Her hand grabbed her mallet to make an instinctive defensive move.

And her instincts—as was obvious by the three

previous broken engagements—weren't worth an anthill of beans. She lost the first game seven-zip. And the game after that. And the game after that.

A crowd of teens gathered around the table. She couldn't understand exactly why until Matthias barked something to one of them and she realized they were checking out her backside. Apparently the place—not to mention the young men—was sorely lacking from a dearth of the female gender. It did smell like a gym after an afternoon of six-man dodgeball. On a rainy day.

Following her three losses she conceded defeat, hoping they could go on their way, but when she stepped back from the table, a stringy-bodied, stringy-haired teenager stepped up in her place and slammed his quarters on the edge of the table. Lauren gathered it was some sort of challenge and, like a scene out of an old Western, Matthias's eyes took on a new gleam and he slammed his quarters down in return.

The competition was on.

And on.

Without a word being spoken about it, as Matthias defeated each challenger, another came to stand in his place. He met each one with the same ruthless intensity as the contender before: his sleeves pushed up to his elbows, his face a mask of concentration, his stance wide and aggressive. At first Lauren was amused and then a bit admiring—the muscles of his forearm flexed in a purely masculine manner—and then…and then she was alarmed by the obvious ferocity of his desire to win.

After a while it was clear he wasn't aware that she was there or aware of where he was or aware of anything but slamming that puck into the goal, over and over and over.

"Matthias…" she ventured.

He didn't flick her a glance as another player stepped in to replace the one he'd defeated.

"Matthias."

No response.

"Matthias!"

He started, then his head swiveled toward her. She saw him blink as if coming out of a fog.

"Assume success, deny failure?" she asked.

He frowned. "What?"

"Is that what this is all about? Victory at all costs, no matter what?" She tried to make light of it, but the way he looked when he played wasn't funny. The way he was looking at her now wasn't funny either.

"What's wrong with wanting to win?" His voice was puzzled. "What's wrong with hating to fail?"

Nothing, unless that was *all* you'd been taught. If you'd never learned that it was okay to fall down sometimes and how to pick yourself up if you did. Lauren thought of her three unsuccessful attempts at marriage.

Losing was something she wished she didn't know so much about.

She cleared her throat and changed the subject. "I thought we were going back to the house."

"There's a competitor…" His voice trailed off as he looked across the table at the scruffy boy who was no more than four feet tall. "It's a kid."

"Matthias, they've all been kids."

He looked around at the faces ringing the table. Then with a half-smile that was more a grimace, he stepped back from the table. "Um, all done for today. Thanks for the games."

He took Lauren's arm and started for the front door. "Okay. I admit it. I got a bit carried away."

Outside the place—named The Game Palace, she now saw—they both paused, adjusting to the bright sunshine. "I thought you'd forgotten all about me," Lauren said, her tone light. "I guess I'll need to take air-hockey lessons to keep some of your attention."

She was teasing, of course, but when he turned to face her, she could see that he was serious again. "Sweetheart, after last night, I know you don't need lessons in the kind of thing that will keep *all* of my attention."

The flush moved up her body this time, a warm wash that surely covered her face to the roots of her hair. "Matthias…"

"Lauren…" His voice echoed hers as he drew a fingertip from her earlobe to the corner of her mouth. "Let's go back now. Let's take the time to learn everything we can about each other."

"Does that mean you're going to tell me all your secrets?"

His finger paused in its wandering. "That might take a while."

She had a while. She had a lifetime, if he was the right man. And suddenly she realized that she was stronger than she'd first thought. Yes, he was sexy, charming and vulnerable in a way that tugged at her from many different directions, but she wasn't going to let those qualities tumble her immediately into his bed.

"Let's go back to the house," she said. "But once we're there, we need to discuss some rules."

"I don't like rules," Matthias cautioned, slanting her a glance from his corner of the living-room couch.

Lauren grimaced. After their return from Hunter's Landing, she'd managed to keep her fiancé distracted for a while by exploring the grounds and then the interior of the luxurious log-and-stone house. It had been built under the auspices of the Hunter Palmer Foundation and, once all of the Seven Samurai had completed their month-long stays, the place would be turned into an R&R retreat for recovering cancer patients—something Hunter himself had understood the need for, presumably, as he'd died of melanoma.

While a couple of the bedroom suites were decorated, as well as most of the living spaces, it was obvious that there was some decorating yet to be done. Still, the whole setup was incredible and it didn't surprise her that her business-oriented fiancé had been drawn to the state-of-the-art office that occupied the loft on the third floor. When she'd made noises about wanting to relax and read for a bit, he'd immediately headed up the stairs with his laptop and didn't come down until the hands of the grandfather clock in the foyer announced it was five o'clock.

After a brief stop in the kitchen, he'd found her in the great room. He'd handed over one of the glasses of wine he was carrying before taking his seat, from which he made that *un*surprising announcement: *I don't like rules*.

Lauren inspected herself for any imaginary lint as

she debated how to answer. While he was mired in work, she'd finally recollected and then retrieved from her car the small weekender bag she'd packed in anticipation of visiting her former college roommate in San Francisco. Now she wore a fresh pair of jeans and a cream-colored cashmere sweater she'd bought in Paris.

"My little sister Kaitlyn has rules that govern just about everything."

"You have a sister?"

Lauren looked up at him in surprise. "You've met her a couple of times, remember? Thirteen? Braces?"

"Of course." Matthias's gaze shifted from her face to the window. "I wasn't thinking…"

Lauren took a breath. "That's where I want to do things differently, Matthias. I want to think before I leap."

"You're doubting that the fourth time's a charm?"

Her face heated at his reference to her three botched engagements. "I'm talking about this…this attraction between us. I'm doubting whether it's smart to act on it and tumble into a sexual relationship so quickly. Aren't you willing to applaud my caution? After all, it's your marriage, too."

Matthias's gaze shifted away again. "Tell me about Kaitlyn and her rules."

Lauren smiled. "Besides the old standbys about avoiding sidewalk cracks and lines, these days she approaches her mirror backward, only whirling around when she's ready to see herself. According to Kaitlyn, true beauty only comes upon you by surprise, so…" Her hands rose.

"If she looks anything like her sister, the question of beauty isn't any question at all."

"Thank you." The compliment pleased her more than she wanted it to. "You've seen Kaitlyn for yourself. No matter how pretty we tell her she is, she's at that hyper-self-critical age. You remember thirteen, right?"

"Yeah." He took a swallow from his glass. "Come to think of it, when my brother and I hit thirteen our father laid a whole list of rules on us."

This was the kind of thing she wanted to know! That his kiss was divine, that he smelled like heaven, that his hands on her was something she desired more with each passing minute—that kind of knowledge was pleasing, but it certainly didn't promise a happy marriage.

She circled her forefinger along the rim of her glass. "What sort of rules?"

"We had chores, everything from the upkeep of our rooms to taking care of our bikes, then later our cars. At our weekly 'academic accounting' meeting with dear-old-Dad, the twin with the highest GPA was declared that week's winner. The loser had to take care of all the combined chores by himself, with the winner supervising. Then Dad supervised *him,* so that if he didn't come down hard enough on the working twin, he was punished."

Lauren stared. Matthias had said his spiel without emotion, but she could barely hold hers back. It formed a lump of appalled sympathy in her throat that was thick enough to bring tears to her eyes. "I—I don't know what to say," she finally managed to choke out.

"We were forced into competition over sports, too. At our weekly meetings he would tally up who had scored the most points in soccer, basketball, lacrosse, whatever the particular sport of the season was. Whichever one of us had done the most for the team that week got a free pass."

She swallowed, hard. "From?"

"A three-page, single-spaced book report. The loser had to read from a selection of nonfiction titles— Machiavelli's *The Prince*, *The Art of War* by Sun-Tzu, current books penned by the superachieving CEOs of the day—and then sum it up in three pages that would pass the muster of our Donald Trump of a dad. After, of course, being graded on the essay by the higher-scoring twin."

Lauren could only state the obvious. "I suppose that didn't foster much brotherly love."

His response was flat. Cool. "After our mother died, the Barton house was devoid of love."

Okay. Wow. There was the getting-to-know-you-better chat and then there was the really getting-to-know-you-better chat. What her fiancé had just told her went a long way to explaining not only his workaholic ways, but his strained relationship with his twin. They'd been raised as warriors in opposing armies instead of brothers who could rely on each other for support.

When was the last time the man sitting two feet away had felt as if someone was on his side?

Without thinking, she scooted along the couch so that she could touch him. She couldn't help herself from wanting to make contact with him, skin to skin. Her hand found his strong forearm and she laid her fingers on it and stroked down toward his wrist, trying to tell him through touch what she wasn't sure she could—or should—say.

I'm here for you. We can be allies, not enemies.

Matthias looked down to her caressing fingers, then back up to her face. "Not that I'm complaining, mind you, but are you by any chance breaking one of your rules already, Lauren?"

She froze, then backed away from him. She was already breaking her rules! She was! How could she have forgotten so quickly how she wanted to limit their physical contact?

Matthias gave her a wry smile, as if he could read her mind. "Don't worry, sweetheart. As to where we're taking the attraction…well, that's all in your hands now, Lauren. As a matter of fact, 'hands' is the operative word here. I promise I won't lay one of mine on you unless you ask."

Oh, terrific, she thought, looking at the beautiful man who had just bared a part of himself to her. He wasn't going to lay one of his hands on her unless she asked.

Just what she was afraid of.

Five

An hour later, Luke still didn't know what had possessed him to spill about what had passed for "childhood" in the cutthroat Barton household. Uncomfortable with his own revelations, he'd jumped up from the couch as soon as he could and strode toward the kitchen.

"There's plenty of food in the freezer and fridge for dinner options," he'd called to Lauren, who'd stayed behind on the great room's couch. "I'll let you know when it's ready."

When he was ready to face her again.

Maybe she'd figured that out herself, because she left him alone to microwave another gourmet meal from Clearwater's, only venturing as far as the dining area to set their places. Smart girl, he thought, as he exited the kitchen with a plate in each hand. She'd put them at the two heads of the long table, leaving a safe distance between them.

He needed that space so that he could keep his mind on what he was doing here with her. He hadn't wanted to jeopardize it when they'd nearly bumped into Nathan and his mayor on the street that morning—he'd had to call his old friend with excuses that afternoon. He didn't want to jeopardize it now.

Their time together wasn't about Luke discussing his ruthless father's way of raising children. It wasn't about exploring the chemistry that she was so intent on making rules about. No, he'd encouraged her to stick around because this was about Matt. It was about how Luke could use this chance encounter with Lauren to get retribution for what Matt had done to him seven years before and for what he seemed to be preparing to do now.

As they finished the last bites of their meal, Luke looked down the length of the dining room table to study his dinner companion. What did Lauren know about what her father and Matt were planning? And what would it take for him to get it out of her?

"So," he said, pushing his plate away from the edge of the table. "How about a soak in the hot tub on the deck?"

Her gaze flew to his. "Um…"

"Warm water. Relaxing bubbles." The perfect location for him to worm from her the combined Conover-Barton intentions.

"I don't…a hot tub…"

From the alarmed expression on her face, he might

as well have suggested doing something X-rated in the middle of Main Street.

He shook his head, smiling a little. "I told you, everything—or anything—physical between us is up to you, Lauren. You can trust me."

"Well—"

"Or at least you can take this opportunity to find out exactly how trustworthy I am."

A smile twitched the corners of her lips. "Not a bad idea, but I didn't bring a bathing suit with me."

He shrugged. "Me neither. We'll skinny dip."

"I'm—"

"Chicken? There isn't any reason to be, you know. I won't turn the deck or hot tub lights on. We can slip outside in towels and slip into the water when the other person's eyes are closed."

"But—"

"You were all set to marry a Frenchman on the top of the Eiffel Tower but now you won't get into a Tahoe hot tub with your fiancé? Where's your sense of adventure, Lauren?"

She scowled at him, and for some reason it made him laugh. "You make it hard for a woman to say no," she complained.

He laughed again. "I take it that's a yes?"

And it was, though half an hour later he doubted his powers of persuasion. Not that she didn't scurry out to the deck wrapped in nothing more than a striped beach towel, but he was doubting the wisdom of what he'd persuaded her into in the first place. As promised, he'd left off the lights but, even with forested darkness surrounding the house, thanks to the moon her bare shoulders gleamed like the surface of a pearl and her blond hair stood out—a pale flame in the night.

He remembered her body beneath the robe, how it was as if it had been constructed to his exact specifications. Curvy breasts, curvy behind—dangerous, dangerous curves.

"Close your eyes," she ordered, approaching the side of the redwood tub.

It didn't matter that he was obedient. Even with his eyes screwed shut, he could imagine everything as he heard the soft plop of her towel dropping to the deck. She'd be naked now. And then he heard the quiet swish of the water and felt the way it lapped higher on his chest as she lowered herself inside the hot tub—calves, knees, thighs, hips, rosy nipples now disappearing from his fantasy view.

His body responded accordingly, part of him rising up as he imagined her dropping down into the wet, silky heat. Even though he knew the night would cover his reaction, he edged away from her on the hot-tub bench.

She exhaled a relaxed little sigh. "You can open your eyes now."

Maybe he shouldn't. Maybe he should keep them closed so he could concentrate on the information he hoped to get from her. *Don't think about her body!* he reminded himself. *Don't think about her wet, naked, curvy body!*

Think instead of saving Eagle Wireless.

And of retribution.

He cleared his throat and slipped a little deeper into the water as if he were unwinding, too. "So," he said, pretending the question was just an idle musing, "how involved are you in your father's company?"

"You mean Conover Industries?"

"Does he have more than one?"

"No." She released a wry laugh. "He needs to have a single company, I guess, if he's going to be as single-minded as he is about business."

"Mmm." Luke tried again for that idle-musing tone. "Does he talk about work at home? You know, about how the company's doing, possible new ventures, that sort of thing?"

"I don't listen when he does."

What? "Not ever?"

"If you think listening to my father drone on to the point of talking over everyone else—including his teenage daughter who wants to share about the new play she's in, or her new teacher, or her new passion for Web site design—is suitable or enjoyable, then you need to eat more meals with the Conover family."

"Ah… Well…"

"You see, in my opinion, the dinner conversation *chez* Conover is pretty much as appropriate as talking about my father and his company on a beautiful spring night in a heated hot tub instead of simply being quiet and appreciating the incredible stars overhead and the inky shadows of the trees around us."

Luke blinked.

If he wasn't wrong, she'd just told him to shut up.

To shut up and relax.

Then he remembered her remark during their exploration of Hunter's Landing that morning. *Haven't you heard of strolling?*

Apparently he was supposed to be "strolling" through this evening as well. Fine. Willing his legs not to fidget, he shook out his arms and raised his gaze. Okay. There were those stars she'd mentioned. That moon.

What the hell is my brother doing right now?

The question popped into his head and he saw spreadsheets instead of sky. He breathed in fire instead of fresh air.

Despite the heat of the water, his muscles went rigid. *If Matt ruins my Germany deal, I'm ruined.*

Luke jumped to his feet. Lauren let out a little shriek. Startled, he fell back to the bench. "God," he said. "You just scared the life out of me. What is it?"

"You. *You* scared *me*."

"Huh?"

She made a vague gesture in his direction. "All of a sudden you stood up and you were, um, wet."

Wet and naked. Hell, he hadn't been thinking about his state of undress. He'd been thinking about his damn twin and then he'd been on his way to his cell phone and a plane ticket to Germany where he would wring Matt's neck.

But he couldn't do that. For the rest of the month, Luke couldn't leave this house, not when it was Hunter's last request.

Swallowing his frustrated groan, he tipped the back of his head against the rim of the tub and tried uncoiling the tension in his neck, his spine, the back of his legs. *Take it easy, Luke. Relax.*

"Are you all right?" Lauren asked.

"No." He grimaced at the clipped sound of his voice.

"Look, I know I invited you out here, but the truth is, I'm not so good at this relaxing stuff. I don't nap, I don't meditate. As far as I know, I don't even take deep breaths."

She laughed. "Is there anything I can do?"

He rolled his head toward her. The starlight caught in her eyes and they gleamed. *So pretty.* "Talk to me, Lauren. Otherwise, I think the silence might make me nuts."

"You just need to get used to it."

This time he didn't hold back his groan.

She laughed again. "All right, all right. What should I talk about? My father, or—"

"Kaitlyn," he said, surprising himself. "Tell me about your sister."

"Ah. Kaitlyn." Lauren wiggled on the bench, sliding a bit lower into the tub. She must have stretched out her legs, because the water feathered against his foot, letting him know she was only a toe or two away. "My infuriating, adorable and genius-IQ baby sister."

"Genius IQ?"

"Mensa genius IQ and then some." Lauren shifted again and this time he felt the brush of the bottom of her foot against the top of his.

He pretended not to notice.

"Kaitlyn terrifies my mother and father."

"But not you?"

"Oh, me, too, but when she points out their foibles and flaws, my parents can manage only to sputter and spit."

As he slid his heel along the slick bottom of the tub, his toes found the little bump of her ankle bone. He gave it a small nudge. "And what does Lauren do?"

"I humbly acknowledge she's right and promise to do better next time."

She went silent, so Luke nudged her again. "Don't leave me in suspense. What's her latest critique of your character?"

"Let's just say she's not fond of junior bridesmaid dresses."

Little sister Kaitlyn thought Lauren's marriage to him was a bad idea.

No. Her marriage to *Matt.*

The reminder annoyed him. "Maybe if the Conovers and the Bartons merge, I'll have to be listening to Kaitlyn myself. Does she have ambitions regarding your father's company?"

"She has ambitions to take over the world. Global peace for the masses and Justin Timberlake for all teenage girls." Her leg moved again and a silky swipe of calf met his own hair-roughened one. "But seriously, I can see her being the CEO of Conover in the not-so-distant future."

He stretched a little more in order to hook his foot around her delicate ankle. They were twined together, now, but it didn't appear to bother her. "What about you?"

"What about me what?"

Did she sound a little breathless? "Do you have any interest in getting involved in the family business?"

Her laugh was short. "You're kidding, right? My father wouldn't find use in Conover Industries for my skills in French and Spanish."

But what about German? Could she speak that, too? Luke remembered he was supposed to be digging for anything he could find about his brother's business instead of finding her sleek leg in the warm wetness. "Lauren—"

"You can't be surprised. I'm sure my father made it clear. The first and only time he's ever approved of me or anything I've done was when I agreed to marry Matthias Barton."

Lauren wished she'd never mentioned the word *marry*. It had sent Matthias catapulting from the hot tub with only a curt "Close your eyes" warning. While wrapping a towel around his hips—of course she'd watched through her eyelashes!—he'd mumbled something about bringing them back some wine before disappearing into the house.

She'd spooked him with the wedding talk, which was weird, because she'd come to the Hunter's Landing house spooked by the idea herself. Yet now…now the idea of being with him gave her an odd feeling of rightness. Odd, because she'd never sensed it on those other occasions when she'd been with him. But the feeling itself was familiar.

The day she'd met her freshman roommate in college, she'd known they were going to be friends for life.

Her senior year, within an hour of interning at the publishing company she still translated for, she'd understood at some cellular level that she'd found her place.

Did it work like that with the man one married?

And if it did—then why hadn't she known when she'd danced with Matthias at the Jewel Ball or when she'd passed him the basket of dinner rolls at her family's table?

Maybe it was her glimpses of all his wet muscles

that had turned the tide. Face it, both sides of his body were spectacular. He might be a workaholic, but some of those long hours must be spent working out. While the wide set of his shoulders might be genetic, it took effort to create the sleek round of muscles supporting them. And then there were his pecs—she'd never considered herself a connoisseur of a particular male body part, but she might have to change her own opinion of herself. Could be she was a chest girl after all.

Yes. After looking at those defined, yet not overdone plates of pectoral muscle gleaming with water in the moonlight, she'd definitely discovered their allure.

And she'd peeked at his butt as he was wrapping that towel around his hips. *Bad Lauren!* But she'd merely been checking out his shoulders from behind and then her gaze had coasted down all that wet skin toward his waist and from there it was just a little *whee!* of a slide to his cute, contoured backside.

So maybe that was it. Maybe her marriage *no* had been transformed into a marriage *maybe* by something as shallow as the way her fiancé looked wearing nothing but H_2O.

Except that didn't explain why she'd felt so drawn to him last night. How much she'd enjoyed breakfast and their walk that morning, even counting the way he'd exposed his hypercompetitive streak at The Game Palace. He'd laughed at himself about it and that kind of humorous self-deprecation held as much charm for her as his smile, as his interest in Kaitlyn, as his understanding that she didn't want to fall right into his bed without getting to know him better, engagement or no.

No engagement. That's what she'd wanted, but now

she didn't want to make *that* mistake either. Now she wanted to be with him.

And so where was he? Surely a simple bottle of wine wouldn't take this long?

A niggle of unease tickling her spine, she scrambled out of the hot tub and swiped up her towel. When he still didn't appear, she took herself and her terry cloth-wrapped body through the French doors. "Matthias?" she called out. "Everything okay?"

Their stemmed glasses were on the countertop in the kitchen along with a bottle opener. But no wine and no man. Recalling the location of the wine cellar from her earlier tour, Lauren headed in that direction.

Her bare feet were silent on the carpeted steps that descended to the lower level. A right turn took her into the small room lined with shelves stocked with bottles. A small table stood in the middle of the room and what looked like a merlot rested on one corner. It was clear that Matthias had forgotten all about it, his attention now focused on dozens of photographs fanned across the wooden surface.

She thought of the framed photos in the hallway upstairs. She hadn't done much more than glance at them enough to gather they were various shots of scruffy young men whom she presumed were the Samurai. She suspected these were more of the same.

Gripping the doorjamb, Lauren called softly in order not to startle him. "Matthias?"

Her fiancé didn't turn around. "He's right here," he said, tapping a photo.

"Hmm?" She ventured farther into the room. "That's a picture of you, you mean?"

He froze, then whirled around, his hands going wide as if he was trying to hide what he'd been inspecting. "Oh. Sorry. I left you out there, didn't I?"

Curious, of course, she drew closer to the table. "That's all right. What're you looking at?"

For a second he didn't move and she wondered why he was so protective of what lay on the table.

"What?" she said, trying to peer around him. "I didn't uncover you admiring your stash of secret blackmail material, did I?"

A ghost of a smile broke over his face. "Close. More college photos of the Seven Samurai. I stubbed my toe on the box."

It was beneath the table now, the white cardboard neatly labeled "Hunter-Samurai." She shifted her gaze to the top of the table. "May I look?"

She had the distinct feeling he wanted to refuse, but then he sidestepped to give her access.

"I'm not going to be shocked, am I?" she asked as she moved in.

He shrugged. "You tell me."

Even with his earlier admission about not doing well with relaxing, there was no missing the new, tighter tension in his body, just as there was no missing the lack of reason for it—at least from her first, cursory inspection of the photos. "Hmm," she said, peeping at Matthias through the corner of her lashes. "If I had to guess I would say you seven majored in beer, basketball and busty co-eds."

Truly, though, there was nothing she could see that would put him on edge. There were plenty of grins, some boozy, on the faces of young-faced college boys who posed with their buddies and some long-legged girls—was every female long-legged at the age of twenty?—in various combinations.

Matthias was in many of them, most often with a sandy-haired, good-looking boy with a buzz cut and a laugh in his eyes. His charisma came through paper, space and time. Lauren lifted a close-up of the smiling face. "Let me guess. Hunter?"

"Yeah." A corner of his mouth hitching up, Matthias took the photo from her hand. He ran his thumb along the edge. "Hunter. He could make an all-night study session an adventure. He'd set an alarm for every hour and when it went off he'd announce some crazy item we'd have to scavenge for in ten minutes or less. The quick break combined with the adrenaline rush would hone our focus for the next fifty minutes of studying."

The easy way he talked about the other young man told Lauren it wasn't memories of Hunter that had agitated him. She looked back at the photos, pushing some aside with her finger to reveal another, larger one, beneath.

And then it struck her, something she hadn't thought through during her cursory view of the photos upstairs. On the table were plenty of shots of a younger Matthias but, looking at this particular picture, she realized they might not all have really been of him. Because this photo showed two faces mugging for the camera. *Two identical faces.*

Of course he had a twin, Luke. But until this moment she hadn't thought to determine how closely they resembled each other. And now she knew. Picking up the photo to hold it closer, she confirmed her first thought. They looked exactly alike.

And in this picture, at least, they looked pleased to be in each other's company. From the corner of her eye, she noted Matthias was studying her face instead of the photo she held. She turned it his way. "Which one is you?"

He shrugged without looking at it. "Doesn't matter."

She shrugged, too. "I guess not. You both look equally…"

"Drunk?"

Her gaze shifted back. "I don't think so. There's a basketball in your hands and it appears you've just finished a hard game."

He nodded. "Hunter likely took that one then. We were a team in a huge three-man basketball tournament. We came out on top."

"You and your brother were a team?"

"With Hunter."

She pressed. "You and your brother were on the same side?"

"We seemed to be in college."

For those years, they'd somehow left behind that sick competition their father had fostered during their childhood. Had it been Hunter's influence, or just a natural brotherly love allowed to find the sunshine away from their father's presence?

"What happened after college?"

"You don't want to know about all that."

Like heck she didn't, particularly because her sudden shiver underscored the new cool tone in his voice. This was exactly the kind of thing she wanted to know all about.

"You're chilled," he said. "Let's go back to the hot tub."

She was chilled *and* naked. He was still just in a towel, too, and there was quite a bit of male muscle to admire. But it didn't stir her even one iota at the moment, not when the sort of nakedness she was interested in right now was the emotional kind—the kind a man shared with the woman who had promised to become his wife.

"What happened between you and your brother, Matthias?"

"Matthias," he muttered under his breath. "Damn. Matthias and Luke. Luke and Matthias. It might as well be Cain and Abel."

"Matthias—"

"Forget it, okay?"

"No. I—"

"I said, leave it alone." He strode toward the doorway. In a moment he would be gone.

The moment would be gone.

"Wait, wait. Just answer me this."

He paused in the doorway, his back still to her. "What?"

"Why? Why do you hate your brother?"

He didn't turn around to face her. But she didn't need to see his expression because she could hear the frigid anger in his voice. "It's because, God help me, he so often has what I want. Now leave it alone."

With that, he left *her* alone in the wine cellar. Alone and with one sure thought. She'd wanted to get to know him better and now she did. Now she knew that talk of his twin was off-limits.

With a sigh, Lauren left the wine and the photographs scattered on the table. Unfortunately, she suspected it was his relationship with his brother that her man needed to open up about most.

At 2:45 a.m., Lauren gave up on sleep. Her light-weight cotton-knit travel robe lay across the end of the bed and she slipped it over the matching nightgown and barefooted it downstairs. The house was silent and dark, but her fingers managed to find the kitchen light switch to flip it on.

"Huh!" A startled male grunt and a liquidy thud told her she wasn't alone. It took her a moment to blink past the fluorescent dazzle of the overhead fixture, but then she saw that Matthias stood at the sink, an empty glass in one hand. A half-gallon carton of milk had landed in the sink, but enough of it had geysered from the open top upon being dropped that there was a big puddle on floor at his feet.

"I'm sorry!" Lauren hurried forward. "Don't move or you'll track the milk all over the place."

With a wad of paper towels in hand, she knelt to soak up the liquid on the floor. "You didn't hurt yourself, did you?" she asked.

"I'll survive a milk bath," Matthias grumbled. "You surprised me, that's all."

"I'm sorry about that, too." She rose with the dripping paper towels and dropped them in the sink. "I couldn't sleep."

"Me neither."

What was the cause of *his* insomnia? "I'm sorry—"

"That's not your fault either," he answered, wiping off the sides of the carton with a wet sponge.

Reaching around him, Lauren wet clean towels then kneeled again to wipe the floor. As much as she regretted being the cause of the mess, she was glad for the opportunity to talk to him again after what had happened earlier. She didn't want the awkwardness of it lingering between them.

A swipe of dry cloths later, the floor was once again pristine. The used towels went in the garbage. "You're free to move now," she said to his back.

He turned to face her.

"Oh." She tore another towel off the roll. "Not quite done after all." Her arm reached out to wipe away the drops of milk that were sprinkled over his chest.

His bare chest. Revealed in all its lovely male perfection thanks to the low-slung pair of pajama pants he was wearing as his only sleep attire. The pants were really cute—a soft olive cotton with all-business pinstripes. All-business pinstripes that didn't appear the least bit Brooks Brothers when they were slung so low they were doing that whole mouth-drying, hormone-heating, hanging-by-the-hipbones thing.

Lauren realized she was standing there, staring.

And that he was staring at her staring.

And that the temperature in the room had turned so warm that the milk on his miles of bare chest had to be in danger of evaporating into latte steam. Clearing her throat, she reached farther to dab at his chest with the paper towel. At the touch, goose bumps broke out across his collarbone and she saw the centers of his copper-colored nipples tighten into hard points.

She swallowed her squeaky moan and tried breaking the sudden sexual tension with her usual MO—babbling.

"I really am sorry about surprising you in here, Matthias," she said, as she continued stroking spots on his skin. "And that you're having trouble sleeping. And then there's the milk that went on the floor, not to mention all over these gorgeous muscles on your hunky chest…"

Her voice petered out as the sound of her own words reached her brain. Her hand froze and her gaze dropped to their bare feet. "Oh, tell me I didn't just say out loud what I think I said out loud."

She felt his laugh through her fingers. "Lauren, Lauren, Lauren." His hand came up to cover hers and then he guided it lower so the towel bumped over the sculpted muscles of his abdomen.

Her fingers opened. The paper wad dropped to the floor. The tips of her fingers absorbed the heat of his skin and he drew them lower, lower. Now she felt the soft fur of the hair below his navel. Now her fingers grazed the waistband of his PJs.

His free hand at her chin, now he tipped up her mouth and looked into her eyes. More heat. And need.

And then that undeniable, oh-so-puzzling but oh-so-welcome feeling of rightness.

"Lauren," he said again, his thumb brushing over her bottom lip. "Didn't anyone ever tell you not to cry over spilled milk?"

Six

Didn't anyone ever tell you not to cry over spilled milk?

The words echoed in Lauren's mind as she looked up into her fiancé's face. Did that mean she shouldn't cry over broken rules, either?

In particular, the one regarding not falling into bed with Matthias until she got to know him better?

Spilled milk. Broken rules. The parallel between the two didn't make real sense, she could admit that, but nothing was making sense lately. Not the strength of this attraction she had to him and not the way it had suddenly come upon her the moment he'd opened the door to her on that rainy night.

"Oh, boy," she whispered, knowing she was in trouble. Her fingers curled, her nails scratching at his bare belly skin. She felt his muscles flinch and his cheeks hollowed as he sucked in a sudden breath. "Oh, boy."

"Oh, man," he corrected, with a faint smile. The hand he'd cupped over hers guided her palm a tad lower until she wrapped his rigid flesh. It twitched at her touch. "Oh, *man*."

Her mouth curved as his lips lowered. She couldn't help but smile into his kiss.

But it turned serious the instant her mouth parted and the tips of their tongues met. Heat rushed across the surface of her skin and she went on tiptoe to press harder against him. His wide hands splayed against her back and drew her nearer.

Her head fell back as she surrendered to his deepening kiss. His tongue plunged inside her mouth and she echoed the motion by sliding her hand down his shaft. His whole body stiffened in reaction and, after a pause, he withdrew his tongue in a slow, deliberate movement.

She mimicked the action by gliding her hand high again. He thrust inside her mouth, she stroked down. He groaned and, loving the sound, Lauren palmed his erection in a seductive caress.

On another sound of need, he tore his mouth from hers. "Witch," he whispered, his eyes glittering. "Beautiful witch."

Hauling in much-needed air, Lauren wondered if the oxygen would bring back her common sense—or at least her sense of caution. But both seemed to have fled for good—or at least for the night. She wanted this man. She wanted, wanted, wanted him.

His head bent again to kiss her cheek, the side of her neck, and then he tongued the whorls of her ear, making her shiver. "Beautiful witch, are you going to let me have you?"

More shivers trickled down her neck. Have her? Would she let herself be had?

She'd wanted to know him better before acting on her desire and the truth was, she did understand him more. Though she didn't know how deep they went, she was at least aware of some of his wounds. And then there was the fact that she was hurt, too. Three times she'd been rejected as she stood on the curb of lifelong commitment and she knew those rejections had affected her confidence in herself, in her femininity and her own appeal as a sexual being.

By giving in to this man who made her heart beat so fast and her blood run so hot, to this man whose own desire for her she was holding in the palm of her hand, wouldn't she be getting so much else back?

And it still felt so right.

If nothing else, Lauren decided, she could regard going to bed with Matthias as a test. Perhaps the "rightness" was just a trick of the mind to pretty up something as simple as lust. And when the lust was sated, then the "rightness" would disappear and she'd no longer be fooling herself about it being something so much more… Something maybe even worth marrying for.

He caught the lobe of her ear between his teeth. Her fingers flexed on his shaft. They both groaned.

His mouth found hers again. He parted her lips and plunged inside and she twined his tongue with hers and crowded against his body, rubbing his erection, rubbing her aching nipples against the hot, naked flesh of his chest.

One of his hands slid from her back to cover her breast. He squeezed and the pressure felt so sweet— oh, fine, *so right*—that she had to bury her face against his neck and ride out the tremors of reaction. Kissing her temple, her cheek, any place he could reach, he continued molding the soft flesh in his palm and used his other hand to pull away the fingers she had around his own straining flesh.

"Can't take it right now, honey," he said, placing her palm on the bare skin of his torso. "It's too early for the fireworks."

She lifted her face and linked her hands around his neck to draw down his mouth. "I'm seeing sparklers everywhere."

They shot into wild arcs of heat and light as they kissed again, a wet, deep kiss that was a whole Fourth of July show unto itself. She lost herself in it, lost herself in his taste and his strength, until his thumb grazed her nipple.

Then flames shot up around her. Her body jerked in his arms and he slid his other hand to the curve of her bottom while his fingers found that tight bud and made maddening circles around it. She jerked again, her hips butting up against his erection, tilting to make a place for it as desire caused a liquid rush between her thighs in preparation for him.

He pushed back, nudging against the notch of her body with the head of his penis. With only thin layers of cotton between them, he was able to insinuate himself between the petals of her sex, the tip of him discovering her sensitive kernel of nerves. She cried out, unable to hold back the sound, and he responded by rubbing there again.

"You like that, sweetheart?" he murmured, looking down into her eyes.

She could hardly breathe and her nerves were humming like a tuning fork. "I—I like you."

He smiled and then the hand on her bottom started drawing up the material of her robe and nightgown together. Cool air washed over the back of her knees and then the back of her thighs and she shivered again, overloaded with sensation. When he had the hem of her clothing in his fingers, he drew up his hand and held his fist at the small of her back.

That cool air now found her naked bottom.

Wet heat rushed between her legs again.

Then in a quick movement he dropped the robe and nightgown—his hand now beneath them. His big male palm now covering her round, bare bottom cheek. Goose bumps prickled over her skin.

"You ready for me, sweetheart?" he whispered.

Ready? How could that be a question? She drew his head down for another kiss. His hand reached between her legs and just as his tongue plunged into her mouth, a long finger slid into her body.

Lauren gasped, then softened against him, opening to his intrusion by hooking her ankle around the back of his calf.

"You *are* ready for me," he murmured against her mouth and there was no way to deny it, no reason to deny it, when he was stroking in and out of her wetness with his clever, clever finger.

Then two fingers. She shivered, sucking on his tongue because she loved the feeling of fullness. Of being open then filled by this beautiful, beautiful man.

It still felt so right.

He lifted his head, his gaze narrowed, a pronounced flush on his cheekbones. "Counter or comforter?"

His fingers were deep inside her body. The tip of his erection was pressed tight against the pulsing ache at the top of her sex. She had no idea what he was talking about and couldn't care less.

"You have to decide, Goldilocks," he said.

She shook her head. She'd decided minutes ago, hadn't she? It was time to ease her lust, to test that sense of rightness, to get over those three rejections that had battered her heart.

"On my bed or on the breakfast bar?"

His question startled a laugh out of her which turned into a tiny groan as it shifted her body against the sweet invasion of his fingers. "You don't have to make the choice sound so romantic," she said, smiling to let him know she was teasing.

"And you don't have to make me so crazy with wanting you that I'd cover you out in the cold, lonely rain if that was the only way I could have you."

That's when she realized the weather had turned again. She could hear the sound of raindrops pattering down and she shivered a little, remembering how frozen she'd been last night. "By a fire," Lauren said. "Take me by a fire."

"Then wait here," he replied, removing his touch so that she wanted to cry with the loss of it. "Wait here until I tell you that it's time for me to have you."

Have you. Cover you. Take me.

As she waited alone in the kitchen, trembling with wanting and anticipation, the phrases ran in a loop through her mind. *Have you. Cover you. Take me.*

Primal, man-woman words of possession.

And she was possessed by the idea of having him, too. Of having him in her body. Of having sex with this particular man who might be the last man in her life if they survived the test.

His voice reached her in the kitchen. "Lauren, come upstairs."

She didn't remember the journey from the hardwood floor to the carpeted steps. She didn't remember mounting them or how she knew to go into the master bedroom with its half-closed door.

It was as if she heard Matthias's voice and then she was in his bedroom—that decadent bedroom, now made even more decadent with the light from a fire burning in the fireplace and casting yellow, orange and red tongues of light across the rumpled bed.

He stood to one side, still in his low-slung pajama bottoms. Lauren felt the heat of his gaze and the heat of the fire and the heat from wearing too many clothes when all she wanted between the two of them was the palpable desire that filled the room.

Her gaze on his face, she loosened the tie of the sash of her robe. She shrugged and the material fell to her feet. As she stepped away from it, her hands rose to the spaghetti straps of her gown. She pushed them aside and stepped forward again after the nightwear shimmied down her naked skin.

And then she stood before her fiancé, offering him all she had.

The poleaxed look on his face made her smile.

Have you. Cover you. Take me.

That could work both ways and it surely seemed as if it was up to her to jumpstart the rest of the event, now that her man appeared lust-stunned by the sight of her. At least she thought he was lust-stunned…

Uncertainty licked a cold line down her spine. Maybe what had been feeling so right to her wasn't mutual. "Is there…is there something wrong with…with…"

"With what?" Matthias said, a frown flickering over his face.

And the word popped out, driven by anxiety. *"Me?"*

He laughed, low and sexy, and her uncertainty and anxiety were chased off by the seductive sound. "The only thing wrong with you is that you're too far away, sweetheart."

His arms reached out and swept her up against him. The contact of their naked torsos made her gasp, but then he muffled the sound with his mouth, taking her into a kiss that turned up the heat all over again.

He backed up and when he fell onto the bed, she fell onto his chest, breaking their joined mouths. She sucked in a breath. "Are you okay?"

Sifting his fingers through her hair to push it away from her forehead, he laughed again. "I'm the most okay I've been in years."

She smiled, but then it died as Matt circled her waist with his hands and lifted her up his body so that he could nuzzle the valley between her breasts. Her palms slid across his crisp dark hair and her fingernails bit into his scalp as he turned his head to catch her nipple in his mouth.

Her back arched into the delicious sensation. He curled his tongue against her, gentle and tender, then sucked hard with a raw, male sound of need coming from deep inside his throat. His sound of pleasure only added to the agony of almost unbearable pleasure that arrowed from her breast to her core.

His head shifted and he plucked at the wet nipple with his fingers as he gave her other breast that arousing attention with his mouth. Lauren could hear her shallow breathing and even when she closed her eyes she could still see the shadows and firelight in the room.

It was like the two of them, that darkness and those flames. Though there were still things they didn't know about each other in the shadowed corners of their souls, that didn't stop the fire from burning between them, from consuming her doubts, from lighting the way to a future that felt so…so…right.

Always so right.

Matthias flipped their positions. Suddenly she felt the sheets at her back and on top the hardness that was his sinew and muscle and bone. She spread her legs to make a place for him, but he ignored the invitation to draw back and stand beside the bed.

With half-closed eyes, she watched his hands go to the drawstring at his waist and she let her gaze drop down to the erection straining behind the cotton.

"So pretty," Matt said, his voice almost harsh.

Her gaze shifted to his face, its angles made even more stark and beautiful by the flicker of the light. He was studying her, his eyes tracking over her breasts and down her parted legs.

Instinct caused her to bring them together again.

"Don't," he said softly. "Don't hide anything from me. Please."

And because she wanted that, too, she slid her heels along the smooth cotton and held out her arms in her own plea. "Come to me."

He shucked his pants in one swift move, then reached into the drawer of the bedside table for a condom. She had the brief impression of thick strength and then he was off his feet and in her arms, his shaft nudging at her entrance even as he took her mouth in yet another devastating kiss.

Lauren twined her arms around his neck and tilted her hips, asking for all of him, and he leaned more of his weight into her, taking her body one inch at a time. She stretched around him in degrees, going from breathtakingly tight to deliciously full.

He lifted his head as he joined them that last little bit. Her eyes closed with the goodness of the completion.

"Don't," Matthias whispered to her. "Don't shut me out like that either."

Smiling, she lifted her lashes. "Doesn't it feel good?"

He rocked a little into the cradle of her body. "What do you think?"

"I think it feels…feels…"

"Just right, Goldilocks," he said. "Not too hot, not too cold, not too hard, not too soft. Just right."

And of course those were her exact thoughts. And of course to hear them from his lips, in his husky heavy-with-desire voice, only made her more certain that she was in the right place with the right man.

Finally.

She tilted her hips to take him deeper, and he groaned, his head falling back. Then he drew away from her, almost to the brink, before sliding forward again. Her muscles tightened to hold him there, it felt so wonderful, but he pulled back again before another slow glide of penetration.

It was a rhythm she tried to fight and yet didn't want to fight. It felt so good to be filled by him and yet she had to let him go for him to come back to her. Her legs wrapped around his strong hips and he found a different angle that made goose bumps break across her skin.

"Oooh," she moaned, as he dropped his head to place openmouthed kisses against her neck. "Please."

"Please what?" he whispered against her ear. "Please what?"

As he continued to stroke in and out of her body, Lauren couldn't think of what she wanted more than this, just this, the play of reflected flames on his wide, powerful chest, the gleam of fire in his eyes, the blissful joining as the two people that were Lauren and Matthias became a single, indivisible whole.

His mouth found one of her nipples again and her body responded by tightening on his. He groaned, and the rhythm altered as both their bodies drove harder toward climax.

"I'm afraid I don't deserve this," he whispered against her mouth.

"I do," she returned.

He half laughed, half groaned and then his hand crept between their bodies and he touched her there, right at the spot that pulsed like another heart.

Gasping, Lauren lifted into the touch and his fingers grazed her again. And again.

"Let me have you," he whispered. "Go over, Goldilocks. Go."

Let me have you.

And she did, shuddering against him, around him, taking his own climax into her body. *Take me.*

As the last of the tremors wracked both their bodies he collapsed over her, heart to heart. *Cover me.*

And oh, Lauren thought. Oh, yes. It still felt so right.

It was hard to regret a nanosecond of what had just occurred, Luke decided, with Lauren's cheek resting on his chest and her blond curls drifting across his shoulder.

Who was he kidding?

It was *impossible* to regret the way her curves had looked, lapped by the light from the fire. It was impossible to regret the way her kisses had burned, the way her breasts had felt cupped in his palms, the sweet little noises she'd made when he'd taken their hard peaks into his mouth.

Hell, even as sated as he was, just remembering that made his blood run south again.

He pressed his mouth against her temple. "Lauren, are you all right?"

"Mmm." She snuggled closer against his side. He smiled at the contented noise, surprised to realize that he felt exactly the same way as she sounded.

But the guilt should be stabbing at him, right?

"Are *you* okay, Matthias?"

Ah, there was that guilt, he thought, wincing. Matthias. She'd gone to bed with him, thinking he was Matt.

He stroked his palm over her soft curls, wondering if he would be able to look at himself in the mirror come morning. "I didn't plan this. I didn't mean for us to end up here tonight."

"I know."

The two words didn't absolve him, though. He finger-combed her hair away from her temple. "I intended to honor my word to you."

"You did honor your word. You promised that whatever happened between us would be up to me, and as you'll recall, I walked in here of my own free will."

There was a hint of annoyance in her voice and he smiled. "You took off your clothes of your own free will, too. I particularly liked that part."

She let out a soft snicker. "You should have seen your face. You looked like a cartoon character after being hit by a frying pan."

"Are you laughing at me?" He reached down to pinch her curvy little butt.

She yelped. "Yes." Then laughed as he pinched her again. "Ouch! That hurts."

Without feeling an ounce of contrition, he rubbed at the spot, reveling not only in the satiny sensation of her skin, but in the relaxing, intimate laughter. Had he ever before found this combination of humor and sex? Before Lauren, he wasn't even sure he remembered the last time he'd laughed with anyone about anything.

At the thought, the guilt-knife stabbed again. Deep. She'd given him herself, laughter, this unfamiliar sense of contentment, while he'd been pretending to be her fiancé.

"Still, Lauren, I can't help but think this shouldn't

have happened. You aren't sure about the engagement, and—"

Her warm fingers pressed against his mouth. "Let me tell you something, okay? Something important."

He nodded, and she drew her hand away from his lips.

"When I was a little girl, I remember asking my mother how I would know the man I should marry."

"And she said…"

"She said I shouldn't worry about it. That she and Daddy would know and then tell me when they found him."

Luke had a sudden flash of insight. "For some reason I'm thinking that Mom and Dad weren't the ones to single out the surfer, the mechanic or even Jacques Cousteau."

"Jean-Paul," she corrected, then sighed. "But yes, you're right. You're my first family-picked fiancé, and you'd also be right if you guessed that I'm not entirely comfortable with the idea, either."

"So…"

She shifted to stack her hands on his chest. Resting her chin on them, she gazed straight into his eyes. Her pale hair frothed wildly around her face, the fire lending it the colors of sunrise and sunset.

"So I'd like to take the engagement off the table for the moment, okay? Instead, can we just be two people enjoying each other's company and nothing more? Can we do that?"

"Yeah," he said slowly, aware he couldn't have asked for anything more, though he likely deserved so very much less. "We can do that."

"Good."

He couldn't help but smile at the new, carefree sound of her voice. He couldn't help but feel carefree himself—once again, so unfamiliar but so damn wonderful. With a twist, Luke took her under him again. "So why don't you let me start enjoying you again, Goldilocks, right this minute."

Seven

Lauren left her lover sleeping in the rumpled covers of his bed. She tiptoed back to her own room, showered, then dressed and tiptoed again, this time heading downstairs to make coffee as quietly as she could. Something told her that Matthias didn't often let himself sleep late and she wanted to give him the opportunity.

Even as she worried about wanting to give him too much.

As she measured out grounds and water, she noted the new look of her bare left hand. Before taking her shower, she'd removed her engagement ring and she intended to keep it off. Last night, once he'd started making guilty noises about breaking his promise to her, she'd needed to say something to get him off that track. But once she'd made her proposition—that their engagement was now off the table—it actually had made sense to her, as well. As right as things were still feeling between them—last night neither that nor lust had been burned out—it was way better to proceed with caution.

She wasn't going to think of Matthias and marriage in the same sentence for the rest of her stay.

As she poured herself a cup of coffee, from her purse sitting on the corner of the counter came the sound of her cell phone ringing. Upon flipping open the phone, she grinned at the tiny screen, then held the piece of equipment to her ear. "What's up, Katy can-do?"

Her little sister got right to the point. "Connie called. You're not in San Francisco. Is everything okay?"

"Oh." Lauren made a little face at the mention of her former college roommate. Though she'd been hazy about her arrival time at her best friend's condo, she should have called to say she was postponing the visit. "I'll phone and tell her I'm staying here in Tahoe for a while."

"With Matthias?"

Lauren hesitated. "Promise you won't say anything to Mom and Dad."

The Mensa-moppet let out a deep groan. "Nooooo. That doesn't sound good. You said you were going there to break things off with him."

"I know." Lauren worried her bottom lip. "Look, Katy, you've been very eager for me to end this. Do you think…do you really think he's a bad guy?"

God, she sounded like *she* was in junior high, but who else could she speak to about him? Her parents were prejudiced, obviously, and Connie hadn't met the man. And to be fair, aside from her fixation on Justin Timberlake, her little sister happened to be a good judge of character.

"I never said he's a bad guy," Kaitlyn said with a little giggle. "I think he's funny. Have you ever watched him trying to work his BlackBerry?"

Lauren frowned. As a matter of fact, she'd seen him take a call on it when they were walking beside the lake the day before. She didn't remember anything remarkable. "I don't get it."

Her sister giggled again. "It was ringing one time when he was over at our house and he didn't know what to do. He had the most befuddled expression on his face and his fingers kept punching buttons until he'd set the alarm so it was both buzzing and ringing at the same time. I thought he was going to throw it into the deep end of the pool until I grabbed it away."

"Well you must have been a good teacher, because he doesn't appear to have any trouble with it now."

"Really? He didn't seem like a very good pupil and he told me he relies on his assistant to work all things technical."

Though that wasn't consistent with what Lauren had observed herself, she shrugged it away and pressed her sister again. "But despite that, you truly like him?" she asked.

"As a husband for you?"

"No, no, no." Remember? She wasn't supposed to be thinking of Matthias and marriage in the same sentence. "Just as a…as a person."

"I told you what I think. Yes, I like him. But wait a

minute." Kaitlyn's voice lowered. "Lauren, are you having sex with him?"

"What?" Her voice rose and she tried to soften it as she strode out of the kitchen and farther away from the man sleeping upstairs. "That is none of your business."

"Why?"

Lauren shot a glance up the stairs to the second floor and scurried down the other set of steps that led to the lower level. In the wine cellar, she closed the door and leaned her shoulders against it. "Why what?"

"Why won't you tell me if you're having sex with Matthias?"

Her fingers pinched the bridge of her nose. "Hasn't Mom taught you not to ask questions of that kind?"

"Yes, but after your stay in Paris, I thought you might have lost some of your American puritanism."

Lauren closed her eyes. "It is not puritanical to refuse to discuss sex with one's thirteen-year-old little sister."

"Then how am I supposed to learn anything about it?"

"Like the rest of us," Lauren retorted. "When you're much, much older."

"Puritan," Katy muttered under her breath.

Lauren pinched the bridge of her nose again. Not that she was going to discuss this with her sister, but last night pretty much proved she was not, in any way, shape or form, a puritan. Sex with Matthias had been pretty spectacular, if she did say so herself, and her heart gave a little jump-skip thinking about indulging in those kind of fireworks for a lifetime. Imagine—

No. She wasn't supposed to be thinking of lifetimes with him.

"So does this mean I'm going to have to wear one of those grody junior bridesmaid dresses after all? Mom found this one that I could *maybe* live with. It's pale blue with a darker blue satin sash…"

Lauren's mind spun away. Kaitlyn would look so pretty in blue. She could see it now, her little sister in a tea-length dress. Lauren herself in something simple and white, with a low, scooped back that would look demure from the front but would give Matthias that same hit-by-a-frying-pan face when he—

With a silent groan, she pushed away from the door. She walked over to the table in the middle of the wine cellar, idly picking up a photo in order to replace in her mind that prohibited matrimonial image. It was the shot of the twins she'd studied last night and, in looking at those two identical faces, she was struck by a new resolve.

"I've got to go now, Katy," she said, already starting to sort the pictures into two piles. There was something she had to do.

The truth was, with or without the engagement ring, with or without her declaration that their wedding was off the table, there was no way she was going to be able to get the idea of marriage and the man upstairs separated in her mind. But she wasn't going to take the notion seriously yet, either. At least not until she understood more about the two so-similar men smiling at her from the stack of photographs in her hand.

* * *

From the angle of the sun in the room, Luke knew he'd slept past his usual 6 a.m. start. Turning his head, he inhaled Lauren's flowery scent on the empty pillow beside his and smiled. He didn't stretch, he didn't even move, he just lay against the soft sheets and let himself wallow in the unfamiliar combination of satiation and relaxation.

Contentment. Yeah, that's what it was called.

And he intended to hold on to it with both hands.

Luke closed his eyes and conjured up Hunter's laughing face and mischievous eyes. *Thanks.* Without his late friend's will, he wouldn't be here in this house.

With this woman.

Thinking of Lauren again got him up and out of bed and into the shower. Once dressed, he found himself whistling as he made his way downstairs.

He *whistled?* Who knew?

Grinning at his own surprise, he helped himself to coffee in the deserted kitchen and took a few moments to gaze out the window and into the verdant forest surrounding the house. He couldn't whistle and swallow coffee at the same time, but his lighthearted mood didn't die.

No wonder. A guilt-free night of great sex with a great woman.

Lauren had given him a free pass on the engagement issue, which in turn gave him freedom from the identity problem. *Can we just be two people enjoying each other's company and nothing more?* she'd asked. *Can we do that?*

Yeah, they could do that.

Luke topped off his mug and then went in search of the woman he very much enjoyed enjoying. But she wasn't in any of that level's living spaces and he knew she wasn't in any of the bedrooms. He wandered downstairs and didn't find her in the wine cellar or using the equipment in the home gym.

Worry took a small bite out of his good mood as he trotted back up the stairs. Pulling open the front door, he saw her car still sitting in the drive. All right, he thought, his disquiet abating.

She hadn't found him out. Surely if she'd discovered who he really was she would have either left him or left him for dead.

But Lauren was still here and he was still alive.

He was certain of that when he finally found her standing in the loft-level office space, her back to him. His heart gave a weird clunk in his chest as his gaze ran from the springy denseness of her blond curls to the heels of the suede boots on her feet. It took him only four silent strides to reach her, it took only a breath to set down his mug on the desk in front of her, it seemed only right to sweep away her hair and press his mouth against the scented skin at the back of her neck.

She gasped, then relaxed as his hands cupped her upper arms. When he lifted his mouth, she turned her head to smile at him over her shoulder. "Good morning."

He returned her sunny smile and caressed her with a stroke of his thumbs. "I woke up alone," he said, trying on a mock ferocious frown. "Maybe I should have tied you to the bed."

"Then who would have made the coffee?" she asked, nodding at the steaming mug he'd slid on the desk.

"There's that." He reached around her body for the hot beverage then held it to her lips as she turned to face him. "Want some?"

"Mmm." Her hands cupped his as she tilted it for a sip.

Luke found himself staring at the way her pretty lips parted and then at the glimpse of wet, pink tongue he saw between them. Her gaze jumped to his over the rim of the mug and he felt the tug on that thread of sexual tension that was, as usual, running between them.

It added a spicy little kick to the warm contentment still oozing through his veins. Maybe it was time they went back to bed. "Lauren. Sweetheart…" He smiled again and let her see the wicked intent in his eyes.

Her pupils flared and she edged back, knocking something off the desk. He bent to retrieve it, then froze as he glanced down at what was in his hand.

One of those college pictures. Matt and Luke, looking… His fingers tightened, crumpling the photo. Looking happy, the way he'd been feeling until two seconds ago.

"Why the hell do you have this up here?" he demanded, his voice harsh.

Lauren snatched the snapshot away from his brutal grip. "Look what you've done," she scolded, placing the photo facedown against her jean-covered thigh, trying to smooth it out from the back.

"You didn't answer the question."

She gestured behind her. "I thought I'd make a collage on the corkboard of some of the college photos. There are several in the hallway but I like these, too."

His gaze followed her gesture. The long desk sat

facing the wall and on that wall was a rectangle made of corkboard tiles already peppered with pushpins, convenient for holding a calendar, take-out menus, or a montage of pictures that were at least ten years old. And that were mostly of Luke and his brother.

Staring at them, he felt anger surge through his system, flushing away that whistle-inspiring happiness that had been inside him only minutes before.

Lauren touched the side of his face. "Don't look like that. I'm sorry if seeing them bothers you, but I thought…"

"You thought what?"

She linked her fingers with his. "I've told you about the bad exes. I thought maybe you could tell me about…about…"

He couldn't seem to wrench his gaze from yet another photo of him and his twin, this one freezing forever a moment with Matt balanced on Luke's shoulders, ready for some ridiculous dorm-wide chicken fight. They'd laughed their asses off…and together taken on all comers and won.

Lauren squeezed his hand. "Matthias?"

Luke started at the sound of his brother's name on her lips. He wanted to get away from those photos and from the damn memories. He wanted her to be in his arms and take all the old anger and frustration away. Drawing her closer against him, he slid his cheek down the side of her face. "What do you say we leave the past up here and find a more pleasant way to spend our present?"

Kissing her neck beneath her ear, he felt her shiver. As she pressed herself against him, the warmth of his previous mood returned, along with a quick spike of sexual heat when her mouth rose to kiss his.

"What happened between the two of you?" she said against his mouth.

Closing his eyes, he pushed her away from him and took a couple of steps back. "Don't."

"Matthias." Her voice was full of disappointment. "*Matthias*."

That other name jabbed at him like a sharpened stick. "Lauren—"

"Please, Matthias."

"All right, all right." He shoved both hands through his hair. "You're not going to leave it alone, are you? You're not going to leave *me* alone."

He crossed to the room's small sofa and dropped onto it. Maybe if he told her then they could go back to that quilt-covered bed and forget everything but each other. His fingers combed through his hair again.

"My father's will went like this…" he started, and then he told her about Samuel Sullivan Barton's last contest. About how whoever made a million dollars first inherited all the family holdings. About how Matt had won everything and left Luke with nothing.

"You mean you," Lauren said, her hand rubbing against his thigh. Somewhere during the telling, she had found her way beside him on the couch.

Shaking his head, he looked into her concerned, sympathetic face. "What did you say?"

"You said that you were left with nothing. But it was Luke who lost that last competition and you, Matthias, who won."

"Right." He nodded. "That's the way it was. Matt

won. Luke lost." Looking away from her face, his gaze found those damn photos again. Basketball. Chicken fights. There'd been a short time when the Barton brothers had been an unstoppable team.

To avoid the thought, he jumped to his feet. "Let's get out of here," he said, pulling her up. "We'll do anything you want. Lady's choice, I promise, as long as it involves the bathtub or the bed."

But she wasn't looking at him in a sexy or steamy way. There was a frown between her eyebrows and more questions on the tip of her tongue. To stymie them, he leaned down and kissed her, thrusting deep inside her mouth until she moaned and clung to his shoulders.

Yeah. That contentment was just around the corner.

But then she broke away from him and stepped back. "Matthias…"

Always damn Matt. "What?"

"There's one thing I don't understand. If you received all the family wealth thanks to the terms of your father's will, why are you and your brother still estranged?"

"What do you mean by that?"

"Once you took over the Barton holdings, didn't you offer your brother half?"

He stared at her. "That's not the way my father wanted it."

"So?" She crossed her arms over her chest. "Are you saying you *didn't* ask him to join you in running everything together?"

Damn it, why was she pressing him on this point! "Yes. Yes, I offered him half of everything. I offered him joint authority and…and he refused." Luke would never forget how angry he'd been at Matt that day. To think that his twin could act so generous by offering to share what he'd actually stolen from him!

"He refused?"

Damn right, Luke had refused. "Yes." He grabbed her hand and started drawing her toward the door. "How about I find us some soap bubbles?"

She dug in her heels. "The story still doesn't make sense. If you made the offer and he refused, why are the two of you still not on speaking terms? Surely you both realize that it was your father who put you into that competition and not each other?"

Luke dropped her hand and stalked to the window. He stared out through the trees at that beautiful blue lake, but no matter how stupendous the view, it couldn't make over the truth. "We don't speak because Luke thinks I cheated in order to become the winner. He…he believes I bribed a supplier to favor me instead of him."

There was a moment of stunned silence. "You wouldn't do such a thing!"

His head whipped toward her. "What makes you so sure?"

"It's obvious. Your father raised you brothers to win, and neither of you would be satisfied to achieve victory through some sort of dirty trick."

For a moment, a weird emotion churned inside Luke's belly. Doubt? *Neither of you would be satisfied to achieve victory through some sort of dirty trick.*

But she didn't know Matt as well as she thought. And she didn't know the details of the events that had occurred seven years before. Luke knew. Luke knew what his brother had done to him. Didn't he?

Neither of you would be satisfied to achieve victory through some sort of dirty trick.

The words looped through his head again. And then again.

Staring at Lauren's big, blue eyes and flushed-with-righteousness face, he couldn't forget how she'd leaped to the—correct—conclusion that Matt had offered up half his winnings. He couldn't forget how she'd instantly assumed Matt wasn't a cheater as well.

Luke couldn't help but remember that he was bamboozling her right now, by pretending to be the very man whom she was so eager to defend.

Images of the night before scattered like more snapshots in his mind. Lauren's eyes, wide and darkening, as she lifted her hand to daub the milk from his chest.

The look of her kiss-swollen mouth as she laughed when he demanded she decide between the bed and the breakfast bar.

Her perfect body, all pale curves, rosy nipples, blond curls as she let her nightgown drop to her feet.

Later, when she'd let him look his fill, taking in all the female enticement of her petaled sex between her splayed, satiny thighs. She'd blushed, but she'd opened to his gaze and opened to his body.

Luke's body, but she hadn't known that.

Maybe he should tell her. Explain. Reveal the whole ruse before it went any further. As Luke, he could woo her now. Win her this time as himself. Then there would be nothing to threaten the contentment he could find in her arms.

"Lauren…" He crossed the room to cup her cheek in the palm of his hand. She edged closer and nuzzled into his touch and her trust struck him like a blow. His voice lowered. "Sweet Lauren…"

At his hip, his BlackBerry buzzed. He grimaced at Lauren, who let go a little laugh.

"Is that a bumblebee," she said, making it obvious she could sense the vibration, "or would someone be happy to reach you?"

His hand was reluctant to let her go, but business instincts ran deep and when he checked the screen he knew he would have to take the call. "Excuse me," he said, stepping back. Then he brought the device to his ear and acknowledged his assistant. "Elaine? What do you need?"

"I've been talking to Ernst in Stuttgart."

The supplier Eagle Wireless had been in talks with. And if those talks were successful, they'd take Eagle a nest or two up in the world. If not… Muting the phone, he looked over at Lauren. "I'm going to take this call downstairs, okay? Will you excuse me for a few minutes?"

She shook her head. "You stay here. I'm going to the kitchen to see what I can do about breakfast."

"Did I mention I don't deserve you?"

On tiptoe, Lauren pressed her lips against the corner of his mouth. "Just what I like. A man with a debt to pay."

He watched her sashay out the door, then returned his attention to the phone call. "Elaine? What's up with Ernst?"

"He's chilly."

The European had never been a particularly cheerful sort. "Any idea why?"

"If I had to guess, I'd say he has a second suitor for those components we've been talking to him about."

His hand tightened on his BlackBerry. "Do you know who?"

"I have my guesses."

"Yeah," Luke said. "Me, too." Matt. Matt was in Germany. Luke had suspected it before and now it didn't take a huge leap to deduce that Matt was his rival in the deal with Ernst. Damn Matt.

Luke's eyes closed as tension tightened like a vise around his head. See? Lauren was wrong for leaping to his brother's defense. And though that was no surprise, it shocked the hell out of him how his brother's betrayal could still hurt. He didn't have to open his eyes to see those college photos once again. Remembering each one opened yet another old wound.

For a short time they'd been so close. Together with Matt, Luke had felt as if nothing could vanquish him. How he missed that.

Opening his eyes, he strode to his laptop, closed on one corner of the desk. Seating himself in the nearby leather chair, he rolled it under the desk at the same time that he pulled the computer toward him. "I'm going to book a flight to Germany."

"I thought you had to stay in the house."

Luke's fingers froze on the keys. "I'll think of something." He was going to have to say goodbye to Tahoe and goodbye to Lauren, too, but it couldn't be helped. "Business comes first."

"Unfortunately for both of us," Elaine said, "and I say 'both of us' because I know what kind of mood you'll be in when I tell you this and that my poor, tender ears will be forced to bear the brunt of your outrage and I'll have to go home to my loving family, deaf in my right ear and thus unable to fulfill my motherly and wifely duties because—"

"Spit it out." Luke braced, because Elaine was nearly as ambitious as he was, and if she said "unfortunate" then it truly was.

"Ernst is going to be incommunicado for the next week. He's attending a big family wedding in the north and will not be available to talk business or do business until he gets back."

Luke blew out a long breath. "Hell. A week?"

"A week."

A week for him to stew over how he was going to save the deal. A week for him to nurture his rage at his brother over the way he was trying to pull the rug out from under the feet of Eagle Wireless.

A week to be with Lauren.

As Matt, damn it. As Matt.

He wasn't going to renege on the revenge he was plotting on his brother, though. No way. Not now. If Matt wanted to be Luke's rival on the Ernst deal, then Luke would continue wooing Lauren just as he had been doing. In Matt's name.

She'd taken off her engagement ring, hadn't she? They were "just two people," not two engaged people any longer.

With that thought in mind, he could still be content with making her happy in bed while waiting for the even happier day when he could watch his brother's face as he learned Luke had had his fiancée first.

It wasn't so despicable, was it? He made her as satisfied in bed as she made him, he was sure of it.

And Lauren had said, after all, she liked a man with a debt to pay.

Luke had a hell of a disbursement to lay on Matt.

Eight

Days passed, and Lauren didn't manage to coax Matthias into talking about Luke again—and to be honest, she didn't try very hard, suspecting it would ruin what they'd found. Together, they'd created their own little world within the environs of the log-and-stone house and the tiny town of Hunter's Landing; she didn't want anything to pierce the bubble of what they'd made together. Anyway, they talked about nearly everything else. The places they'd traveled to, the places they wanted to travel to, the interesting characters they'd met in their lives.

Nothing occurred to change Lauren's opinion that Matthias was a workaholic who needed to learn to relax, though, and the forced vacation at Hunter's lodge was the perfect opportunity for him to take his pace down a notch or two or ten. While he complained about feeling lazy, they slept in every morning. And because he seemed to have never taken the time off in the last few years to see even the most popular movies, she managed to persuade him into slow, cozy afternoons and evenings in front of the plasma TV, making headway through the extensive DVD collection they'd discovered.

Shivering, laughing or tearing up at a Hollywood offering was all the sweeter from the warmth of her man's arms. He'd squeeze her tighter when she'd bury her face in his neck as the knife-wielding villain approached the unsuspecting hero. His eyes sparkled when a particular comedy tickled her funny bone. As he'd thumbed away her tears during the denouement of an excruciatingly tragic love story, her stomach had flipped at the expression of tenderness on his face.

"Sweetheart, it's just a movie," he'd said, wiping away yet another tear.

She'd sniffed. "Great love isn't 'just' anything."

Amusement had joined the affection in his gaze as he'd shaken his head. "I'll take your word for it, I guess, but I'm thinking the hero might feel better if he went back to work or at least went out for a couple of beers instead of moping around with his dead lover's moldy nightgowns."

"Back to work. Out for beers. Moldy nightgowns." She'd tried pushing him away, but he'd lifted her like a rag doll and placed her on top of his body so there was nothing for her to do but accept his kiss.

And wonder if she should worry that he didn't appear to believe in love.

Maybe he'd sensed her mood, because then he'd distracted her by issuing a challenge to yet another of their air-hockey rematches. They were quite the regulars at The Game Palace now. She liked the sense of fun the place was now giving Matthias and something of his competitive spirit had begun to rub off on her.

She was the current champion in the twelve-and-under age bracket. It was a feat she was embarrassingly proud of, even though she'd been allowed to compete against players less than half her age only because the younger contenders had stated with a pithy pity bordering on scorn that they would let her play against them because she was "only a girl."

Ha! Now the preteen set had reason to rue the day they'd said those words and she continued to take each and every opportunity she was offered to hone her skills in preparation for beating the big, bad champion of them all—Matthias.

Now, from across the air-hockey table in The Game Palace, he paused, mallet in hand. "I don't like that ruthless gleam in your eye. You used to play with this don't-hurt-me-because-I'm-cute look on your face. Now that's changed."

She wiggled her brows, then gave him her best gunslinger glare. "I don't have to settle for that namby-pamby passive-aggressive stuff any longer. I'm going to start doing things your way—straight up."

A funny expression crossed his face. "I take it you mean you're out to win?"

"Loser buys the lattes."

She was crowing thirty minutes later as they waited in line at Java & More. "I did it. I did it," she started, then paused. "You didn't let me win, did you? Promise you didn't let me win."

He shook his head. "I didn't let you win. Fair and square, you beat me, Goldilocks."

She bounced on her heels, thrilled at the idea. Maybe some would see it as a silly accomplishment, but there was a deeper meaning to it. There was. Her usual response to the kind of aggressive attitude Matt showed toward air hockey was to either find a less-than-straightforward way to fight or to back away altogether. This time, though, she'd held up her head and kept her gaze directly on the prize.

From the corner of her eye, she sent a sidelong glance at Matthias. It had helped that he'd seemed distracted during the game. Though she could admit that, too, it didn't change the fact that she'd learned something from the win. And from him.

Spinning his way, she put her hand on his arm. "Hey."

He looked down at her, his gaze quizzical. "Hey, what?"

"You're good for me."

His muscles went rigid under her hand. "Lauren—"

"What can I get you?" the person at the counter asked.

They both looked up, startled to find themselves at the head of the line. "A medium coffee for me," Matthias answered, "and for Lauren…"

"Lauren?" The man on the other side of the counter blinked, then his gaze switched from Matt to her. He had sun-bleached blond ringlets that hung raggedly to his shoulders and bright blue eyes in a walnut-tan face. "Is that you, Lauren Conover?"

As she looked, really looked at the barista, heat flooded her face and she felt a distinct, needle-like poke. Ouch, Lauren thought, wincing. Ouch and damn. Her happy little bubble had just been pricked.

Beside her, Matthias cleared his throat.

Okay, that was her cue. She should say something. Do something.

Make introductions? Haul off and slap the guy who was supposed to be making their coffees? Curl up and die due to sudden onset of old humiliation?

As the silence stretched longer, Matthias's left hand curled around the back of her neck. His right stretched across the counter. "Matthias Barton, Lauren's…fiancé."

The barista shuffled his feet even as he shook hands. "Uh, Trevor Clark, Lauren's…first fiancé."

The shame of rejection flamed through her again, as hot as it had on the day she'd discovered he'd left on their honeymoon trip without her. She'd been in her bedroom when his note arrived, trying on her grass skirt which rustled every time she moved like the sound of a rodent running through weeds. Knowing it was going to make her mother nuts, she'd been smiling at her reflection in the mirror as Kaitlyn came in to deliver the sheet of paper bearing Trevor's nearly indecipherable scrawl.

For a few moments Lauren had thought he was suggesting they streak at their wedding ceremony. After squinting and making allowances for spelling errors, it became clear he was breaking it off. She could still feel the texture of the paper against her fingers. She could still remember the gossipy whisper of her skirt's grass fronds as she'd dropped to her bed. The guest list had been small, but gifts had already arrived and she could still remember each burning tear spilled as she'd repackaged for return every ten-speed blender and every gleaming set of chef's knives.

Alone.

Unwanted.

Unloved.

Now Trevor turned away to get the drinks and, mortification still coursing through her, Lauren couldn't think what to do next. She tried pretending she wasn't in the shop. Would that work? Was it possible to make believe she and Matthias were back at the house on the couch, in their just-the-two-of-us little world and that this embarrassing encounter wasn't happening?

Except the other half of "just-the-two-of-us" was squeezing her neck and bending close to peer into her eyes. "Are you all right?" His voice was quiet. Kind. Concerned.

She wasn't all right. Not only was it more-than-awkward to come face-to-face with the first man to dump her, but...but... Though a few days ago she'd wanted Matthias to know all about her failed engagements to make it clear what a bad bet she was when it came to marriage, things had changed since then. Now she definitely didn't want fiancé number four contemplating for even two seconds why she hadn't been able to please even a shaggy-haired coffee counter-person.

The only halfway decent option was to get the two

of them out of Java & More and back to the bubble ASAP. When Trevor returned with the drinks, she made to snatch them out of his hands. Who would guess that he'd choose to hold on to them when he hadn't been inclined to keep her all those years ago?

The grim set to his mouth was as tenacious as his grip on the coffees. "Look. I really should explain…" Trevor started.

"No need." On her end, Lauren tugged on the drinks, hard enough to burp a froth of foam from the sippy hole on the plastic top of her latte. Maybe if she pulled harder it would spew enough hot coffee to force Trevor into letting go. Her fingers tightened.

Another set of hands took over the paper cups. A warm chest pressed against her back. "I've got them, Goldilocks," Matthias said. "Let go, baby."

Baby. He'd never called her that before. It sounded sexy. Like a name a man would use for a woman who pleased him in bed. It sounded intimate. Like the way a man would talk to the woman he wouldn't mind keeping around for the rest of his life. Some of her humiliation leached away as her fingers loosened and then her hands dropped to her sides. Matt remained a warm presence behind her.

"Now—Trevor, was it?" he said. "What did you have to say to my wife-to-be?"

At the question, Lauren wanted to duck away, or at least close her eyes and again try that pretend-she-wasn't-in-the-room technique, but with Matthias at her back, she had nowhere to go. Make-believe wasn't working, either. The only consolation she had was that

Trevor looked more miserable than she felt. His gaze flicked to Matthias, then back to her.

"Lauren, I—I've felt guilty about it for years." He pushed his corkscrew curls over his shoulders. "I shouldn't have run off on you like that. With such a lame note and—"

"And with those trip tickets that Lauren had paid for herself?" Matthias sounded so polite.

Still, Trevor's face flushed an unbecoming red against the streaky-blond of his hair. "I'll pay you back someday, I swear. I don't make all that much right now, but I did okay as a ski instructor last winter. Maybe if I get the kayaking job this summer."

As he continued talking, his promises sounded as lame as that note he'd left behind and Lauren didn't know how to respond. Once upon a time Trevor had been the love of her life, and now he just seemed sort of…

"Pathetic," Matthias remarked as they finally exited Java & More. "My God. If this is an example of the kind of man you wanted to marry I'm starting to wonder if all your previous choices were simply a way of rebelling against parents. You certainly weren't thinking with your head. What did you ever see in that goofy, overgrown Peter Pan?"

"I loved him!" Lauren heard herself snap back. "He…he was a free spirit."

"Freeloader, you mean. Did you catch on to the part where he's living with some girl whose daddy owns a local resort?"

"Yes." Her voice sounded glum.

There was a moment of tense silence, then he

wrapped his hand around her arm and swung her to face him. "Tell me you're not still in love with him."

In love with Trevor? Lauren stared off into the distance. Of course she'd been in love with Trevor once, but it was hard to exactly recapture the feeling. It was much easier to remember the grass skirt, the embarrassment of rejection and how relieved her parents had been that she wasn't marrying a man—a boy— with such a distinct lack of prospects and ambition.

Now she looked up at *this* fiancé, noting the expression of irritation on his face. Because he was mad at her first fiancé *for* her, she realized. He'd given Trevor the icy poke about cashing in on the honeymoon, even as he'd stood behind her, a warm and solid presence.

Warm and solid. That described Matthias to a *T*, except it didn't take into account hot and sexy. And sweet and fun, she added, remembering all the sweet kisses as they lay laughing together on the couch and all the sweet moments she'd spent watching his face relaxed, finally, in sleep.

All at once, that bubble they'd been living in—the one she'd thought seeing Trevor had popped—was back. It seemed to invade her chest now, though, filling her so full that her heart crowded toward her throat and her stomach was flattened like a pancake. But then she realized the bubble *was* her heart and it was growing, taking up every inch of space it could find inside of her, because…because love took up a lot of room.

Love.

Swallowing hard, she gazed, helpless, into the dark eyes of the man her parents had picked for her.

"Well?" he demanded.

She swallowed again. Was there a question on the table? "Well what?" It came out a squeaky whisper, her voice box compressed by that unstoppable emotion getting bigger inside of her.

"Do you still love Trevor?"

"No!" Not him. There wasn't room for any other man in her mind, body or heart but Matthias. Yes, there was no doubt she was in love with him. This man.

The one whose ring she'd removed from her finger.

During the past few days, Luke had become accustomed to Lauren's moods. He knew what made her laugh and what made her sigh. He knew what she wanted when their eyes would suddenly meet across a table, a room, the mattress of the bed they'd been sharing.

He liked her moods. Her playfulness amused and distracted him during this period of forced inactivity. When he started stewing over his brother's machinations or when he experienced a resurgence of guilt over playing Matt, they faded away under his new preoccupation with the expressive curve of her lips or the wink of the dimple in her left cheek when she laughed. He found her sentimental side to be excessively girlie, sure, but a romantic movie could make her melt in his arms and who could find fault in that?

She'd become a damn good air-hockey player. Which would have been only a more amusing distraction if she hadn't spooked the hell out of him after their latest match by saying, *You're good for me.*

Good God. *You're good for me,* she'd declared.

He knew that wasn't true.

Luke wasn't any better for her than that loser Trevor who'd left her at the altar.

But she didn't know that, though he couldn't figure out another reason why she'd so suddenly be giving him the silent treatment. All the way back to the house from Java & More, she'd been like a ghost beside him in the passenger seat. Ghost wasn't one of Lauren's regular moods.

He unlocked the front door and she drifted in ahead of him, still surrounded by that unusual quiet.

Why?

She'd claimed to no longer be in love with Trevor, but...

"Lauren." His voice sounded harsh to his own ears.

"Hmm?" She kept drifting ahead of him.

It made him nuts; just as he thought he understood her, now he couldn't read what was going on inside her blond head. And his frustration with that only made him more nuts.

When it came to relationships, he never looked deep. He never cared too much.

Yet now he couldn't help thinking about which wheels were turning in Lauren's mind.

Yet now he couldn't help worrying about how this was all going to end up.

Yet now he couldn't help wondering why the hell he'd gotten himself into such a predicament.

She turned her head to look at him through her incredible lake-blue eyes. Her blond curls floated back and he thought, suddenly, of that fantasy woman he'd dreamed up on his first day in Hunter's house. He'd gotten all the outside specifications right, but he hadn't realized how much there could be on the inside. Warmth. Humor. That refreshing honesty that was like a deep breath of air he never could seem to take.

His hand rubbed against the center of his chest.

She frowned. "Did you need something?" she asked.

"No." He couldn't say it fast enough.

"Okay. I'm going to take a bath." She headed for the stairs without another look.

Which was good, he told himself. Without her around, he could let go of the worrying and the wondering. The examining and the analyzing. Maybe he'd turn on the TV. Find ESPN. An old Western. Lauren always turned up her cute nose to those.

He could lose himself in the tube and turn off this uncharacteristic bend to his mind.

Throwing himself on the couch seemed to help. He stretched out and reached for the remote. Any moment now, he'd be thinking of nothing at all as he surfed endless waves of brain-fogging television.

Good. A rerun of the game show, *Jeopardy!*.

Bad. The first category: "Sexy Blondes."

What was his sexy blond thinking right now?

Why had she been so quiet?

Clicking off the TV, he popped up from the couch. There had to be some way of redirecting his brain from focusing on her. From focusing on *anything*. Luke Barton only gave this kind of single-minded attention to work.

Never to women.

At one end of the dining-room table, they'd dumped out the contents of box holding a thousand-piece jigsaw puzzle. Now, he fiddled with the loose pieces and started sorting all those with straight edges.

Lauren, most likely, would make fun of this orderly method. She'd want to do it the wild way, he guessed, by blindly choosing one cardboard bit and then scrambling through the 999 other choices to find it a partner.

She'd definitely want to do it the wild way.

Luke pressed the heels of his hands into his eyes, trying to dispel the images those words dealt in his mind. He didn't want to be thinking of her.

He didn't want to be thinking of what she was thinking.

Of what she was doing.

She was taking a bath, a voice inside recalled for him.

Hell. Reminded of that, how could he possibly have anything *but* her at the forefront of his mind?

And then he could think of only one logical way to shut down his busy brain.

He took the stairs two at a time.

The flowery scent of the steam curled from under the door in the master bath and yanked him forward as if a hand had grabbed him by the neck of his shirt. Beneath his fingers, the knob turned without a sound.

At the sight that greeted him on the other side of the door he got exactly what he wanted…a sight that knocked everything out of his head.

Lauren in nothing but gleaming skin and soap bubbles.

Her head whipped around to face him. Her forearm crossed over her breasts. The warm-temperature flush on her face deepened. "Is everything all right?"

"No." He stalked closer. "I need…"

Her eyebrows drew together. "What?"

What was he talking about? Luke didn't need anything. Except mindlessness. Except sex, which would drive away all that he'd suffered today.

You're good for me.

Of course I'm not in love with Trevor.

If he knew the first wasn't true, how could he possibly believe the second?

"What do you need?" she asked, drawing back against the side of the tub as he came even closer.

His nostrils flared as he took in another breath of the scented water. He could almost taste her skin on his tongue.

He *had* to taste her skin on his tongue.

His fingers snagged the nearby towel, and he stretched it between his two hands. "Hop out now."

Her gaze jumped to his and *phttt,* a match struck and lit that ever-ready fuse between them. He saw Lauren swallow hard, but he didn't retreat at that sign of nerves. It was too important that they get body-to-body right now so that he could turn off his mind.

You're good for me.

Of course I'm not in love with Trevor.

One of her hands gripped the side of the tub and she pushed herself to her feet. Rivulets of water ran down her sides. Clusters of bubbles the size of cotton balls dotted her pink, naked skin.

Luke watched, fascinated, as one group skated down her belly to pause in the wet curls of her sex. She was blond and pink there, too, and so tantalizing that hunger gnawed at him. He had to have her.

As if he was pulling her on a string, she lifted one leg and stepped out of the tub, giving him a quick glimpse of the heaven between her legs before she was hidden behind the huge bath towel.

He wrapped his arms around her, encasing her in terry cloth. She looked up at him, a faint frown on her face. "I wanted some time alone to think."

"Oh, baby, bad idea."

"You wouldn't go away if I asked you to?"

He inhaled her sweet, sweet scent. "Are you asking me to?"

The answer was in her eyes, in the flare of the flame rising between them as that fuse continued to burn. Wrapped in the towel, she was easy to pick up and carry toward the bed.

She was easy to unwrap there, too, the damp ends of her hair making dark trails against the pale pillow-case. He stared down at all her bath-flushed skin and her scent rose around him as if he was rolling in a rain-dampened, flower-strewn field. It filled his head so that he was thinking only of Lauren, of her luscious skin, of the heat that he could feel radiating from her flesh as he crawled between her legs.

"You're still dressed," she whispered.

"You're not." He licked across her belly button.

Her stomach muscles jittered and he saw her pupils start to dilate. "I think—"

"Don't," he admonished, sipping a stray drop of water that was poised on one of her ribs. "Don't think."

No thinking. This was time for touching, caressing, tasting. This was time for easy, breezy sex.

His palms found her breasts. Her tight nipples poked against them as his mouth opened on the side of her neck. She made a little sound—protest and plea both at once—and he knew exactly how she felt. He sensed everything she was feeling through her shivers and her moans. Through the way her body twisted toward his mouth and twisted into his touch.

He sensed every unspoken word.

Her hips were lifting against his as the silent words clamored in his ears. She was rubbing against his jeans, probably abrading that delicate skin just inside her hipbones and, to spare her hurt, he lifted away despite another sweet yet muffled sound of desire. He calmed her by kissing down her belly and, yes, finding the redness where denim had scraped her delicate skin. With his tongue, he took a moment to soothe the marks and then drew lower, found her center, opened wide her satiny thighs.

She was blushing here, too, all pink and swollen and so inviting that his heart slammed against his chest, knocking loudly to make sure that Luke knew it was time to open this door.

He had to have her here, too.

She gasped at the first touch of his tongue. Her fingers twisted in his hair, but he could hardly feel it, overwhelmed as he was by the sweet, creamy taste of her in his mouth. Heat poured off her skin as he held her open to his feast and his mind spun away as her tension twisted higher. He could feel it through his hands, hear it in her breathless pleas, urge it on with the insistent *bam-bam-bam* rhythm of his heart.

He gave himself up to serving her desire, let it take control of him so that nothing else could intrude. There were no bothersome thoughts, no nagging worries, nothing but Lauren, her skin, her passion, the sound of her crying out in orgasm as his tongue stroked her to paradise.

Still shaking with the aftereffects, she pulled him up to her, her hands insistent now as she yanked at his shirt and pulled at the buttons of his fly. He shoved aside what was necessary, fumbled with a condom, then slid inside all her soft, clutching heat. His eyes closed and he threw back his head at the exquisite goodness of it.

As he began to move, again there were no thoughts, no recriminations, no wondering about feelings or future. Yes. Yes. There was only this sensation. The sensation of Lauren in his arms. Being in Lauren. A puzzle piece and its partner.

When he didn't think he'd survive the flaming pleasure of her body a second longer, she tilted her hips and took him even deeper. Made him helpless to the rocking rhythm they'd begun. Then, with one sharp jolt of bliss, pleasure sank like fangs and dragged him under.

He hoped he'd drown in her.

Somehow though, minutes later, he discovered he'd survived. Lauren was cuddled against his chest, her body as boneless as his seemed to be.

One of her fingers could still move, however, and she was using the tip to draw idle yet intricate patterns on his chest. A maze, he decided, and he let himself get lost in it, his brain still unengaged, just as he'd intended.

"Why did Hunter do it?" Lauren asked, her breath tickling the sensitive flesh at his collarbone.

Luke rubbed his chin against the top of her head. "Hmm?"

"Why did Hunter set up these month-long visits for the Samurai?"

Luke didn't plan his answer ahead of time. He still wasn't thinking. He still didn't want to think. "Because we're now in our thirties? Maybe he figured we'd need something at this time in our lives."

She stacked her hands on top of his beating heart and studied his face. "Well? *Did* you need something?"

"Yeah," he heard himself answer. "I needed you."

And those weren't thinking words. They were just the truth.

Hell.

Nine

It was dawn and Luke couldn't sleep. It was just like the old days—the days before he'd come to Lake Tahoe, when he was constantly revved. Then, he'd always been energized about his work, about making a buck, about proving himself to be a success without needing anyone or anything to back him up.

Now, and all during the night, his mind had flitted between two separate subjects, first picking up one, then the other, figuratively fingering each like pieces of that jigsaw puzzle. His brother, Matt. His lover, Lauren.

Leaving the second focus of his thoughts asleep in bed, he retrieved the box of college photos from the wine cellar and carted them into the kitchen. With the overhead light switched on and the coffee starting to drip, he took a breath and flipped open the cardboard flaps.

His own face stared back up at him. Times two. Lauren had dismantled her collage on the corkboard after he'd told her about the situation between himself and his twin. The photos of Matt and Luke were on top of all the others.

He drew a fistful out and fanned them on the table like a large hand of cards.

When partnered with Matt, he'd always come up a winner.

That's what he saw in the images caught on Hunter's film. Twins, identical enough that he couldn't pick himself out in most of the shots. Each face smiling, triumphant in good health, good spirits, in...brotherhood.

Had it been Hunter's magic that had brought them together during those years? Or a genuine feeling of kinship?

If it had been authentic, how could their father's will have destroyed it?

But the stipulation in their father's will hadn't destroyed it. Matt had. Matt had double-crossed Luke in order to make that first million.

Your father raised you brothers to win, and neither of you would be satisfied to achieve victory through some sort of dirty trick.

Lauren's words. Lauren.

Now he stared at the photos on the table, unseeing, his thoughts shifting to the woman sleeping upstairs in his bed. Without the request in Hunter's will, he wouldn't have taken a weekend, let alone a month, away from work. Yes, he dated when someone striking passed through his world, and he could find willing bed partners when that urge struck as well, but he'd never taken the time to really get familiar with a woman.

To know her favorite kind of movie. How she liked her morning coffee and how that was different than how she liked her evening coffee. The silly grin she wore when she caught him staring at her.

He'd never before found himself interested in the how and the why a woman wound up with three former fiancés and zero wedding bands.

He sat back in his chair, his mind turning things again, trying to understand how the pieces fit. Lauren. Matt.

Matt. Lauren.

A knock on the kitchen door jerked him from his reverie. He looked up from the photos and out the mullioned windows of the Dutch door. His reflection peered back at him.

Startled, Luke jumped, then his surprise ebbed away as the door handle turned and he realized it was Matt, not his own ghost, who was walking into the kitchen.

"Bro," his brother said. "Long time no see."

Luke shot to his feet and leaned against the table, using the shield of his body to hide the old photos from his twin. The last thing he needed was Matt supposing he was sentimental. When it came to his brother, he wasn't going to be stupid enough to reveal any weakness like that. "What the hell are you doing here?"

His twin sauntered over to the counter where he helped himself to a mug of coffee. "I thought I'd check in. See if you needed anything." His gaze circled the room, brushing along the granite countertops and the gleaming stainless-steel appliances. "Hunter did it up right, if the outside of the place and the inside of this kitchen are anything to judge by."

Luke crossed his arms over his chest. "You'll be comfortable enough when it's your month. Now go away until then."

Matt leaned against the counter, mimicking Luke's pose against the table. His head tilted. "You're looking fine, too. Rested."

"There's not much to do here but rest."

"It's more than that," Matt said. "I can't quite put my finger on it, but…"

"But I suppose your assessment of my appearance can be excused from your usual razor-sharpness due to the fact that we haven't seen each other in—how long?"

"Well, we did run into each other last year in that parking garage by the opera house. We both had tickets to…"

"Wagner," they said as one.

"God spare me," came out in tandem as well.

And then they were grinning at each other.

Their smiles clicked off at the same moment, too, as if simultaneously recalling their long-standing enmity.

Matt looked away. "Your date was stunning," he offered.

"Yours, too," Luke replied. "The woman I was with—"

He halted, as he suddenly thought of the woman he was with right now. The woman upstairs, sleeping like an angel in his bed.

Matt's fiancée, Lauren.

Matt and Lauren, two pieces of a puzzle that he definitely didn't want to link up today.

Setting his jaw, he pushed away from the table and headed for the kitchen door. "While it's been so much fun catching up," he said, "now it's time for you to go."

But his brother's gaze had caught on the photographs that Luke had been concealing. His mug firmly in hand, Matt walked toward the table instead of to the door that Luke was pointedly pulling open.

His brother lifted one of the snapshots off the table to study it. "Where'd all that go?" he murmured, turning the photo Luke's way. "You and me laughing together?"

"It went to hell, exactly where I'm wishing you right now," Luke answered, narrowing his eyes at the man who had promised to marry *his* Lauren. He couldn't get it out of his head, the image of her walking down the aisle and into the arms of the one man who always snatched away what Luke wanted. Their father's approval. The family wealth. The woman sleeping upstairs. "Time to leave, Matt."

"Lunkhead, for the last time, I didn't do a single damn thing to you, all right? I know you believe I somehow messed with your chances to win the Barton holdings, but I didn't. And it was *you* who refused your half later."

Luke didn't have time to get into this. There was a tick-tick-tick clicking away in the back of his brain, reminding him that any second Lauren could awaken, smell the coffee and head downstairs to find some…and him.

Two of him.

"Get out, Matt."

His brother appeared to grow roots that sunk into the slick surface of the kitchen floor. "Not until we get to the bottom of this. I'm damn sick of your false accusations and your bitter recriminations hanging over my head."

Anger tightened Luke's chest. False? Bitter? How could his brother dismiss his grievances like that? Still, it wasn't the time—there wasn't time—to hash it out with Matt. His fingers curled into fists and he jerked his head toward the open doorway. "I'm asking you to go."

Matt was shaking his head as a female voice floated down the stairs. "I woke up to an empty bed. Is my favorite man in all the world already up and making my favorite beverage in all the universe?"

Oh, God. Every muscle in Luke's body cramped to charley-horse tightness. *No. Not now.*

He remembered wanting to watch his brother's face when Matt realized Luke had Lauren first. He remembered rationalizing how fitting that would be, how it wouldn't be hurting anyone, not really, except the bastard who had delivered Luke that body blow by cheating him all those years ago.

But he'd never imagined the look on Lauren's face when she found out what he'd done. And he didn't want to see it now. Not until he figured out a way he could explain it to her that made sense—and made him look less like the villain he was suddenly feeling himself to be.

Frozen by his own body and seconds away from disaster, a desperate Luke sent an unspoken message to his twin. It had worked in the old days. The good old days, when they were a team. Real brothers. Maybe it would work now, as long as Matt hadn't recognized Lauren's voice.

Please God Matt hadn't recognized Lauren's voice. *Do what I ask, bro,* Luke silently urged his brother. He managed to jerk his head once more toward the door. *Please.*

Apparently Matt didn't realize who the woman in the house was—and apparently he still had some decency left. It surprised the hell out of Luke, but with a quick nod, his brother set down his mug then strode toward the door.

Luke released the breath he was holding as his twin, with a two-fingered salute, stepped over the threshold.

All right. Crisis averted.

Then Lauren's voice sounded again. Louder. Closer. "Matthias? Are you in the kitchen?"

Luke's brother stilled.

In a slow move, he turned around just as Lauren entered the room.

She stopped up short, her gaze jumping between their two faces. If she sensed the catastrophe in the offing, her expression didn't immediately show it. Instead, her hands tightened the sash of her robe, then she moved forward, her hand stretching for Matt's.

"Good morning," she said, her voice and smile warm.

Yeah, Luke thought, his body still in that frozen state. The looming catastrophe had yet to chill her air.

"It seems you've caught us," Lauren finished.

Oh, hell. She didn't have a clue.

Matt's hand stayed at his side and he just stared at her for a long, tense moment, taking in her short robe and the glimpse of thin nightgown underneath. Then his gaze shifted to Luke, wearing nothing but his pajama bottoms.

Finally, Matt laughed, a mirthless sound sharp enough to cut glass. "I guess I did catch you, didn't I? How long has this been going on? You and my brother, behind my back, f—"

"*No.*" Before that ugliness could make it into the room, Luke's paralysis evaporated and he surged forward to slug his twin in the face. At the blow, his brother reeled back, Lauren shrieked, and the red tide rising in Luke's vision threatened to swamp him. He caught Matt by the shirt before he hit his head on the upper cabinets.

"Don't say that word," he snapped out, holding his brother steady. "That word is not what Lauren and I are about."

Matt's left eye was already swelling, though it didn't hinder its ferocious glitter. "That's not the way I see it," he said. "If there really is a 'Lauren and you,' then I've been royally—"

"Leave Lauren out of this," Luke broke in again, his voice harsh. "She didn't—she doesn't know it was me."

"What…what do you mean?" Lauren's voice. Lauren.

Luke watched his fists tighten on his brother's shirt. He couldn't turn his head and look at her. He couldn't speak another word.

"Damn it, lunkhead," Matt said, stepping back so he broke free of Luke's grasp. "What the hell have you done?"

What the hell *had* he done? It hit Luke, it hit him one brick at a time. Pretending to be his brother. For days and days. Making love to Lauren while she thought he was Matt. Time and time again.

Even with the engagement off the table, even when she'd said "can't we just be two people," it was still the most underhanded, ugly thing Luke had ever done in his life.

A something that, now, in the cold light of this morning, couldn't be excused, no matter what underhanded and ugly thing Matt had done or was trying to do to Luke's business.

Yes, Luke was the villain here. That destructive wolf he'd once imagined himself to be.

Swallowing hard, he forced himself to swing around, his gaze finding Goldilocks, her face pale and her blue eyes shadowed by growing suspicion.

"Lunkhead?" she echoed. "You—you said I didn't know it was you. What didn't I know? What's going on?"

And he had to put the pieces of the puzzle together for her—there were really three pieces, he realized now—as much as he wished they didn't fit. Three pieces: Matt, Lauren and himself.

"I'm Luke," he confessed. "I got a call, Matt wanted me take his month and, then…"

Lauren's hand rose to her throat. "He wanted you to take his fiancée, too?"

"Keep me out of this," Matt said, as he turned to pull a bag of frozen peas from the freezer. He winced as he placed it over his eye. "I was as much in the dark about my twin's little deception as you."

Lauren glanced over at Matt, then returned her gaze to Luke, horror overtaking the confusion on her face. "You…you were…"

A dozen excuses came to mind. Phrases that might, somehow, save the situation. Explanations that might, with luck or with charm or with both, absolve him. But his mouth refused to utter them. His lips would only form three words. "I was wrong."

They were the same three that sent her flying away from him.

In the master bedroom, Lauren worked at erasing her presence from Hunter's house. Maybe, just maybe, if she made it as if she'd never been here, then the past days would be like a dream—a nightmare—that she could wake from.

It didn't mean the monster wouldn't find her one last time, however. Though she'd hoped Matthias—no, *Luke*—would stay well clear of her after what he'd confessed in the kitchen, when she felt a little tingle at the base of her spine, she looked over to find the man who'd tricked her leaning against the doorjamb. Wrenching her gaze away from him, she continued stripping the sheets from the mattress.

"What are you doing?" he asked quietly.

With the bathroom towels in a pile on the floor and the pillowcases already on top of them, she thought he could figure it out. "Don't worry, I'll remake the bed," she said.

The tension in the room leaped higher and when she glanced over at him, she saw the new hard-set to his jaw. "Lauren…" he started, but then gusted out a sigh and stalked off.

She released her breath and rubbed her damp palms on her jeans. Maintaining her dignity while in his proximity was paramount—though next to impossible.

However, she wasn't going to leave until she completed this cathartic little process.

Or stall tactic. Maybe that's what it was. Because though she knew that Luke had betrayed her, it hadn't sunk in quite yet. At the moment she was almost numb…and she liked it that way.

The bottom sheet joined the pile of dirty linens. Then she turned toward the hallway to find clean ones but instead found him barring her exit from the bedroom, his arms full of what she was after.

"I'll take those," she said, sweeping them away.

Her gaze avoided his naked chest, even as the back of her hands tingled from where they'd rubbed against his. Without a word, he disappeared into the walk-in closet, but he was back too soon, now dressed in jeans and a T-shirt.

The Game Palace, it read. Where Guys Go To Get Game.

He'd played her, all right.

The thought jabbed through her anesthetized emotions and made a direct hit at her heart. Ducking her head, she reached deep for calm as she smoothed the bottom sheet along the mattress. It stretched away from her hands and she looked over to see Matthias— *Luke*—pulling it up to reach the opposite corner.

"I can do it myself," she hissed, then felt herself flush, embarrassed at the slip in her composure. *Find the numbness again,* she told herself. *Let him think it meant nothing to you. Let him think you don't care that you went to bed with the wrong man.*

Then how come it had felt so right?

She bit down hard on her bottom lip as she continued making up the bed. What was the big surprise that she'd messed up again? She'd been wrong three times before. The fourth should have been a given. It *had* been a given! She'd come here to Lake Tahoe to break it off, then she'd met Luke and he'd messed up her plans.

Her hands shook as she picked up a pillow. Then she found herself staring at him, across the width of the bed where they'd slept together so many nights. "Why did you do it?"

He shrugged, staring down at the fresh sheet before he looked up to meet her gaze again. "I told you once. I was tired of my brother having everything I want."

He hadn't wanted *her,* though. Not really. He'd merely wanted something of his brother's. She could see that now. "Were you laughing at me?"

His eyes closed. "No. Never." Then they opened, a faint smile trying to quirk the corners of his mouth. "Okay, sometimes, when you cried at those tragic movies."

"That's not funny, Matthias." She groaned at her own mistake, even as she felt hot tears sting the corner of her eyes. "Luke. *Luke.*"

She sank to the edge of the bed and rubbed her forehead with her hand. "Funny, in my mind I started thinking of you as the bad twin. I guess I was right."

"I guess you were," he agreed. "Because I can see now that my reasons—"

"You actually think you have an explanation for this?" Flabbergasted, she stared at him, then wiggled her fingers in a little go-ahead gesture. "I can't *wait* to hear it."

He scraped his hand over his face. "I told you about what happened with our father's will, how Matt cheated a supplier to make his million first."

"That's what you say happened."

"It's happening again now. I've been in talks with a company in Germany over the last few months, putting together something that's make-or-break for my company, Eagle Wireless. Everything seemed to be proceeding fine and dandy and when my brother asked me to do him the favor of taking his month at Hunter's house, I agreed. But then I found out the second day I was here that Matt was in Stuttgart, talking to my guy and trying to take over *my* deal."

And for a man like Luke who hated to lose… She knew all he didn't say, and it amazed her that he'd been able to hide his anger and frustration over the past few days. No wonder he'd found it so difficult to relax. Every minute with her here meant another minute jeopardizing the success of his company.

"But you have to see that this—" he continued, gesturing toward the half-made bed, "—you have to know that this was never something I did to hurt you."

"Well, you could never hurt me," she scoffed. She was numb, remember? Anesthetized. Thank God, because his brother's actions didn't excuse the way he'd used her. "I'm not hurt."

"The engagement—"

"I took that off the table, remember? *I* already broke up with *you,* if you'll recall. I'm not wearing your ring, right?" Then she looked down at her bare hand and laughed. "Oh, but that was Matthias's ring."

It struck her as funny now. So funny that she heard

herself laughing again as she thought of breaking up with Luke who wasn't Matthias. Of going to bed with the wrong brother who had felt so right. Of taking off Matthias's ring so Luke wouldn't feel bad about breaking his promise to her.

Of how she felt about the fiancé who wasn't her fiancé after all. Still laughing, she dropped her face to her hands and gave up any pretense of dignity. It was all too funny for that.

"Lauren?" Luke hurried around the bed and sat down beside her. "Are you okay?"

Her cheeks were wet with tears. "Don't you find it hysterical?" she managed to get out.

"What?" He lifted his hand as if he was going to touch her face, but then it fell to his thigh. "What's making you cry?"

"I'm laughing," she corrected him. It continued to bubble inside of her and she had to hold her palm over her stomach to hold it down. "I'm laughing, because for the first time in my failed career as a fiancée, I fell in love with the man who put a ring on my finger, only to find out he was still the wrong man after all."

She wiped her cheeks with the back of her hands. "Just like everyone else, you never really cared about me."

Too late she heard all that she'd revealed to him.

Too late she realized all the dignity she'd lost.

Too late she recalled almost the very first words he'd ever said to her: *Never show me your weakness, I'll use it against you.*

Luke found his brother in the kitchen, making another pot of coffee. Well, not making the coffee exactly. He had the ingredients at hand but he was frowning at the coffeemaker. The coffeemaker that had been perfectly fine earlier that morning but now had a malfunctioning readout that was blinking an angry red like a malevolent animal.

He shouldered Matt aside. "Let someone with tech savvy take over."

"Kendall always makes the coffee."

"Who?"

Matt dropped into a chair at the kitchen table. "Kendall, my assistant. She brings it to me, too."

Luke rolled his eyes. His assistant, Elaine, would throw the stapler at his head if he asked her to make him a coffee. His brother's actually delivered beverages. "One in a million," he murmured.

A kabillion.

His gut churned with bile. *A kabillion.* He remembered Lauren saying that, saying it was what they could make on their bottled sexual chemistry. Closing his eyes, he gripped the countertop and hung his head, waiting for the nausea to pass.

"So, where's my fiancée?" Matt asked, his voice casual.

His head whipped toward his brother. "She took off your ring."

Matt stretched his legs out in front of him. "When she thought you were me. I can understand that."

"Damn it, she came here to break off the engagement!"

Matt stifled a yawn behind his hand. "You didn't answer the question. Where's my fiancée?"

"She left, all right? She left—"

"You. She left you."

Luke was standing by the counter and the coffee-maker one minute. The next, he was jerking his brother out of his seat, holding him by fistfuls of his starched shirt. "She never wanted to marry you in the first place."

"What are you going to do about it, lunkhead? Give me another black eye? Is that the way you're solving your problems these days?"

Luke shoved Matt back in his chair. His brother's shiner was puffy and red and he didn't feel an ounce of guilt over it. "This is all your fault," he said. "Damn it, Matt, if you hadn't cheated me—"

"Aren't you sick of that song?" Matt rose from the chair, his voice tight. "I told you I didn't cheat you then, I told it to you earlier this morning, but I'm not going to tell you again. Damn it, I'm done with my part of this little tune."

He stalked toward the door, then paused for a long moment. With a tired shrug, he turned back around. "I came here to do the right thing. You took my place in the house as a favor. Do you need me to move in now so you can get back to work?"

I came here to do the right thing. Luke stared at his brother and then Lauren's voice sounded in his head—would he always hear her? *Neither of you would be satisfied to achieve victory through some sort of dirty trick.*

"Well?" Matt prompted. "Are you heading back to work?"

Work. Eagle Wireless. Luke ran his hand over his face. Back at the helm of his company, things would make sense again. There would be meetings, conference calls, engineers who need a butt kick in order to jump-start their latent skills in speaking non-tech English. Best of all, he could immediately board a plane for Stutt-gart and do whatever it took to salvage his deal with Ernst.

With all that on his plate, he'd forget about his time here. He'd forget about Lauren. He'd forget about Matt's betrayal.

Neither of you would be satisfied to achieve victory through some sort of dirty trick.

His gaze lasered in on his brother. "Where've you been?"

"I told you when we spoke last week. Germany."

"Stuttgart? Ernst?"

His twin's good eye narrowed. "You know Ernst?"

Luke laughed. So much for brotherhood. "He's *my* guy, as if you didn't know."

A strange expression crossed Matt's face. "What?"

"You must know I've been working on him to make a deal with Eagle Wireless. So I'm guessing you have a spy in my company. Somebody else you're paying off to your advantage."

"I don't have anyone I'm paying off in your company," Matt retorted, but then his voice slowed. "That I know of."

Luke laughed again. But as that odd expression once more crossed his brother's face, he swallowed his scorn.

Neither of you would be satisfied to achieve victory through some sort of dirty trick.

Luke shoved his hand through his hair. "Look, I've been in contact with Ernst since last fall. When did you hear about him?"

"*Fall?* I've only been talking to Ernst this last month." Matt looked off, his jaw tightening just as Luke's did when he was angry. "Hell."

"Damn it, Matt," Luke said. "Tell me you didn't cheat me seven years ago."

His brother's one-eyed gaze jerked back to his face. "I've told you and told you."

"Just tell me again." Luke grabbed up a few of the photos spread on the table, his gut churning once more as he felt poised on the brink of something big. Something really, really big.

"Here in Hunter's house, swear on the brothers we used to be." He held out the evidence toward his twin.

Matt reached out for the photos, but he didn't look away from Luke's face. "I'd rather chew off my own arm than admit this, Luke, but what you said about Ernst means I have to investigate what's going on. Someone I've trusted may have conned us both out of quite a lot. Believe me, though, on the memory of our good friend Hunter Palmer, on the memory of the kind of brothers we used to be, I didn't knowingly cheat you. I swear."

In a decisive strike, those last two words blew a hole in Luke's defensive wall of bitter anger. Emotions long-dammed up released, pouring relief, sadness and a weird kind of elation into his bloodstream. His brother hadn't cheated him.

He had his brother back.

"Matt." Though he felt dizzy with the revelation, he could breathe easier, he found. After all these years, he could finally take a deep breath. "I believe you, Matt."

A faint smile turned up his brother's mouth. "Say 'I believe you, meathead.'"

Meathead and lunkhead. The names from their childhood when the enemy had been each other.

"He still wouldn't be sorry for what he did to us," Luke said.

Matt knew exactly who he was talking about. Exactly what he was talking about. "Dear old Dad and those destructive games he made us play."

"I hope we can get past him, and them, again." Luke looked at the photos his brother still held. "We did in college."

"You slept with my fiancée."

Lauren. Oh, God, Lauren.

With the emotional dam that had been inside of him now destroyed, there was no longer any protection against the guilt and remorse now coursing through him like a flood. He'd hurt Lauren.

Lauren, who was in love with him.

Lauren, who'd said, *Just like everyone else, you never really cared about me.*

But Luke did care about her. Luke cared a whole hell of a lot, and he couldn't let her go on with her life thinking he was yet another failed fiancé. Except that failed fiancé would be Matt, wouldn't it?

And that made him feel better, even as it struck him again what an arrogant, unfeeling bastard he'd been, using Lauren to get back at his brother.

I'm in love with you. She'd said that.

And he'd broken her heart.

But it would be all right, wouldn't it? Give her a

couple of days and she'd realize his sorry soul wasn't worth her smiles, her laughter, her touch, her heart.

Hell.

He couldn't live with that.

"You're staying here at the house," he told his brother, making a swift decision. "I have somewhere I've got to be."

"Some*one* you've got to *see?*" Matt asked, lifting the bag of frozen peas to his face again.

"You don't love her." As a twin, he knew he was speaking the truth.

"I don't love her," Matt admitted, removing the plastic to gaze at him with both eyes. "But I was talking about Ernst."

"Ernst?" Already Luke had forgotten about flying to Germany. He waved the man's name away. "It's Lauren I'm thinking about." Lauren, who he'd betrayed.

Matt shook his head and replaced the bag of peas. "What makes you think she's going to be happy to see you?"

Luke refused to be defeated by the idea. "I'll make it right with her," he told his brother. He had to. "No matter what. It's the Barton family motto, remember? Assume success, deny failure."

Matt shrugged. "All right. Maybe it'll be okay. Maybe you just need to get your foot in the door."

Luke's shoulders sagged. She wouldn't let him get his foot in the door, would she? By the time she drove home, he was certain she would have convinced herself she never wanted to see him again.

If Luke showed up she wouldn't let him get within twenty feet.

But what if…?

He looked at his brother. "There's something else you have to do for me," he said to Matt. "And I think you're going to like it."

Ten

Dinner hour, *casa* Conover. Lauren looked around the table at her little sister, her mother and then her father who had just seated himself after making them wait while he finished a phone call. Though she'd only been back in the family house a mere twenty-four hours, it was as if she'd never left.

"That bumbling Bilbray," her father muttered as their housekeeper, June, set his steaming plate of chicken Kiev in front of him. "It's as if he doesn't understand the law of supply and demand. Didn't he go to business school? Hasn't he been working for me for more than fifteen years? Do I have to teach him to tie his shoes as well as read a spreadsheet?"

Lauren turned to her sister, raising her voice over her father's continued annoyed ramblings. "What were you saying, Kaitlyn? That Mr. Beall wants to you to design the drama department's page on the school Web site?"

Without waiting for an answer, she swiveled toward her father. "Dad, did you hear that? Kaitlyn's drama teacher is going to be paying her real money for Web site design."

At the word *money* her father paused in his brainless Bilbray-litany and glanced in his younger daughter's direction. "We could use the extra cash now that Lauren's broken it off with Matthias Barton. Though maybe I can do something about that. Maybe I can give that young man a call and—"

"Dad," Lauren interrupted. "I don't want to marry Matthias Barton."

"He'll probably give you another chance, you know. He's as eager to be aligned with Conover Industries as we are eager to be aligned with him, and—"

"Dad, I'm not going to marry Matthias Barton."

Lauren's mother looked up from her chicken Kiev, a spark lighting in her eyes. "Ralph, do you really think you can persuade Matthias to reconsider Lauren? Despite her rash response to another of her Bad Ideas? I haven't had a chance to cancel the reservations for the reception yet—"

"What?" Lauren stared at her mother. "You didn't tell me you'd booked a venue for the reception. We hadn't even started talking about that yet."

Carole Conover waved her manicured fingers. "I've had my eye on this particular Napa winery for years. You could have the wedding there, too, if you'd like, though maybe Matthias would prefer a church service instead."

Lauren shook her head in disbelief. "By all means, let's consult Matthias," she muttered to herself.

Kaitlyn's voice piped up from across the table. "There *was* that pretty junior bridesmaid's dress. I could live with the blue one with the ribbon sash."

Lauren's gaze jumped toward her sister. *"Et tu?"*

Their mother beamed at Kaitlyn. "I think you're right. Definitely the blue one with the sash."

Lauren wanted to scream. She wanted to rent her clothes. She wanted to find a completely unsuitable groom and elope to Lithuania. Ha, she thought. *Maybe Trevor can be convinced to leave his ski-heiress for me. Then* her parents would be sorry.

Which was exactly why she'd agreed to marry Trevor the first time, she realized. And why she'd said yes to her father's mechanic. And why it had almost been oui with Jean-Paul on the top of the Eiffel Tower. Luke had suggested that to her, hadn't he? And now she saw it, too. All her previous fiancés had been perfect-perfect paragons of parental rebellion.

Oh God. Had she really tried standing up to her overbearing mother and father by marrying the wrong man time and again?

And again?

Good God. If that was true, bumbling Bilbray was way more on the ball than Lauren.

"How shall you handle this, Ralph?" her mother was saying. "Maybe keep it simple and tell Matthias Barton that Lauren was just suffering a little case of cold feet?"

During which she'd slept with your brother and fallen in love with the jerk, Lauren finished for her mother. Not that she'd shared with her parents that part of her Tahoe visit. Maybe they'd been right all along. Maybe she had no business deciding what to do with her own life because she just kept on botching it up.

"I've always thought September weddings were special," her mother said with a sigh. "It's a lovely time of year for a honeymoon."

Lauren grimaced. No matter what, no matter who, it wasn't happening in September. "I'm committed to a conference for the publishing house that month, Mom. There's not room for anything else on my calendar then."

Her father waved away her objection with his fork. "Nonsense. You can just quit that silly job if it gets in the way of your wedding."

"Silly job?" Lauren echoed, even as her father went back to his meal. "Dad, I make a good living as a translator. I could even take my skills and help you out at Conover if you'd let me."

"Help me out how?"

"Translating, Dad. You know, what I've been trained for? What I've been doing for several years now. I even have a hefty bank balance to prove it. Other companies besides the publisher pay me tidy sums for my work involving technological and business matters. It's not easy to find people who can not only translate, but translate techno-speak as well."

Her father started to bluster. "We have a company on retainer—"

"Linguanotics. I know them. I know Jeremy Cloud, who does most of their work for you. I'm better. And I'd like to put together a presentation that will show you just how and why you should hire me as a consultant instead. I guarantee you won't be sorry."

Her entire family was staring at her in surprise. Lauren herself felt energized, focused, her senses as honed as when she competed against her arch-nemesis, Luke. This was what it felt like to tackle things head-on with an intention to win, she realized.

And she liked it. It was the one good thing she could lay at Luke's door—that he'd taught her the power there was in assuming success and denying failure.

"Well…I—I—" Her father sputtered, looking over at her mother for help.

"I'm sure your father will give you time for a presentation," Carole said smoothly. "But why don't you wait until after the honeymoon, all right?"

It was straightforward straight talk time once again. Lauren's heart sped up as she gripped the edge of the table and leaned toward her mother. "Mom, you need to listen to me. I'm not going to marry that man. There isn't going to be a wedding in September. Cancel the winery, call off the dressmaker, rip up any other plans you've been hatching behind my back."

"Lauren—"

"There's going to be no wedding," Lauren interjected, her voice firm. "I'm not going to marry Matthias and he certainly doesn't want to marry me."

The sound of a throat clearing had everyone swiveling in their seat. June stood on the threshold to the dining room, clutching the skirt of her apron in her hands. Her face was flushed. "Um…there's someone here."

"Someone who?" her father demanded, his gaze

flicking to the grandfather clock in the corner of the room.

"Mr. Matthias Barton."

Lauren groaned as her mother shot her a triumphant look.

Luke was practically choking thanks to his Matt-tight tie as he was shown into the Conover dining room by the pink-cheeked housekeeper. The first person his gaze landed on was a young girl—Kaitlyn, of course—and he sent her a little grin as she reacted to his face with a wince.

Then *he* winced a little, too, because the smile hurt like hell.

"Barton!" Ralph Conover stood up from his place at the table and reached out his hand. "Have you had dinner?"

Luke hadn't seen the older man in years, but even if he hadn't already recognized him he would have known him by the Lauren-blue of his eyes. "I'm fine, sir, no dinner for me. I'm sorry to disturb you, but I came to see if I might have a word with your older daughter."

He sent her a sidelong glance, but she was staring down at her plate, as if mesmerized by her asparagus.

"Lauren?" her mother prompted. "Why don't you and Matthias go have a nice long chat in the library?"

A moment passed, then, with a resigned nod, the younger woman pushed back her chair. As they exited the room, Kaitlyn called out, "Don't forget the blue dress, Lauren. It's really pretty."

In the library, she shut the double doors behind them, then spoke without facing him. "I left the engagement ring on the dresser in the master bedroom," she said. "I should have told you that before I left. Now, if there's nothing else…"

Luke stared as she started turning the double door-knobs again. She was leaving the room? Leaving his life? "Wait…wait…"

She spun to face him. "What? What is it you want, Matthias?"

He was stupid. He'd had hours with which to figure out what to say right now, and he'd thought of nothing beyond finding a way to be alone with her again. "About my brother…"

"That's quite a shiner he gave you."

"Yeah." Matt hadn't been as reluctant as Luke might have wished to give him a matching punch to the face. But he'd realized he deserved it and more for what he'd done. Most important, he'd been certain that Lauren wouldn't have agreed to see him as himself, Luke.

So he'd gone for the ole twin switcheroo again. Maybe he should feel more guilt over that, but at the moment there was only desperation in his heart.

"Look," he started, still hoping for inspiration to strike. "My brother, he's really sorry—"

"About being as stupid as I was in agreeing to marry a near-perfect stranger?"

"He can be a little single-minded about business, too, and he thought—" Luke broke off, realizing what she'd said. Realizing that she'd seen through the switcheroo. "So you know."

"Fool me once, shame on you," she said, her face expressionless. "Fool me twice, shame on me. What are you out for now, Luke? More revenge?"

His face ached like a hammered thumb and it was all for nothing, damn it. And the pain was making it hard to think. "I wanted to try again to explain what happened."

She crossed her arms over her chest. "Your brother stole something from you and you wanted to steal something from him. I get that."

Luke shook his head. "That thing with Matt…we don't know what happened exactly, only that it was something shady, but I now know he didn't do it to me."

For a moment her stony face softened. "Oh, Luke. You have your twin again."

"Yeah. Maybe. I'm hopeful." His hand went to the egg on the back of his skull. "Though he's gained a powerful punch over the last few years. When he hit me I fell back and cracked my head on the table. I was seeing double from my one good eye until noon, which is why it took me an extra day to get here."

If he thought she might respond to the sympathy card, he was wrong. Her face was cold again and that's how he felt, too, cold with…with…hell, he had to admit it. Cold with fear.

What if he couldn't get through to her?

"But someone robbed something from me, after all," he blurted out.

"I told you where the ring is."

"That's Matt's, and you know I'm not interested in a damn piece of jewelry." The cold inside of him was as icy as the blue of her eyes, and it was slowing his heartbeat to a death knell.

How could he go on without her beside him? Who would he have to watch sappy movies with? Who would give him a pinch when he was getting too competitive?

After Hunter had died, there had been no one to show him the wider, brighter world until Lauren. Even if Matt had his back, who would be at his side?

It had to be Lauren. He only wanted Lauren.

He was in love with Lauren.

The thought ran like a flame through cold snow. Until this moment, he'd never allowed himself to even silently form the words, now he was consumed by them. He was in love with his Goldilocks, with her humor and her sweet disposition. With her knack for relaxing and the way the air heated when they were in a room together.

He was in love with her blond hair and her curvy body, from her short nose to her short toes, and every inch of creamy skin in between. He loved her full breasts and her pink nipples. He loved the almost transparent color of the curls that did little to protect her sex from his gaze. He loved the little sounds she made when he touched her there and found her already wet and her little bud—

"Luke."

From her annoyed expression and flushed cheeks, he figured she'd read just about all of that on his face.

"Luke, why did you come here?"

He squashed his panic at her cold, angry tone. She wasn't just falling into his arms as he might have hoped, but that didn't mean he'd give up. Bartons never gave up, and he sent out a silent prayer of thanks to his father for that. Amazing, that loving Lauren could even give him a new appreciation of Samuel Sullivan Barton.

"Luke—"

"You did take something of mine." The words tumbled out.

Her brows came together in a frown. "What?"

Here it was. Time to hand over the power. In business, he'd taught himself to always hold back, to keep some of his cards to himself, but now...now if he really wanted her he would have to lay it all on the table. He'd never had much faith in loyalty, but now he was going to have to take the risk and believe that this woman would give him hers.

"I don't want back what you took, though," he said, stalling. "You can keep it. You can have it forever."

Her frown deepened. "Well, what is it?"

Here goes. "My heart."

Lauren remembered the time she'd told Luke he looked as if she'd hit him with a cartoon frying pan, and she was certain that was the same expression she wore now. It certainly felt as if something had struck her, knocking the breath straight out of her lungs. "Wh-what?"

"I don't know if you took my heart or if I gave it or when it happened or how I could get so lucky. Maybe it's like Kaitlyn's rule and that true...true beauty only comes upon us by surprise. I wasn't expecting this, Lauren, but with you I see things so much clearer. I have a perspective that I've been missing nearly all my life. With you, I can think about breathing instead of about winning. With you, I can forget about my business and the constant hustle to make the next buck."

It was the longest speech she'd ever heard him make.

His voice, a little hoarse, a little breathless, rang with sincerity. Shaking her head, she flattened her hands against the creamy white paint of the doors and stared at him, trying to understand. Luke's eyes were serious, their expression intent.

Again, sincere.

But…but…

"You…your brother…you always want what he has," she reminded them both. "Now you're only trying to get back at him for that Stuttgart thing."

"This isn't about Matt anymore, Lauren," Luke said. "Please, please believe me, though I know I don't deserve your trust."

He *didn't* deserve her trust! "You seduced me under false pretences."

"Yes."

"You came here today, doing the same all over again."

He grimaced. "Yes. And I'm sorry, so sorry. Not so much about today, though. I needed to do whatever it took to see you again. To try to explain—"

"You shouldn't have bothered," Lauren said, bitterness giving bite to her words. "While it might be difficult for me to forgive you, believe me, I understand. I'm Ralph Conover's daughter, remember? I'm accustomed to the lengths a man will go for his business."

Her father's single-mindedness had been something she'd always half-joked about, but it had rankled her entire life. Even more as she grew older and saw how it affected Kaitlyn. The whole family had lost out on so much during his ruthless drive for the all-mighty dollar.

After the way Luke was raised, it was no surprise he was filled with the same competitive, cold-hearted zeal.

"So go away," she said, turning her face so she could avoid his. "Get on the first flight to Stuttgart and beat out your brother that way."

There was a long moment of silence, then Luke spoke again. "Lauren." It sounded strained. "Lauren, please look at me."

That was a mistake. Because despite his competitive, cold-hearted zeal, he had the appearance of a man who was more worried about losing than consumed with winning.

"I could *be* in Stuttgart right now if that's what was important to me," he said. "Matt's at Hunter's house to fulfill the stipulation of the will and if I wanted I could be in Europe, working on Ernst. *Without* a hell of a shiner, I might add, and without a bump on the back of my head bigger than a baseball. I didn't go to Stuttgart. I came to you."

Her heart jolted, one hard thump against her ribs. For the second time her breath was knocked right out of her.

Luke hadn't gone to Stuttgart.

He hadn't left Hunter's house at the first instant he could to shore up his business deal.

How could this be? How could competitive, cut-throat, cold-hearted Luke have abandoned the most important thing to him in the world?

She said it out loud, just to be sure. "You didn't go to Stuttgart." Her voice came out a whisper.

"I haven't given Germany another thought since you walked out on me," he replied. "I didn't go to Stuttgart because I wanted to be with you. I want to be with you because when we're together I actually enjoy the life that Hunter is no longer here to share. I finally figured out why he arranged that situation for the Samurai— or at least why he arranged it for me. I needed to reconnect with people again, Lauren. I needed to realize that I'm actually one myself, a person with emotions, and needs, and fears…and…and love. I'm so in love with you."

He was in love with her! Lauren felt her stomach fall toward her knees. He was in love with her? Before, he'd said she had his heart, but she'd still been trying to convince herself he didn't have one. But to say this, to say he was in love with her. And to give up his important business deal so that he could…

It was true. It must be true.

Oh, Luke.

She took a slow step forward. He froze, just watching her with those serious, worried eyes, as if afraid to believe what he was seeing.

She remembered dozens of sweet hours in his arms. Dozens of conversations about movies, travel, nothing at all. It hadn't mattered one wit what he called himself. It was the man, and not the name, she'd fallen for. Taking another forward step, she remembered again the exact moment she'd realized it, when he'd been angry, for her, at Trevor.

Her forward movement halted, her feet digging into the carpet.

Luke must have read the renewed reluctance on her face. For a second his eyes closed as if he experienced a sharp pain. Then they opened, and she could see that pain in his eyes.

Tears stung hers.

"What is it, Goldilocks? What's coming between you and my arms?" The tightness of his voice showed his strain. "I love you. Don't you believe me? Don't you believe that the man who was with you at Hunter's house, whether his name was Matt or Luke, was a man who fell in love with you?"

She shook her head, mute. That Luke hadn't hurried off to Stuttgart proved the strength of his feelings. The problem, at the moment, wasn't him.

"What can I do?" he asked, hoarser now. "What can I do to make you mine? I want to marry you, Lauren."

"I'm afraid," she said. Thinking of Trevor had opened the door to it. "I've been engaged three times before. Each time the decision was wrong."

"Make that four times, sweetheart." Luke grimaced. "Remember? I'm not Matt."

Her eyes widened and she felt them sting again. "You're right. Four mistakes. Luke…"

His hands fisted at his sides. She could see him holding himself back. Luke would always be one who reacted with action, whose first instinct would be to take matters into his own hands and force the results he wanted. But here he was, letting her come to her own conclusions. It made her love him more…feel even more unsure of what she should do about it.

"Lauren, sweetheart." He blew out a breath. "Trust yourself."

"*Myself*? Trust *myself*? What kind of reasoning is that? I'm the one who picked Trevor and Joe and Jean-Paul."

"You know what I think about them? I think you picked those three with your parents in mind, and if

that's the case, then they were exactly the wrong men—
which was exactly right for what you were after at the
time."

Oh, God. That was true. Hadn't she acknowledged
it during dinner? They'd been perfect men for her
perfect parental rebellion. Luke knew her so well. And
yet still loved her. How could she turn away from that?
Four fiancés should have taught her *something*.

"This time, Goldilocks, if I might make a suggestion,
why don't you pick the man who is just right for you."

Lauren loved the library. As a little girl, she used to
tuck herself away behind one of the leather wing chairs
and pour over old atlases that listed exotically named
countries such as Persia and Wallachia and Travan-
core. She dreamed of the people who lived there and
the sounds of their spoken languages.

Later, she dreamed of visiting those places with a
man who would share her curiosity and who would
make her spin with dizzy happiness—like the globe
sitting on the table in front of the mullioned windows.

Of course, she'd never imagined she'd be cradling
her love's head on her lap while applying a bag of
petite white corn kernels to his battered face—but she
crooned sympathetically to him in French and Spanish
as a way of making up for it.

He opened his good eye. "Did you just call me a little
toad?"

"Only because of all these new lumps on your skull,"
she said, trying not to laugh. Laughter jostled her legs
which in turn put pressure on the bump on the back of
his head. "Are you sure you shouldn't see a doctor?"

"Your mother won't let me out of the house, not now that we've convinced her *our* engagement isn't a big hoax to get back at her for not taking your career seriously."

"Thank you for making that point to her when she started going off on a September wedding date again. I'm determined to manage her in just such a straightforward manner from now on." Lauren leaned down to press her mouth lightly to his.

When he tried to take the kiss deeper, she pulled back. "No. You're supposed to be resting."

His eye closed and his lips curved up in a smile. "We'll go back to Hunter's house tomorrow and rest up for the remainder of my month."

"I'm a little afraid to let you go to sleep, though," Lauren said. Her gaze traveled over the face that had become the map to her happiness. "What if, thanks to that bump on your head, when you wake up you don't remember me?"

He opened his good eye again and the expression she read there made the love inside of her expand until there wasn't room for breath.

"Then we'll become acquainted all over again, Goldilocks, because the Big Bad Wolf has finally caught the pretty girl—and he isn't ever letting her go."

Lauren and Luke were making a final walk-through of Hunter's house before they left it for the last time. She peered under the bed and spotted a penny on the carpet in the very middle—too far to reach even if she got down on her hands and knees.

With a little smile to herself, she left it where it lay.

Maybe the coin would bring the next Samurai the same good luck Luke swore he'd found here.

On her last sweep of the master bathroom, she discovered a note taped to the mirror. Luke's handwriting was as dark and aggressive as he was, and, no surprise, he didn't waste time with greetings or goodbyes. It only read:

> Dev: Remember the talk we had about women on New Year's Eve our senior year? We were wrong, man. So wrong. We didn't have a clue.

Luke came up behind her as she read over the words. She looked up to meet his gaze in the glass. "Well?" she asked.

His lips twitched. "Well, what?"

"What's it mean? What didn't you two have a clue about?"

Tenderness replaced amusement in his eyes. He twirled a curl of her hair around his finger. "You'll meet Devlin Campbell someday very soon, Goldilocks. And then you can ask him."

* * * * *

THE ROYAL
WEDDING NIGHT

by
Day Leclaire

Dear Reader,

This is the final book in THE ROYALS trilogy and I can't tell you how sorry I am to be leaving the amazing country of Verdonia. I hope you've all enjoyed visiting it as much as I've enjoyed writing the stories. I think this final Royal book may have been my favourite. There's something about a man and a woman stranded together that has always appealed to me. Maybe it's the heightened emotions that solitude can create as two people are forced to depend on each other while they confront their deepest conflicts. Or maybe it's the inevitability of a stolen romance, far from prying eyes. Whichever, I loved every minute writing this book, particularly as I redeemed Brandt.

Though I don't have any more Royal books planned, I hope you'll enjoy visiting with Joc Arnaud (Juliana's brother from *The Prince's Mistress*) in my June 2008 release, *The Billionaire's Baby Negotiation*. It would seem that Lander's wish is granted and Joc finds himself in a similar situation to the one he forced on Lander!

Please visit me at my website: www.dayleclaire. com. I love hearing from readers!

Best,

Day Leclaire

DAY LECLAIRE

is the multi-award-winning author of nearly forty novels. Her passionate books offer a unique combination of humour, emotion and unforgettable characters, which have won Day tremendous worldwide popularity, as well as numerous publishing honours. She is a three-time winner of both a Colorado Award of Excellence and a Golden Quill Award. She's won a *Romantic Times BOOKreviews* Career Achievement Award and a Love and Laughter Award, a Holt Medallion, a Booksellers Best Award, and she has received an impressive ten nominations for the prestigious Romance Writers of America RITA® Award.

Day's romances touch the heart and make you care about her characters as much as she does. In Day's own words, "I adore writing romances and can't think of a better way to spend each day."

To True Love… To Matt and Adrienne.
Happy first anniversary.
Wishing you another fifty just as happy!

One

Principality of Avernos, Verdonia—
How it all began...

"No. No way, no how. You're not doing this, Miri. I don't care what you say or do. I won't have you involved in any of this."

She threw off her cover-up to reveal the wedding gown she wore beneath. She didn't care how much he loomed over her, she wasn't about to back down. Her other royal stepbrother, Lander, had long been dubbed the "Lion of Mt. Roche." But Merrick reminded her more of a golden leopard than the king of beasts. Maybe that had something to do with his being whipcord lean and sleek, and deadly silent until he moved in for an attack. Not to mention possessing a speed and agility she'd never seen bested.

"It's too late, Merrick. I'm already involved."

His mouth compressed at the sight of her gown, and he pinned her with a merciless gaze. "Only because you listened in on a private conversation." He nodded knowingly. "Yes, you damn well should blush. Hell, Miri. I'm the head of Verdonia's Royal Security Force. If I'd caught anyone else doing what you did, I'd have thrown them in the deepest, darkest pit I could find. Worse, if anyone in a position of authority had found out you'd spied, I'd have been forced to act. My own sister!"

"You need my help," she insisted stubbornly.

He gripped her shoulders and gave her a gentle shake. "Listen to me, honey, this is serious. Abducting a woman…it could mean jail for everyone involved."

"Then it means jail." She shot Merrick a stony glare, utilizing every ounce of logic she could summon—a difficult proposition when raw emotion held her in its grip. "Think about it. You're planning to abduct Princess Alyssa minutes before her wedding. Don't you think the groom's going to notice when his bride goes missing? You need someone to take her place at the altar. To fool people just long enough so you have time to get away."

He thrust a hand through hair streaked every color from blond to umber. "The operative words here are 'get away.' I get away. My men get away. Even Alyssa gets away, if not by choice. You're the one left at von Folke's mercy. What do you think will happen when he unveils you—literally—and discovers you're not Princess Alyssa Sutherland, political ally. Instead, he's married Princess Miri Montgomery, sister of his political foe. Or have you forgotten that von Folke and Lander are rivals for the throne of Verdonia?"

She dismissed the question with a sweep of her hand. "Of course I haven't forgotten. But do you really think Prince Brandt will have me arrested? Throw me into prison? How will that look five short months before the election to choose our next king?"

"Von Folke isn't going to be happy," Merrick replied, before adding beneath his breath, "and that has to be the understatement of the year. There's no question in my mind that he'll take out his unhappiness on someone. I don't want that someone to be you."

"Brandt wouldn't hurt me. At least…not the way you mean."

"You can't be certain of that." Merrick started hammering away again. "He might find another way to get even for the theft of his bride. I won't allow him to use you for that purpose. Not when I'm the one responsible."

"Nor will I." She stood in a copy of another woman's wedding gown, trembling from a combination of fury and heartbreak. "I have it all planned out. When it's time for the unveiling at the end of the ceremony, I'm going to refuse to allow it. I'll fake an illness, if I have to. I'll ask them to take me to my room—Alyssa's room—until I can recover. And the instant I'm alone, I'll change into whatever of hers fits and leave."

"Just like that? You don't think anyone will stop you?" Merrick folded his arms across his chest. "You can't be that naive."

Miri lifted an eyebrow. "Why would anyone stop

me? After all, I'm just a guest at the wedding, not the bride. It'll be Miri Montgomery who strolls out the front door, not Princess Alyssa Sutherland von Folke. Now, stop arguing, Merrick. If you don't like my idea, then work on perfecting the plan. What can we change so it will work?"

"There's no point in perfecting or changing anything. I won't allow you to go through with this."

"You'll do it." She played her final card. "You'll do it, or I'll tell big brother what you're planning."

She may have pushed him too far. Anger sent twin flags of color flaring across his cheekbones. "You'd involve Lander?"

"In a heartbeat."

"If you tell him, if you involve him in this, he'll lose any chance at the throne. He'll be an accessory."

She grasped Merrick's hands in hers. "Then let me help you. If your plan succeeds, Lander will sit on the throne. Isn't that what you want?"

"That's not why I'm doing this," he instantly denied. "All I want is a fair election. That won't happen if von Folke marries Princess Alyssa. If he gains her as a political ally, the throne is as good as his."

"Fine. We're both doing it for the good of Verdonia. I just want your plan to succeed and I'm the best person to make sure that happens. Now, are we through here?" She gestured toward the door. "Do we go switch brides now, or do you want to waste more time arguing?"

Sheer stubbornness turned his eyes a molten gold and for a full thirty seconds she was certain she'd lost. Then he gave an abrupt nod and Miri allowed her breath to escape in a silent sigh of relief. She turned toward the door, but he stopped her before she could open it.

"Not so fast." Drawing her deeper into the room of the cottage he'd rented, he examined her appearance with a critical eye. "What the hell did you do to your hair?"

She touched the loose curls self-consciously. "Your man said Alyssa was a blonde. I figured my disguise would hold up a little better if I bleached it."

"Can you turn it back…after?"

She actually managed to smile at the hint of alarm in his voice. "Yes, I can turn it back. You like it dark better than blond?"

"On you, yes."

How ironic. From the day her mother had married Merrick's father, King Stefan, she'd wanted to look like the rest of the Montgomerys, all of whom were tall and athletic and striking, their streaked hair and hazel eyes kissed with golden sunshine. Her coal-black hair and pale green eyes had always made her feel like an outsider, as did the fact that she was a princess by adoption and proclamation, rather than birth. Only with Brandt had she ever felt—

To her relief, Merrick broke in before she could complete the thought. "It just might work," he conceded reluctantly. "From the photos I've seen, you're close in height and body shape."

"That was my biggest concern."

"It's not mine," he retorted, a sharp edge to his words. "When it's time for you to leave as Miri Montgomery, people might wonder why you've bleached your hair blond, especially when they see you exiting Alyssa's room."

"You think it'll rouse suspicion?" She shook her head. "They'll think I've made a poor fashion choice, that's all. It won't occur to them it's because I took the bride's place at the altar. As for being in Alyssa's room…I was helping the bride, poor dear. Something she ate didn't agree with her, I suspect. She's asked that no one disturb her for a bit. Just give her an hour or two to rest and she'll be fine. Oh, and perhaps you'd deliver a message to Prince Brandt? Tell him that his bride is looking forward to joining him a little later this evening, after she's had some private time to recover."

Merrick looked far from happy. "It might work."

"It *will* work."

"Don't get cocky, Miri. You're not a perfect match. And it's far from a perfect plan."

"So, I'll improvise. With luck no one will notice the discrepancies, especially not beneath a veil. You'll need to give me Alyssa's. If I wear a different veil…that is something women will notice."

"I'll make sure you have it." His voice turned gruff. "You look—You look incredible, sweetheart. I just wish this were real, that you were standing here dressed for your own wedding, instead of for this farce."

His words struck like a blow, though he couldn't possibly have known. She forced out a careless smile and prayed her voice would hold steady. "Thank you. But I'd need a fiancé for that, wouldn't I?" Too bad the man she'd had in mind was no longer interested, despite what he'd once claimed.

An odd expression drifted across Merrick's face, one she could have only described as "brotherly." Tucking a strand of hair behind her ear, he shrugged. "You're only twenty-five. There's plenty of time to fall in love." He made a production of checking his watch, then gestured toward the door. "Time to go. We're cutting this close as it is."

Miri preceded her brother from the cottage he'd rented as a command center and allowed him to help her into the passenger seat of a silver-gray SUV. Behind them his men piled into a matching black one, which tailed them at a circumspect speed through the hilly roads of Verdonia's northernmost principality of Avernos. Nerves prevented her from attempting idle chatter, not that she'd have had any opportunity. Merrick spent the entire trip filling her in on every detail he'd uncovered about Princess Alyssa, no matter how minor. Half an hour passed before the two cars turned down a narrow country road. Less than a mile farther along they veered onto a dirt shoulder.

Leaving the car to idle, Merrick swiveled in his seat to look at her. "Listen to me, Miri. This shouldn't take long. No more than twenty minutes." He tapped the car clock. "If we're not back in that time precisely, you are to get behind the wheel and drive away. Head straight south from Avernos all the way through Celestia until you reach Verdon, and don't stop until you get there. Don't come looking for me. Don't call anyone. Just get the hell out. Are we clear?"

"Clear."

He shook his head. "I'm serious, Miri. I want your

word of honor. If I don't return in twenty minutes, swear to me you'll leave without intervening in any way."

They were the two most difficult words she'd ever spoken. "I swear."

He nodded in satisfaction. Climbing out of the SUV, he signaled to his men. The four of them, all dressed in melt-into-the-shadows black, slid ominous hoods over their heads as they trotted across the expanse of grass beside the road and headed toward a small ridge half hidden by a dense expanse of deciduous forest. Miri inched forward in her seat and kept her gaze glued on the car clock. The seconds crept by, one by one, until after an hour—or what seemed like an hour—a mere fifteen minutes had piled up onto the clock.

At nineteen minutes, thirty seconds, Merrick emerged from the woods. He held a woman in his arms, a woman wearing a silver gown that proved a close match to Miri's. A flowing lace and tulle veil sat askew on her long blond curls. Princess Alyssa Sutherland. She was absolutely stunning, Miri noted with a sinking heart. And a bit shorter than she, herself, was. But that shouldn't present a problem. She'd brought an extra pair of shoes to cover just that eventuality. Switching the ones she wore for the pair with the lowest heels, she opened the car door and headed toward Merrick.

"It's time," he said, as she approached. "You don't have to go through with this. You can still change your mind."

"I can't and I won't. There are…reasons."

She didn't dare explain further. If Merrick knew the truth, he'd never have agreed to involve her. At the sound of her voice, Princess Alyssa stiffened. She started to turn her head to look, but his grip tightened, preventing her.

"Quickly, Merrick," Miri warned. "We have only moments until her disappearance is discovered."

Ripping the voluminous veil from Alyssa's head, he tossed it to Miri. "Will this work?"

"It's perfect. From what I can tell our dresses are nearly identical. The veil will definitely conceal any discrepancies." She shot a wary glance toward Princess Alyssa and switched from English to Verdonian. From what Merrick had said, the woman had been raised in the United States and, until she'd flown out to marry Brandt, hadn't been in Verdonia since she was a toddler. Chances were excellent she didn't speak the language.

"Be careful with this one," she warned, nodding toward the woman Merrick held. "I know how you are around beautiful women. She's liable to turn you from a grizzly to a teddy bear."

Merrick gave a short, gruff laugh. "Don't worry about me. Worry about yourself," he said in a surprisingly tender voice. "Compared to von Folke, I really am a teddy bear. Go now. Head straight through the woods. There's a chapel about a hundred yards in. You'll find a guard unconscious in the garden just beyond the chapel walls. Put on your veil and sit next to him. When he comes to, tell him he passed out. Tell him whatever you think will work, but don't let him report the incident."

She nodded in understanding. Without another word, she hurried into the woods, picking her way as swiftly as possible through the underbrush, careful to make certain that the layers of skirting didn't snag on any of the shrubs. If she didn't get to the unconscious guard before he woke, her subterfuge would be pointless and Merrick would be caught before he'd gotten more than a mile down the road.

Emerging into the clearing, she saw one of Brandt's guards laying spread-eagle in the grass near a stone bench. To her consternation, she noticed a small dart protruding from his neck. Shuddering in distaste, she plucked it free and tossed it in some nearby bushes.

After assuring herself that no one had noticed the exchange—at least, no one had raised an alarm—she took a seat and pulled a handful of pins from a small pocket she'd sewn into her gown. Sweeping her hair into a similar style to the one Alyssa had worn, she carefully anchored the veil in place before arranging the layers of lace and tulle so it completely concealed her features. And just in time. At her feet, the guard stirred.

"What…"

She swiftly crouched beside him, silver chiffon skirting flaring around her. "Are you okay?" she asked in a soft voice, praying she sounded similar to Princess Alyssa. Why, oh, why, hadn't she asked Merrick to make the woman speak so she'd have a better idea of accent and intonation? It was a foolish mistake. "You tripped or passed out or something. Are you ill? Should I call your superior and tell him you fainted?"

A dull red swept across the man's cheekbones and alarm filled his brown eyes. "No, no, ma'am. I'm fine."

"I think they want us inside." She slipped a shoulder beneath his arm and helped him to his feet, which only increased the spread of embarrassed red across his broad features. "Are you sure you don't need help? Maybe I should request a doctor for you."

"Please." His voice lowered to a whisper. "Don't tell anyone this happened. It could mean my position in the Guard."

"Oh, dear. That would be terrible." She infused a wealth of sympathy in her voice. "I'll tell you what. We'll keep it our secret. After all, no harm done. I'm right here, safe and sound."

The guard nodded in relief. "Yes, Your Highness. I'm grateful that you didn't attempt to run off when the opportunity presented itself."

Run off? Her brows pulled together. Why would the guard suspect Alyssa might run, unless… Miri's breathing hitched. The comment suggested that Princess Alyssa wasn't a cooperative bride, that the guard wasn't here as an honorary attendant, but in an official military capacity. But why? What was going on? Was Brandt forcing the marriage? Her eyes closed in anguish. If so, why was he doing it? Was he so desperate to be king that nothing else mattered?

She found that difficult to believe. She knew Brandt. He wasn't like that. She couldn't equate the man who'd go to such extreme measures with the one she'd known since the tender age of seven, let alone the Brandt of one short month ago. Tears pricked her eyes. The Brandt she'd fallen in love with.

"Of course I didn't run off," she murmured. "After all, where would I go?"

Together they crossed to the gateway separating the expanse of garden from the inner courtyard of the chapel. Guards formed a corridor of uniformed muscle from gateway to chapel entry and she ran the gauntlet without a word. She stumbled as she entered the vestibule, blinded by a combination of the dim interior and the heavily tatted veil.

Her escort slipped a hand beneath her arm, steadying her. "Your Highness?"

"I'm fine, thank you," she murmured.

A bevy of bridesmaids in a rainbow of pastels surrounded her briefly, before reorganizing themselves into pairs for their trip up the aisle. One fluttered to Miri's side, dipped a curtsey and handed her a bouquet of cascading calla lilies, the lilac color a beautiful complement to the silver tone of her gown. It made her want to cry. This should have been real. This should have been her wedding day. It shouldn't have been this…this lie.

Why, Brandt?

Drawing a deep breath, she moved to stand beneath the archway that led into the sanctuary. At her appearance, a massive pipe organ thundered out the first few triumphant notes of a wedding march prelude. She knew she was supposed to move forward, to take slow, gliding steps up the aisle. Instead, she stared at the man standing, waiting, in front of the altar.

He made for a striking figure. Tall. Commanding. Ebony-eyed with hair as dark as a starless night, no one would have labeled him as handsome. Not like Merrick and Lander. Brandt's features were too austere for conventional good looks, the planes and angles of his face hard and uncompromising. Intimidating. Until he smiled. When he did that, his entire expression changed.

And that's what he'd done when they'd run into each other right before King Stefan's death. He'd smiled at her and she'd fallen. No, not fallen. Tumbled, helplessly, endlessly, passionately, forever in love. She thought he'd felt the same, that he loved her every bit as much, and she'd planned to go to his bed, to allow what she felt for him to take physical expression. But before they could consummate their relationship, she'd received the call informing her of her stepfather's death, and had immediately flown home.

To her eternal shame, she'd left Brandt a note. One almost incoherent in its odd combination of love and grief. In that note she'd detailed, in no uncertain terms, precisely how she felt about him along with her hopes and dreams for their future, painting her childish picture in broad, vibrant, adoring strokes. What a fool she'd been!

She glared at the man waiting for her at the altar. That's what came from being so impulsive—a character trait she'd never been able to overcome—and for flinging herself headlong at a man who saw life in shades of gray, never in color. A man without emotions, who put ambition ahead of everything else. Tears threatened and Miri forced aside the pain and anguish in favor of anger, needing that blinding fury in order to hold all other emotions at bay and get through this next hideous hour.

Taking a deep breath, she moved forward, heading step by step toward a revenge she'd never thought herself capable of. And all the while memories washed over her. Memories of how it had all started.

* * *

She was a fool. A total and utter fool.

Here it was well past midnight and she'd managed to lose the group of friends she'd been vacationing with on the tiny Caribbean island of Mazoné. They'd all gone to the grand opening of a new club that had been tucked a few blocks off the main drag. It wasn't until she'd enjoyed several hours of dancing that she'd discovered she'd lost them. By then the noise and crowd had become overwhelming and she'd decided to head back to the hotel on her own.

It had been a huge mistake. She'd never been accused of having much sense of direction when she actually knew where she was going. In a strange city, late at night, she'd managed to prove to herself just how bad it was. She'd headed out, certain she knew the way back to her hotel. But in just a few short blocks, the ambiance had gone from upscale party scene to dark and threatening. Worst of all, she hadn't a clue how to get back to where she belonged.

She clipped down the street in a ridiculous pair of four-inch heels at a I-know-where-I'm-going-don't-bug-me pace, praying she'd come across whatever served as local law enforcement, a cab, or a knight on a white charger. Even a knight *in* a white charger would do. Anyone who could point her in the right direction or—better yet—escort her there.

Instead of any of those things, she heard a noise that sent chills shooting through her, the scurry of stealthy footsteps, rapidly approaching. The sound echoed through the empty streets behind her, her first warning of impending danger. And then came confirmation that she was in serious trouble, a single voice that commanded, "Get her!"

Without hesitation, Miri hastened around the next corner she came to, kicked off her heels and took off running. Adrenaline screamed through her system, threatening to numb her mind. Her heart pounded so loudly she couldn't hear over the desperate thrumming. Were they still behind her? Closing? A sob choked her, making it difficult to breathe. She fought against the fear, fought against caving to sheer panic, fought even harder to remember everything Merrick had taught her about self-defense.

She forced herself to focus. Elbows. Elbows were the strongest point on her body. If her attacker got close enough, she'd use them. Then nails to the eyes. A fist to the nose. But first she'd toss her purse toward them, hoping that would satisfy long enough for her to get away. The credit cards and few dollars she had on her could be replaced.

Other things couldn't.

Rounding another corner, she ran straight into a wall of muscle. *Oh, God. Please, please, please! Don't let this be happening.* Somehow they'd surrounded her, cutting her off front and behind. Bouncing backward a couple steps, she tossed back her waist-length hair so it wouldn't impede her and threw a punch—one the man casually blocked. So was her knee to his groin and her elbow to his midsection. Each countermove was accomplished with an economy of movement and a smooth grace that spoke of long practice. The realization that she didn't have a chance against this man filled her with unmitigated terror. She opened her mouth to scream, but to her horror all that escaped was a pathetic whimper. Parrying a final blow, the man caught both of her wrists in his hands with terrifying ease.

She twisted her arms in an attempt to break his hold, an exercise in sheer futility. "Please—" The word escaped in a sob. "Let me go."

Two

"Relax." The man's voice rumbled from six full inches above her. "I won't hurt you."

"Then let me go." She spared a swift glance over her shoulder. "Please!"

"Stop fighting me and I will."

A thread of amusement drifted through his comment, and there was something about his voice that struck a chord deep inside, some quality that she would have recognized if she weren't so terrified. Before she had an opportunity to respond, footsteps skittered behind her. It had to be whoever had been chasing her earlier. They came to an abrupt stop when they caught sight of her and who she was with, and hovered uncertainly. The man holding her released her wrists. Sweeping her behind him, he turned to confront her pursuers.

"Don't be afraid. I'll take care of this," he murmured. Raising his voice, he called to them. "This little one is mine now. Turn around and walk away and I won't have to hurt you."

She peeked out from behind his back, wincing when she saw there wasn't just one or two, but three of them. Heaven help her! She wouldn't have stood a chance. They shifted and bobbed, reminding of her of a pack of hyenas working up the nerve to attack.

"Maybe I'll just run," she offered apprehensively.

He shook his head. "They'd only give chase."

She heard it again, that quality in his voice. But before she could analyze it, he glanced over his shoulder at her. She caught a brief glimpse of a hard, hawklike profile and the glitter of cold, determined dark eyes. It matched the rest of him and she shivered, realizing that this man could very well prove more dangerous than all three at the end of the block combined.

He had Lander's impressive height, but was built more like Merrick. Lean and sinewy, she could feel tense, well-defined muscles through the jacket of his tux. Why hadn't she noticed before? He was wearing a *tux*. She supposed there could be the occasional well-dressed assailant out there. But she seriously doubted anyone interested in offering her harm would run around attacking women while wearing formal wear. For the first time since she'd gotten herself into this mess, she breathed a little easier. But only for a moment.

The three men at the end of the block were talking quietly. At a guess, they were discussing their options. Maybe working up their courage. She knew the instant they'd reached a decision. In unison, their heads swiveled toward her, their smiles shining bleached-bone white in the darkness. As one they came, swift and assured, forming a wide half circle as they moved forward. A pack of predators circling their prey.

The man she cowered behind didn't so much as twitch. He simply stood and waited. "Aren't you going to do something?" she asked nervously, plucking at the back of his tux jacket. "Maybe we should run."

"Do as I say and you won't get hurt. Stay behind me and keep out of the way." He shot her a swift warning look. "Don't run."

Right before the three were on top of them she caught the distinct flash of steel in each of their hands. She called out a warning—ridiculous, as well as pointless, considering he could see far better than she what they held. Nor did her warning do any good. He still didn't react. The assailants took two more swift steps forward and that's when the man protecting her responded. The explosion of movement lasted less than thirty seconds. A short, chopping blow. A kick. A punch. And all three were down, sprawled in a disjointed heap while their weapons clattered discordantly to the pavement.

Pivoting, the man dropped an arm around her shoulders and urged her away from the scene. As soon as he realized she was shoeless, he slowed the pace and helped her avoid anything that might cut or injure her feet. "Where do you belong?" He ushered her down a dark alleyway and onto a street that actually held traffic. Up ahead she could see the welcome glow of lights. "What's the name of your hotel?"

She swallowed against the dryness in her throat, struggling to get her brain functioning again and her breathing slowed now that the crisis was over. "I'm staying at the Carlton," she said, naming the only five-star hotel on the island.

He inclined his head in a courtly manner. It was one she'd seen countless times before at royal functions and public occasions, and one that held her riveted. "As am I."

And that's when it hit her, why his voice had struck such a chord, why even his mannerisms seemed familiar. "I know that accent. You're Verdonian!" They stepped from shadow into light and she caught her first good look at him. "Brandt." His name escaped in a soft gasp of wonder and delight. The realization that she'd escaped almost certain disaster without injury—thanks to this man, no less—made her almost giddy with relief. She'd always considered him a knight in shining armor. Tonight he'd proved it. "Brandt! It is you, isn't it? Don't you recognize me? It's me. Miri Montgomery."

Brandt stared at her, not quite able to equate the awkward teen he vaguely remembered with this vibrant, gorgeous woman he'd just rescued. "Miri?"

"Oh, thank you." Lifting onto tiptoe, she threw her arms around his neck and kissed first one cheek and then the other, before planting a gentle, lingering kiss on his mouth. Her lips were petal-soft and warm, not quite as skilled as his last lover's, but experienced enough to know what she was doing—and what she was offering. Pulling back, she gave him a broad smile. "Thank you so much for saving me."

His hands settled at her waist, a tiny waist covered

by a mere slip of a dress. Damn it! She was practically naked. What the hell was she thinking, running around like that? And who had let this...this *child* loose in one of the most dangerous sections of Mazoné? When he found out, he'd make the man regret it to his dying day. Instead of returning her smile, he frowned in disapproval. "What are you doing here, Miri?"

"I'm on vacation." She slipped her hand through his arm in a companionable gesture, seemingly unaware of the way her grasp pressed her breasts tight against his sleeve. "How about you?"

He fought not to react to her as a woman. It wasn't right. She was practically family, not to mention far too young. "No, I mean, what were you doing in the part of town where I found you? You could have been hurt...or worse."

"I got lost."

Anger vied with concern. "Where's your family? Where are your brothers? Who's looking out for you?"

She blinked up at him. As soon as she registered his annoyance, her chin rose and she gave him a level stare from bottle-green eyes. He'd forgotten how stunning those eyes were, how they reflected her every thought and emotion. Confusion. Irritation. Affront. "I'm looking out for myself," she replied evenly. "It's been so long since we last saw each other, you've probably forgotten there's only seven years between us, Brandt. I turn twenty-five next month."

Was it possible? Had so many years passed since he'd last seen her? His gaze swept over her once again, seeing the woman who'd ripened from the child he remembered. It only served to fuel his anger. "That makes you old enough to know better than to wander through a dangerous section of town at two in the morning without an escort."

She waved that aside. "I'm old enough to take care of myself."

"Is that what you were doing when you were running from those men? Taking care of yourself?"

She released his arm and dipped into a practiced curtsey, somehow managing to imbue it with amused sarcasm. "You always did do intimidation well, Your Highness. Tonight you excel at it." Her smile flashed again. "Come on, Brandt, stop acting like my hide-bound old uncle. You're not. Nor do I want you to be."

He lifted an eyebrow. If she found him intimidating, she didn't show it. He'd have to see what he could do about that. He approached, crowding her. "What would you have done when those three caught you?"

Without shoes, she barely cleared his shoulders. She tilted back her head and a waterfall of silky black hair swirled around her hips. "I'd have scratched their eyes out. Kicked. Screamed." She shrugged. "Merrick taught me how to defend myself."

"Yes, it worked so well with me." He deliberately caught her wrists in his, as he'd done earlier, holding her with ease. "And I didn't even have a knife."

He scored with that one. She flinched as though she could still see those knives gleaming in the moonlight. Hell, he could still see them. Wickedly serrated. Purposeful. Glittering with the promise of serious injury, if not death. The thought of them scoring her tender flesh made him want to howl in fury. She wouldn't have stood a chance against the three who'd been chasing her, even if they hadn't been armed.

Something of his thoughts must have shown in his face and for the first time she did appear intimidated. "Let go, Brandt."

"Make me. Prove you could have defended yourself against even one man."

Instead of fighting him, she stepped forward and rested her forehead against his chest, leaning into him. "You're right. I couldn't have." She sounded exhausted. "Let me say it again. Seriously, this time. Thank you for saving my life. I do know that if you hadn't been there, tonight would have ended far differently."

Her words hit like a blow, succeeding where defiance never would have. Releasing her wrists, he forked his fingers deep into the rich mass of her hair and tilted her head upward. The moonlight caught in her eyes, turning them iridescent. "I wouldn't want anything to happen to you. I'd never forgive myself." His mouth tilted to one side. "I doubt your family would, either."

Instead of pulling free, she continued to stand within his grasp, her body locked tight against his. "Do you know that I was madly in love with you when I was a child?" she asked him with an impulsiveness he'd always found disconcerting. "Wildly, crazily, deliciously in love, or as much as a child can be. Crazy, huh?"

For the first time that evening his features relaxed and a found himself smiling. "Were you now?" Unable to resist, he traced the curve of her cheek with his thumb. The smooth, creamy skin proved as soft to the touch as it looked. "You always were a reckless child. I'm not sure much has changed since then."

"Maybe not," she conceded with a shrug. "One thing's changed, though."

"And what's that?"

She grinned up at him. "In case you haven't noticed, I'm not a child anymore."

He couldn't help it. His gaze wandered over her, taking in the short, spangled dress, wishing he could do more than look. He wanted to gather her up and carry her back to the hotel. Even more, he wanted to strip away that handful of silk and bare her. Touch her. Take her. No matter how wrong it might be. He did none of those things, allowed none of what he felt to show in his expression. Gently, he set her away from him.

"You're right," he murmured. "You are all grown up. But this isn't the time or place. Let's get you to your hotel."

"Okay."

Instead of stepping back and continuing on toward the Carlton, she tilted her head to one side and held him with those clear mountain-lake eyes, eyes that reflected a desire so strong, it roused the most primal instincts he possessed, instincts that demanded he take what she so blatantly offered. Take here and now, giving no quarter. How he managed to hold himself in check, he never recalled.

Tucking her hand into the crook of his arm once again, she gave him a final verbal shove, one that shot him straight over the edge. "So, tell me, Brandt," she said as casually as though they were discussing the weather. "When and where would be the right time and place? I want time, date and location, if you don't mind. I want to finish what we've started."

The memory faded and Brandt forced himself to watch his bride drift toward him while the pipe organ thundered out the processional, as though volume could drown out what everyone gathered today whispered— that this ceremony was little more than a farce. His gloved hands collapsed into fists before he forcibly relaxed them.

Those whispers were all too accurate, not that it made him any happier about the situation. As for his memories of Miri and those amazing weeks together, they were just that. Memories. Bittersweet moments-out-of-time that were no longer possible and never could be again. He fixed his attention on his bride and kept it there. He couldn't afford to lose focus, not when so much depended on him.

Princess Alyssa approached, not a scrap of her visible beneath a traditional Verdonian veil of lace and tulle. Just as well, all things considered. All he needed to make this travesty complete was a bride weeping her way through the ceremony, something Angela, the mother of the bride, was handling quite capably, thank you very much.

The organ music continued even after the bride had reached his side, creating an awkward few minutes. Finally, it died away and the ceremony began. The minute Alyssa opened her mouth to whisper the vows being forced on her, Brandt thanked divine intervention for her voluminous veil. She didn't sound at all like herself, whether from anger or tears he couldn't quite tell, but he'd just as soon not have to witness either one.

When his turn came to speak his vows, he did so without hesitation in a calm, carrying voice that held not a scrap of emotion. Duty didn't require emotion. And he did have a duty. A burdensome one. To the principality he governed. To the country he loved more than himself. But especially to the people of that country.

No matter how much he might wish this bride were someone far different than Alyssa Sutherland—in fact, a woman almost her polar opposite—that choice had been taken from him when he received the reports about the Montgomerys' malfeasance. They'd stolen from Verdonia, from the country they'd sworn to protect. After that, there had been no other choice available to him except this one. And he'd fulfill his responsibilities, no matter how distasteful he found them.

With a start he realized the brief ceremony was drawing to a close, the benediction gravely intoned over their bowed heads. Next came the traditional declaration of their union, words of permanence that held endless complications. "From this day forward, until the end of your reign on this earth, may you forever and ever remain husband and wife." A pause followed, a pointed acknowledgement of the pragmatic nature of the ceremony just performed, before the final words of the ceremony were pronounced. "Your Highness, you may kiss your bride."

Brandt reached for Alyssa's veil, but she took an unexpected step backward, her hand pressed to her middle. "Please," she whispered. "I don't feel well. I think I'm going to be sick."

Perfect. The perfect end to a perfect wedding. Just as well. He had no more desire to kiss her than she had to kiss him. As a way out, illness worked fine for him. He turned to the congregation with a calm smile. "My bride knows Verdonian tradition well. She has requested that I unveil her in private, so I'm the first to set eyes on her as my wife."

There was a wave of uncertain laughter drowned out by a recessional more thunderous than the processional. Offering his arm to Alyssa, Brandt escorted her down the aisle, through the vestibule, and into the sun-dappled courtyard. Off to one side, a small wooden doorway stood ajar and, without waiting for an escort, he led her into the tunnel that ran from chapel to palace.

"Hold on just a few minutes longer," he murmured. "We'll get you to your room."

"Thank you."

The words echoed strangely in the tunnels, softening the broad American tones that normally flavored her voice. He couldn't help comparing it to a different sort of accent, still American-born, but with an underlying hint of a Verdonian lilt. Teasing. Impulsive. Filled with laughter. Just the sound of it had broken through layers of pomp and circumstance, allowing him to feel human, if only for those brief days he'd spent on Mazoné.

The tunnel emerged at a central courtyard in the palace and he escorted Alyssa—his *wife,* he forcibly corrected himself—to a doorway that connected the courtyard to a corridor not far from the suite of rooms he'd given her, rooms that adjoined his own. She would have disappeared inside without a word or backward look, if he hadn't stopped her with a hand to her shoulder.

Alyssa froze beneath his hold. "Don't" was all she said.

"I know you want an explanation."

She spun to face him, her illness apparently forgotten, assuming she'd been feeling sick in the first place. "Yes, I would."

"And I also explained that I couldn't give you one. Not yet. I'm sorry, Alyssa."

He could feel the frustration radiating off her. "So am I. You must want to be king very badly."

Hell. He should have known he couldn't keep that quiet. "Who's been speaking to you about that?"

"No one. I just assumed…"

"You claimed not to know anything about Verdonia's political situation," he cut in. "Or was that a lie?"

Her hands wrapped themselves in the folds of her gown, betraying her nervousness. "It's just something one of my bridesmaids said," she murmured. "I don't understand how marrying me will accomplish your goal to be king, but apparently it does."

"It's complicated."

"Why don't you uncomplicate it?"

He stilled. Up until now Alyssa had always been soft-spoken. Almost timid. The only time she'd confronted him had been out of concern for her mother's safety, one of the more despicable methods he'd used to coerce Alyssa into this travesty of a marriage. Though it was something he'd spend the rest of life regretting, he deliberately shoved the memory away, compartmentalizing it for another time, after he'd met his duties and obligations.

She must have realized she'd said something wrong

because she edged away from him, pressing her back to the door. "I'm sorry. I shouldn't have asked. I'm not feeling well and I'm upset."

"You deserve to know, Alyssa." He reached past her, trying not to take it personally when she flinched from him. "Go on in your room and rest. I'll send your mother to you."

"No! Please don't bother her."

Now he was certain something was wrong. His eyes narrowed. "You've done nothing but ask to see her since you arrived. Now that you can, you don't want to?"

"I…I—"

"Alyssa? Baby?" Angela appeared at the far end of the corridor and hurried toward them. "Are you all right?"

"Fine, er, Mom. I'm fine."

Brandt shoved the door open and gestured to the two women. "Why don't we go inside where we'll have a little more privacy."

Since he had both women together, he'd take the time to explain as much as he could about the current political situation in Verdonia. He signaled to a pair of his men stationed nearby. Immediately, they took up positions on either side of the doorway.

Once closeted inside Alyssa's suite, he regarded his wife and mother-in-law. The two stood next to each other, speaking in soft murmurs. To his consternation, Angela looked ready to burst into tears again. She kept darting swift, apprehensive looks from him to her daughter and every scrap of color had fled her cheeks. Hell. What a predicament.

Crossing the room, he tried not to take offense when

the two stiffened in alarm. He caught the trailing end of
Alyssa's veil and lifted it. "Here. Let's get this off you.
I'm sure you'll be more comfortable without it."

Three

"*No!*" Miri snatched the veil from Brandt's grasp. "Don't." She backed away, tripping over the hem of her gown in her haste. "I'd rather keep it on."

His eyes narrowed in blatant suspicion. He sensed something was wrong, and if she didn't act fast, he'd figure it out. She was amazed he hadn't already. Some problem must have him preoccupied, otherwise a man as intelligent as Brandt would have put two and two together by now.

Angela had known instantly she wasn't Alyssa. It had only taken two words for mother to tell an imposter from her daughter. Thank goodness Brandt didn't know his wife quite so well. And thank goodness he'd given the two women a few seconds for private conversation. It hadn't given her much time, but it had been long enough to reassure Angela that her daughter was safe and beg the poor woman to remain silent about the switch.

Miri fought to regain her focus. Okay, one problem at a time. The most pressing concern was to distract Brandt while keeping her veil firmly on her head. "Please…I think I'm coming down with a migraine." She did her best to mimic Angela's voice, in the hopes it would sound similar to Alyssa's. People had always thought Miri's voice identical to her mother, Rachel's, and often confused them on the phone. With luck, the same held true with Alyssa and her mother. Based on Angela's amazed reaction, the attempt must have passed muster. "I get headaches sometimes when I'm stressed. Noise and light make them worse. The veil is actually helping."

"Migraine," Angela parroted, babbling nervously. "Please, she needs to keep her veil on."

Judging by Brandt's expression, he didn't believe her excuse for a single minute. To her relief, he didn't press the issue. With a shrug, he stepped back, giving the two women some breathing space. "If it makes you more comfortable to leave it on, that's fine," he said to Miri.

The gentleness of his voice had her blinking in surprise. Did he attribute her insistence that she remain veiled to fear? If so, she'd run with it. "Thank you. I feel so much better with it on."

She shot a quick glance in Angela's direction in the hopes of gaining some hint as to how to proceed. But the woman stood transfixed, staring in blatant panic, so Miri spun to confront Brandt. No, not confront. Clearly, that wasn't typical of how Alyssa had dealt with him up to this point. She'd ask. Politely.

"Please, Your Highness. You promised to explain what's going on to me and my mother." She crossed to Angela's side and took the woman's trembling hand in hers. "Why did you force me to marry you?"

He folded his arms across his chest and contemplated the two women. "I need your mother's assistance in order to get all the facts straight."

Miri spared Angela a swift glance. She looked on the verge of passing out. "What does my mother have to do with any of this?"

"She needs to tell you who you are. You haven't, have you?" he asked the older woman.

Angela shook her head, her breath escaping in a shuddering sigh. "She doesn't know anything."

"If I may?" He waited for her reluctant nod before continuing. "What your mother has neglected to tell you is that you were born Princess Alyssa Sutherland, here in Verdonia. You're the daughter of Prince Frederick, who died a few years ago, and the half sister of his son, Erik. When you were a year old your mother divorced your father and left the country with you."

Okay, if she were really Alyssa, she'd be surprised by this information. "Is this true?" she demanded of her "mother."

"Yes." Angela's grip on Miri's hand spasmed. "I'm sorry I didn't tell you before."

"Why? Why didn't you?"

Angela caught her bottom lip between her teeth. "I just wanted to start over. To leave my past in the past." She shot a reproachful glare in Brandt's direction. "That didn't work very well."

"No, it didn't," Miri agreed. "Which leads me to my next question. What has my heritage got to do with—" Her gesture encompassed Brandt and the palace around them. "With why I'm here and our marriage?"

He frowned as though debating what to say next. "Do you know anything about how Verdonia's monarchy works?"

Miri hesitated and sent another quick glance in Angela's direction, who hastened to answer the question. "I haven't told her anything about that, either."

Brandt nodded, as though not surprised. "I'll see if I can keep this simple." He crossed to the writing desk positioned in one corner of the room and helped himself to a piece of paper and pen. Drawing a rough map of the country, he handed it to Miri. "Verdonia is divided into three principalities, each ruled by its own prince or princess. The northernmost principality—mine—is Avernos. The central one is Celestia, where your brother, Erik, most recently ruled. And the southernmost is Verdon and is governed by Lander Montgomery."

"Go on."

"Unlike most monarchies, we elect our kings and queens by popular vote from the three royal bloodlines, rather than allowing the crown to pass along hereditary lines. Until six weeks ago, we were ruled by King Stefan Montgomery. With his death, the people of Verdonia will choose his successor from the eldest eligible prince and princess of each principality."

"Are you one?" She already knew the answer, but it seemed an appropriate question.

"Yes."

"Am I?" Another reasonable question, one she'd neglected to ask Merrick and one he hadn't thought to volunteer. Though perhaps he hadn't known for certain.

Brandt shook his head. "Normally, your brother, Erik, would have been a candidate. But he abdicated his position immediately after King Stefan's death. Though you're qualified at any age to govern your particular principality—in this case, Celestia—you're not eligible to rule all of Verdonia because you won't be twenty-five at the time of the election."

She'd heard about Erik's abdication, if not the reason for it. A question for Merrick once she got out of here. "What I still don't understand is why the marriage? You haven't explained that part."

"Since neither you nor Erik is eligible to rule Verdonia, the choice is between me and Lander Montgomery." His dark eyes lost all expression, his voice taking on an emotionless quality. "Remember we're dealing with a popular ballot. Our citizens tend to vote the prince or princess from their principality. That means Verdon will throw in with Lander, and Avernos with me. If it were just a contest between the two of us, Montgomery would win since the population of Verdon is largest. But there's still Celestia to consider."

Even a child could figure out where this was headed. "Whichever way Celestia votes, so votes the country." The map crumpled in her hand. "Because of our marriage, Celestia will want to remain loyal to its princess and vote for her husband—namely, you. Celestia plus Avernos equals a crown."

"Yes."

Tears filled her eyes at the unapologetic acknowledgement. She'd been so certain there was more involved in his decision than simple greed. How could she have been so mistaken about the man she loved? "Then the woman I overheard is right," she stated numbly. "You married me to be king."

He didn't bother to deny it. "Yes," he said again.

"You bastard." The accusation came out in a low hiss, full of feminine fury. "How dare you?"

Angela stepped hurriedly between them. "My daughter isn't feeling well. Please. Could you give her some time to rest? I'm sure her headache will be better in a few hours."

Brandt inclined his head. "Yes. I'm sure it will. Unfortunately, we need to deal with this here and now, headache or no." He glanced at Angela. "Would you excuse us, please? You and Alyssa can spend the day together tomorrow and get caught up then. Today…your daughter and I need to come to terms."

It was clear Angela didn't want to leave, and equally clear she couldn't bring herself to confront him. "Yes, Your Highness," she murmured after an extended pause. Sparing Miri a single anguished look, she exited the room.

Brandt approached, silent and determined, and Miri took a hasty step backward, not that it did any good. Taking her forcibly by the hand, he lifted her fingers and brushed them with his mouth. "None of what I've told you changes anything."

"You have to be kidding," she protested, remembering just in time to alter the sound of her voice. "It changes everything."

"I warned you what I expected from this marriage. And the first thing I expect is to find you recovered by this evening."

Her eyes widened. Surely he didn't mean... Even through the dense layers of lace and tulle she could see his expression well enough to know he meant precisely that. "Oh, no." Maybe the veil gave her the courage to be so confrontational. Under normal circumstances, she'd have watched her tongue. "That is *not* going to happen. No way, no how."

He simply smiled. "I warned you before that this would be a real marriage. Nothing has changed since then."

"Everything's changed. You're using me to win the throne. That's outrageous!" She kicked her skirts out of her way as she strode across the room. "I notice you were careful to keep that detail from me before the wedding."

"For cause."

She paused before him, relieved that he couldn't see her expression, that he couldn't see the grief and anguish glittering in her eyes. "You married me for cause," she repeated. "What cause? Explain it to me. Explain that there's something more going on than some clever plan to steal the throne."

Anger shredded his emotionless facade. "I'm not stealing the throne."

"No? What do you call it?"

"Saving Verdonia from the Montgomerys."

She flinched as though he'd slapped her. "I don't understand."

"And I can't explain. Not yet. Just trust me when I

say that it wouldn't be in Verdonia's best interest to have another Montgomery on the throne."

"You're doing this to ensure Prince Lander isn't elected king?" He fell silent at the question and Miri knew from experience she wouldn't get any more out of him. Still, she had to try. Any information she could bring back to Merrick would be useful, possibly vital. "Has he offended you in some way? Caused some sort of trouble that would have an adverse effect on Verdonia?"

He simply shook his head. "Eventually I'll be able to justify my actions. And I promise, you'll agree there's cause for concern. In the meantime, we have more important issues to deal with." He smiled, a slow curve of his lips that had melted her on more occasions than she could count. Even now, she could feel that smile working and struggled to steel herself against its pull. "Today's our wedding day. I'd like to see if we can't find a way to make our marriage work."

She wanted to agree, until she remembered that he wasn't speaking to her, but to Alyssa Sutherland. His *wife*, or at least the woman he thought he'd married. Miri took a deep breath. "I'm supposed to forgive what you put me through? What you've done to my…my mother? I'm supposed to forget about all that and turn into a happy, eager bride? You've lost your mind, if you think that's going to happen."

"I wouldn't have hurt her or you. I forced the issue because it was urgent that we marry."

"For the good of Verdonia."

"Yes."

More than anything Miri wanted to drag off her

veil and confront him as herself. To demand an explanation. But that wasn't possible. There was more at stake here than assuaging her pride. She struggled to draw a decent breath, feeling smothered beneath the layers covering her. Not just smothered, but tired and hurt, too. Crossing the room, she sank into the nearest chair.

"I need some time alone." She lifted her hands to rub her temples before realizing she couldn't. "I really do have a headache."

"Very well." He indicated the door next to her chair. "If you need me, I'll be in my room. I've arranged for a tray to be delivered in a few minutes, just some tea and a light snack."

"Thank you."

He approached, standing far too close. "And I've ordered a private dinner for later this evening. I'll expect you to join me." He touched the trailing edge of her veil. "Without this."

He didn't bother to wait for her response, which was just as well, since she had none to offer. The minute the door closed behind him, Miri burst into tears. It was a foolish indulgence, but one she couldn't seem to prevent. She gave herself two full minutes to cry it out, then another minute to regain her composure, all the while forcing herself to face facts. She'd learned as much as she could from Brandt. It was time to get out of here.

A soft knock sounded at the door leading to the outer corridor and a maid peeked into the room. Seeing Miri sitting there, she slipped in, carrying a tray. "Tea and sandwiches, Your Highness. Shall I serve you?"

"No, thank you," Miri murmured. "Just leave them, please."

The girl had been well-trained. With a minimal amount of fuss, she arranged the contents of the tray on a nearby table, and with a quick curtsey, exited the room. The instant Miri was alone again, she ripped the veil from her head. Tangled streams of hair tumbled free of the pins, the sight of those sunny blond curls threatening more tears. The color was a painful reminder that the man she loved had chosen someone else, someone who looked as different from her as night from day.

She would have sworn her time with Brandt on Mazoné had been serious, that he was incapable of the type of cold-blooded acts he'd committed over the past several weeks. Her jaw firmed. But now she knew the truth. Brandt had married to be king. He'd married to prevent her brother from gaining the throne. Standing here weeping over might-have-beens was both pointless, as well as foolish. She needed to leave. Now.

Crossing to the walk-in closet on the far side of the room, she yanked open the doors. She found the selection less than impressive. Alyssa hadn't come to Verdonia with much of a wardrobe. Either she'd planned to replace it when she'd arrived, or she hadn't planned to stay long. Miri's mouth tightened. Until Brandt had changed her mind.

Flipping through the choices she selected a plain navy skirt and ivory shell. Not quite the sort of finery a guest would have worn to a wedding, but it should pass muster for getting her out of here as Miri Montgomery. She slipped the clothing from the hangers and draped them over the chair before reaching for her zipper. It was then that she remembered her gown didn't have a zipper. Not a zipper or buttons, or any other easy way out of her clothing.

She'd forgotten she'd been sewn into the darn thing, as tradition dictated, the workmanship too skillful to even rip her way free. Someone would need to help. Either that or she'd have to find a pair of scissors or a knife and cut her way out. Her gaze drifted toward the table where her meal waited, the gleam of silver catching her eye. Hurrying over, she examined the utensils. Sure enough, there was a knife, but a blunt one lacking even the hint of a serrated edge, intended for nothing more onerous than buttering bread.

It was the last straw. Sinking into the chair, she buried her face in her hands. More than anything, she wanted to go back to how it had been before her stepfather had died, to those amazing carefree weeks when her day revolved around falling in love with Brandt. Most of all, she wanted to return to that last perfect day they'd shared on Mazoné. To go back and relive those final happy moments over and over again.

"How far is this place?" she panted.

"Not far," Brandt replied. "We just need to follow this river up into the mountain a short way."

Scrambling behind him, Miri paused at the next outcropping of rocks to gaze at the heavy foliage that tumbled down the mountainside in an unbroken cascade of green. The river flowed beside the path they took, chattering over heavy black boulders on its passage to the ocean. Ferns and lianas overflowed the banks, while huge flower blossoms peeked at them with faces containing a variety of shades more spectacular than a rainbow. A flock of parakeets burst from the brush on one side and streamed in a flash of yellow, blue and green through a gateway of orange heliconia that bordered the far side of the stream.

"Move it, Montgomery. You can't be out of breath already."

The path drifted deeper into the jungle from where she stood, away from the river. Wiping the perspiration from her face, she hiked up the last forty feet. But when she'd reached the spot she'd last seen Brandt, he was nowhere to be found. "Hey, where'd you go?"

"Through here."

His voice came from the direction of the river, well off the path. Shoving past endless ferns and palm fronds, she stepped into a clearing and stopped dead. Wordless, she simply stared. To her left, a fifty-foot cliff towered above them, the river pouring off it in a silver sheet to form a wide circular pool at their feet. A narrow channel to her right sent the river continuing on its way downstream. Flowers and foliage grew in and around the tumble of rocks, forming a brilliant explosion of color.

But most glorious of all were the butterflies. Hundreds of them floated in the misty air, like flower petals swirling on an endless updraft. She'd never seen such a riot of color before, luminous jewels of every hue given flight on iridescent wings.

Brandt grinned at her amazement. "What are you waiting for? Strip, woman." He lifted an eyebrow at her hesitation. "You are wearing a bathing suit under your clothes, aren't you?"

"Yes, of course."

"Too bad."

Miri choked on a laugh, but her amusement didn't last long, fading beneath an intense longing she couldn't disguise. Not from herself, nor from Brandt. She wanted him, had wanted him almost as long as she could remember. Her gaze locked with his and without a word she kicked off her shoes and slipped off her shorts and tee, allowing them to puddle at her feet. He followed suit.

Then, he took her hand in his, holding it for an impossibly long moment. It was a large, strong hand with powerfully corded ligaments and tendons that were far more suited to a laborer than a pencil pusher. He held her with tempered strength, the moment stretching before he helped her into the pool.

The next hour passed like a dream, the two of them playing and splashing in the water together. Laughter rang across the glade. Finally, exhausted, they levered themselves up onto a flat rock close to the waterfall. A soft spray misted them, cool and refreshing beneath the hot Caribbean sun. Miri sat cross-legged on the rock, combing her fingers through her hair.

To her surprise, Brandt's hands joined hers, working with her to free the tangles. "I wish...I wish I could stay in this moment forever." She tilted her head to watch the colorful dance above them. "The butterflies. The waterfall. The flowers and pool and—" Her voice dropped. "And you."

"I've discovered nothing lasts forever, no matter how much I might want it otherwise."

"That sounds like something your grandfather would have said."

Brandt shrugged. "Not surprising considering he raised me."

"As I recall, he had a saying for every occasion, especially when I'd get into trouble." She shifted in place at the memory. "He made me so nervous the first time I met him."

"Finally. Someone who intimidates you."

"Cut me some slack. I was all of seven. My mom had just married King Stefan and I was feeling very much out of my element. Then I literally ran into this tall, gruff man at one of Verdonia's royal functions, a man who looked even more like a king than my stepfather. How would you feel?"

Brandt lifted an eyebrow. "I assume you weren't intimidated for long."

"Heavens no. Not once I got past his tough exterior to the marshmallow center." She smiled fondly. "Your grandfather was very kind to me. Gracious. Charming. Encouraging. He treated me like a real princess. And his homilies, though painful at times, stuck."

"What was the first homily he taught you?"

"That's easy." For some reason she felt the sting of tears. "A Verdonian is born from the heart, not from the land."

"Ah." Brandt's voice turned gentle. "You must have been feeling out of place."

"Very much so. I'd just been told in no uncertain

terms that I wasn't a 'real' princess. And more than anything I wanted to belong to the country I'd adopted as my own."

"He made quite an impression on you."

"Oh, he did. A lasting one. As did you." She narrowed her gaze on Brandt's face. "Now that I think about it, you two look a lot alike. He was gruff and craggy and those eyes—"

"Piercing."

"Again. Like yours." She cupped her chin, leaning her elbow on her knee. "Thank goodness he was there for you. It must have been difficult, losing your parents at such a young age."

"I don't have any real memories of them. They were killed when I was a baby." So calm. So accepting. "But I always had my grandfather. He taught me everything I needed to know."

"Let me guess. Honor. Duty. Responsibility. And…" She screwed up her face in thought. "And sacrifice. Am I close?"

"On the money. Though I might have said 'choice' rather than sacrifice, though it adds up to the same thing. The choices we're expected to make are for the good of the country rather than for our own betterment."

"And when the two are at odds?" she asked, curious.

"No contest," he answered promptly. "Verdonia wins every time."

She shook her head in exasperation. "You're so pragmatic."

He accepted the observation with a shrug and a slow smile. "And you're so…not."

She loved that smile. In fact, she'd worked hard over the past two weeks to win as many from him as she could. Considering how rare they were, she regarded them as more precious than gold. He continued to gaze at her for an endless moment. Something in those deep, dark eyes sent a shiver of awareness darting through her.

How old had she been when she'd first fallen in love with this man? Eleven? Twelve? Granted, it had been puppy love. But even then she'd been drawn to him, had been aware of him on some intuitive level. She'd almost forgotten those unbidden feelings, the sense that she'd finally found someone who fit her when she so clearly didn't fit in with the Montgomerys.

Tossing her damp hair over her shoulders, she shifted so she could watch Brandt's expression while they talked. Nothing would make his face a thing of beauty. It was too hard, too austere, with eyes so grave and intent that most people had trouble meeting his gaze. Their intensity had never bothered Miri. She'd always been fascinated by them, and on some odd level, reassured. They were trustworthy eyes, eyes that didn't lie, no matter how tough the question or unpleasant the truth.

Right now, she wanted to hear the unvarnished truth. "I'm wondering what happens when we go home. Between us, I mean."

If her question threw him, he didn't show it. "What do you want to happen?"

"I want to continue the way we are now," she answered promptly, before correcting herself. "No. I take that back. I want more."

"More." He regarded her impassively for a long

moment and then she saw a slow burn gathering in the ebony depths of his gaze, a burn that gave her hope. "Define more."

"Tell me something first. Is this just a fling we're having, or what?"

He settled back on his elbows, his features schooled to patience. "I don't think our relationship qualifies as a fling, no."

"Because we aren't sleeping together."

She scored another smile, this one wider than before. "You are blunt, aren't you?"

"It helps if you consider me refreshing. That's how my family describes me. Refreshingly honest." She linked her fingers together. "And you haven't answered my question. Are we having a fling?"

No equivocation. No hesitation. Just a simple "No."

"Oh." She cleared her throat. "Would you like to?"

He continued to lounge on the rock, resembling nothing more than a great sinewy panther. But underneath that casual manner, she could sense his gathering tension, as though he were ready to react to the least provocation. "What are you doing, Miri?"

"Don't you know? Can't you tell?" She was poking a big, dangerous cat with a stick. Brilliant.

"You're playing with fire," he warned, confirming her suspicions.

Not that his warning had much affect on her tongue. "I wouldn't mind seeing some of that fire," she informed him. "I sense it's there. Well hidden, but there someplace."

He moved with a speed and deadly intent that caught her by surprise. One second he lounged casually beside her, and the next he'd scooped her into his arms and flipped her onto her back. He leaned over her, his shoulders so wide they blocked out the sun.

"Shall I show you?"

Four

"I think this might be the 'something more' I had in mind."

"Might?" It took every ounce of Brandt's self-control to keep from taking her then and there. "I'd say it was definitely the 'something more' you had in mind. At least, it's the 'something more' *I* had in mind."

Miri stared up at him, her sea-green eyes soft and luminous. "Then why have you waited? Why haven't you tried to make love to me before this? Is it because of who I am?"

He wouldn't lie to her. "Yes. Who, what. There are warnings and conditions stamped all over you and I'd be a fool to ignore them."

"That's funny. I could have sworn the stamps had your name on them and maybe a small warning that says, 'Open with care.'"

"I wouldn't do it any other way." She was too precious for anything other than care. "Not with you."

He'd never been one to take advantage of a woman, and he didn't plan to start with Miri. All Brandt's previous lovers had known the score, he'd made certain of that. For the most part they'd been experienced women interested in a mature relationship. Since he refused to put an offer of marriage on the table, that's all he had to offer them. But with Miri, instinct warned him to tread carefully. She was a Montgomery. A Princess of Verdonia. He couldn't take a woman like this for his mistress, not without all hell breaking loose.

Miri's mouth curved to one side, a teasing look he'd become intimately familiar with. She loved to give him a hard time, and he found, much to his surprise, that he thoroughly enjoyed being on the receiving end of her ragging. "Tell me the truth. Do these warnings you claim to see scare you?" she asked, draping her arms around his neck.

"Without question."

"What if I gave you permission to ignore them?"

He released a frustrated bark of laughter. "I don't understand you. I never have."

Sooty brows drew together. "What's to understand?"

"Most people find me off-putting."

"Really?" Her eyes widened in mock innocence. "I hadn't noticed."

"That's the sort of thing I mean. They wouldn't have the nerve to tease me the way you do."

"And you've used that reaction to your advantage, haven't you?"

"It would be foolish not to." He cupped her face. "But it never worked with you. You were always perfectly comfortable around me. Why is that?"

"Because I know you. I recognize you. I did from the first moment I saw you." Her arms tightened around his neck. "And I've learned something during our time here on Mazoné."

"I'm almost afraid to ask."

"I've realized how right this would be. Us. Together like this. Don't you feel it, too?"

He did. But it was too soon, with too much still unresolved between them. Once he took her, they'd be indelibly connected, joined in a way he didn't think she was prepared for. Theirs wouldn't be a casual fling, regardless of what she might think. He knew better. Taking this any further would bind them irrevocably.

Before he could set her aside, she lifted upward and sealed his mouth with hers. Her lips parted and she breeched inward for a delicious seduction, offering heat and passion and a burning desire. She left no doubt as to how much she wanted him. The sweet truth of it was there in her kiss, one that gave him every bit of herself, unrestrained, leaving herself open and vulnerable to rejection.

Not that he could reject her. He forked his fingers deep into the silken weight of her hair and deepened the kiss. A sigh of delight slipped from her mouth to his, a sigh that filled him with her essence, invaded every sense, overriding sensibility. He could take her here and now, and she wouldn't offer a single word of protest. She'd submit. Hell, she'd more than submit. She'd welcome his possession.

"Miri, we need to stop." But even as he said the words, he slid his hand from her hair and followed the sweep of her neck to the edge of her bikini top. He traced the plunging line with a fingertip. "We can't let this go any further."

She shivered beneath the delicate caress. "Finish what you're doing and then we'll stop."

"Good plan."

He pinched the clasp between her breasts and a bubbling laugh escaped her. Peeling back the triangles of her top, he exposed her breasts. They were perfect, fitting into his palms as though made for his touch. The deep rose nipples tightened in reaction and he bent down to savor them. A musky woman's scent rose up to greet him. Her scent. A scent more erotic than any perfume.

He should stop. This was the wrong time, the wrong place, even if it was the right woman. If they took this the next step, he wanted a better understanding between them, to deal with the ramifications beforehand rather than with regret afterward.

"We can't." He shuddered with the need to finish what they'd started. "We can't do this now."

She peeked at him through lowered lashes. A delicate flush warmed the sweep of her cheekbones and gave a rosy glow to her breasts. "If not now, then when?"

He closed his eyes. "Tomorrow."

"Not tonight?" He could hear the disappointment in her voice.

"I have a business meeting. I don't know how late it'll run. And we need to talk before we take this any further." He looked at her then. "I'm not interested in something temporary. Not with you."

She smiled radiantly. "Neither am I."

Brandt drew a deep breath and refastened her top. Forcing himself upright, he held out his hand and pulled Miri to her feet. "Time to go."

He gathered her close and kissed her a final time. It was a kiss of longing. Of celebration. Of promise. Soon she would be his. And once she was, he'd have everything he'd ever wanted. Finally, he released her and she started to slip back into the pool. Brandt reached out and stopped her at the last minute.

"Tonight," he stated.

She didn't bother to ask what he meant. He could see in her eyes that she knew, her gaze promising a moondrenched night filled with unforgettable passion. Or at least, he thought so, at that point.

By later that evening, King Stefán was dead and Miri had returned to Verdonia. Of course, she left a note. But it was too late. By then, everything had changed. What had seemed so certain, would never be. His grandfather had taught him well. Honor. Duty. Responsibility. And one thing more. He thought he'd also learned choice at his grandfather's knee. But Miri had been right, after all.

What he'd learned was sacrifice.

Night had fallen on Brandt's wedding day hours earlier and the only light in the room came from a small fire blazing in the fireplace across from his chair, a fire he'd deliberately built for a single purpose. Opening the letter Miri had left for him on Mazoné, a letter creased from more readings than he could count, he traced the words written there. A bittersweet smile twisted his mouth as he reread it.

Miri's handwriting epitomized her perfectly—passionate and grief stricken. After explaining that she was on her way to the airport to fly home after learning of King Stefan's death, she'd then addressed her hopes for their relationship. Her feelings for him poured from every scrawled word, painting a beautiful, if impossible, future.

Once upon a time he thought he could have it all. A life with a woman who adored him, who wanted nothing more than to love him. To bear his children. To grow old with him.

He closed his eyes, picturing what would never be. He'd given himself these few hours to indulge in foolishness, something he couldn't afford to do again. This was his wedding day. Instead of marrying Miri Montgomery, as he'd once thought possible, he'd taken Alyssa Sutherland as his wife with a cold-blooded deliberation that he'd learned at his grandfather's knee. Well, he'd made his decision, and he wasn't a man for second thoughts or half measures. He'd committed himself to Alyssa and he'd live up to that commitment, no matter how difficult.

Up until now, he'd considered the Sutherland woman a nonentity. A tool. He drew in a deep breath. That would have to change now that she was his wife. He couldn't simply dismiss her from his mind and life because he would have preferred a different bride. She would be an integral part of his future and the future of Verdonia. As much as he resisted, she deserved answers. And soon, he'd offer them to her and see if they couldn't establish a marriage of compatibility and affection, if not love.

A hint of honeysuckle and coconut wafted upward in the quietest of protests. Not Miri's perfume. The sunscreen she'd worn on that last day by the waterfall. His smile faded with the memory. It was time. Time to bind himself to his wife. Time to move forward and never look back again. Leaning toward the fire, he allowed Miri's letter to slip from his hand. It floated in the air for a brief moment before swirling above the flames in the grate. The paper blackened and then the oils on it caught fire and in a soft whoosh it exploded in a shower of sparks. He waited until the last ember died, before closing his eyes.

"Goodbye, Miri," he whispered.

Miri froze in the private doorway between Brandt's suite and hers, watching as the letter she'd left for him in Mazoné drifted from his hand into the fire.

She covered her mouth with a hand to keep from crying out. He was breaking her heart, a heart she'd already thought broken beyond repair. Yet, seeing the undisguised despair lining Brandt's face she conceded that his decision to marry Alyssa hadn't come easily, and that he'd chosen this time alone to say goodbye to what they'd once shared.

Slowly, carefully, she drew in a deep breath. Then another. In the hours she'd been sitting in her room lost in memories, she'd reached a decision. She'd track him down and confront him. Demand an answer. But standing here, watching him, she realized he'd already given her that answer.

He'd married Alyssa—thought he'd married Alyssa—in order to win the throne. What more did she need to know? Not that his plan would work. Merrick would see to that. If Brandt became king, it would be in a fair election against Lander, not through an illicit marriage to Alyssa Sutherland.

It was pointless to stand here, expecting more from him, expecting something he couldn't give. She should leave now. Her job was done. She should return to Alyssa's suite and search the place for a paring knife or sewing shears and cut her way out of her wedding gown. Chances were she'd be able to slip away with no one the wiser.

But she didn't leave. Instead, she bowed her head and faced the painful truth. She didn't want to go. She wanted an opportunity to say goodbye, just as Brandt had. Looking up, she stared into the darkened room. The fire had died to a faint glow. The only other light came from a sliver of moon slipping in one of the windows to form a tight halo around the chair in which Brandt sat. Just one night, that was all she asked. One night to say farewell.

Not giving herself time to consider the foolishness of her actions, she entered the room. Silently, she crept across the carpet until she reached his chair. Once there, she crouched, staying well clear of the moonlight.

"Brandt," she whispered, doing her best to imitate Angela's accent, hoping she was correct in assuming it came close to matching Alyssa's.

His head jerked up and he glanced at her. A full minute ticked by before he spoke. "You surprise me, Princess."

"Why's that?"

"You're here. I thought I'd have to track you down."

She gave a careless shrug. "You might have, except for one thing."

"Which is?"

She allowed an exasperated note to enter her voice. "I can't get out of this stupid dress."

His features relaxed ever so slightly. "My apologies. I'd forgotten it would be necessary to cut you free. Another Verdonian tradition you may not be familiar with."

"Would you mind? It's getting late."

He stood, and so did she, her skirts rustling as she took a quick step backward, allowing the shadows to swallow her more fully. Bypassing her, he walked to a door leading to the outer corridor. Opening it, he spoke quietly to whomever stood outside. When he returned he held a dagger.

"Your men are well prepared," she commented faintly.

He shrugged. "It's part of their uniform," he said, reaching for a light switch.

"Don't." She fought to modulate her voice. "Please, I'd rather you didn't turn on the light."

"I need to see what I'm doing." She couldn't think of a reasonable response to that, but to her relief, she didn't have to come up with one. "But I won't turn it on if you'd rather I didn't. Let's see if this will work."

Returning to her side, he dropped a hand on her shoulder and guided her into the moonlight. She was careful to keep her back to him, terrified that he'd catch a glimpse of her face. Even though Merrick must have gotten far away by now, any extra time she could give him would only help. Not that her plans for this evening had anything to do with helping her stepbrother.

"Hold still," Brandt instructed, sweeping her hair off her back. "I don't want to cut you."

She felt a slight tug at her bodice before it loosened. Inch by inch it sagged forward, slipping from her shoulders. Folding her arms across her chest, she held the gown in place. The silence grew deafening, broken only by the harshness of her own breathing.

When he finished cutting her free, he didn't step away. "Your skin is amazing." He traced a path from the nape of her neck to the base of her spine. "The moonlight has turned it to silver."

"What are you doing?" she whispered.

"You know what I'm doing." He continued his stroking touch, sending shivers shooting through her. "We can make this work, Alyssa."

Alyssa. Miri closed her eyes against the sharp bite of pain. "You really expect me to consummate this marriage?"

He continued to stand close, so tall he made her feel tiny. "Do you want romantic words? I can give them to you if you wish. But they wouldn't be true. Because the truth is, we need to consummate our marriage in order to make it legal." His hands tightened on her. "That doesn't mean it has to be an unpleasant experience or that we can't enjoy the physical part of our relationship. How we proceed from here is up to us. This can be a beginning, for both of us."

"You'd find it that easy?" It hurt unbearably to think so. "A tap to turn on or off? Is that how your emotions work?"

"No. No more than with you. But I'm determined to make our marriage work, if you're willing."

"We're strangers. You know nothing about me. And I—" Her hands clenched, her nails biting into her palms. "And I know nothing about you." She'd only thought she did. But she'd been wrong. So horribly wrong.

Sliding an arm around her waist, Brandt spooned her close, her spine tight against his chest. His hand splayed across her abdomen, warm and heavy and possessive. The warmth of his breath washed over her as he traced the curve between her neck and shoulder with his mouth. She shivered beneath the delicate caress, relaxing into his embrace. The instant she realized what she'd done, she stiffened in his grasp. Taking a hasty step forward, she edged farther into shadow.

He followed, maintaining contact. His fingers trailed along the path his mouth had followed, gently easing the gown off her shoulders. The sizzle from that stolen touch burned like fire, igniting a shockwave that caused the beadwork on her loosened gown to glitter in agitation.

"Slow and easy, wife," he attempted to soothe. "We have all night."

She'd thought she could do this, thought she'd steal this night with him with no one the wiser and no one hurt. But hearing him call her by another woman's name, having him address her as *wife* was killing her by inches.

"Maybe we should wait until tomorrow." The suggestion escaped in a breathless rush. "Wait until we've had a chance to get to know each other better."

"Nothing will have changed." He sounded so gentle, so caring. Almost tender. "Come tomorrow, we'll still be married. We'll still be relative strangers. And your apprehension will have another day to take root and grow."

"So we're better off getting it over with?"

"Better off discovering that you have nothing to fear."

"I'm not afraid," she instantly protested.

And she wasn't. She wanted to make love to Brandt. She just wanted him to know who he was loving, though she didn't dare reveal her identity. But perhaps… perhaps there was a way she could turn this around. If she could reach him on some level, if he recognized her—even subconsciously—maybe it would be enough. He'd still be responding to the uniqueness of her touch. To her personal scent and taste. To a kiss only she could give. In the end, he'd be making love to her, not to Alyssa, and she'd have to hope that some small part of him realized it.

Slowly, she lowered her arms, allowing her gown to slip downward. He accepted her silent surrender without comment. His touch remained gentle, careful. He eased the gown to her waist, then hooked his thumbs in both skirt and petticoats, and guided them down her hips. His palms swept the upper slopes of her buttocks, lingered, then moved on. Dropping to one knee, he helped her step free of the voluminous layers of silk.

Before she had time to feel self-conscious, he stood and turned her in his arms, taking her mouth with his. She remembered this kiss, had longed for it ever since that day by the waterfall. And she found herself returning it, tentatively at first, and then with mounting passion. His lips hardened, grew more forceful. But rather than protest, she met his demand with one of her own.

She barely felt the give of her bra, wouldn't have noticed if he hadn't feathered his fingertips from the sensitive sides of her breasts inward to the burgeoning tips. He stroked her with excruciating precision, as though he knew just where to touch in order to elicit the most intoxicating pleasure.

And just like that she realized what he was doing. He was seducing her, step-by-dispassionate-step. Moonlight slashed his face, revealing the remote determination in his eyes, as well as the calculation in his expression. And now that she understand what he was attempting she could feel it in his studied touch.

Miri shook her head. She didn't want him to make love to her, not like this, not with cold-blooded intent. Somehow she had to find a way to break through to the passion that lay beneath that carefully controlled exterior, like she had beside the waterfall.

"Wait," she whispered. She had to repeat herself before he broke off his siege. "Slow down."

She found his reluctance to release her encouraging, but it wasn't enough. She wanted an emotional bonding as much as a physical one. The moonlight had fled across the room and she shifted away from Brandt to follow it, standing so it cut across her from the nape of her neck to her calves. She could literally feel his gaze, like a line of fire tracing her spine. She drew a deep breath, aware that this next part would be the hardest thing she'd ever done.

With as much casual grace as she could muster, she removed first one glistening stocking, then the other, deliberately dipping and swaying as though to some private song. Next came her garter belt, a flimsy bit of silk in bridal white. And then all that remained was her thong. Gliding it down her hips, she gave a slow shimmy to send the scrap of lace floating to her ankles. Shaking her bleached hair back so it tumbled toward her hips, she half turned and glanced over shoulder.

From deep in the shadows she could hear the harsh give and take of his breath. Feel the want. Practically taste the desire that scented the air. Without a word, he ripped off his clothes with impressive haste. When the last piece of clothing hit the floor, he came for her, fast and determined, stepping from shadow to moonlight. And finally, finally, he allowed his emotions free rein.

His eyes heated, filled with an urgency she couldn't mistake. In response, her own body warmed with forbidden hunger. He paused when he reached her and touched a spot on her left hip. "What's this?"

Her breath caught. She'd forgotten all about that. "It's a tattoo." One she'd gotten after that memorable day by the waterfall.

"It's a butterfly."

"I like butterflies."

"I...I used to."

"Not anymore?" she dared to ask.

He shook his head, his mouth tightening. He ended the discussion by sweeping her up in his arms and carrying her to the bed. The sheets were cool against her back, a distinct contrast to the liquid heat coursing through her. Rolling onto his back, he lifted her on top of him. His hold remained light, more embrace than grip. She wanted to wrap herself around him. Devour him. Drive every thought from his head but one.

Sinking downward, she covered the breadth of his chest with kisses. Her hair draped over and around them like the softest of cloaks and he shuddered in reaction. He reached for her, impatient, sliding her upward until she found his mouth again, and took it in quick, desperate kisses. It wasn't enough. Not nearly enough.

He must have felt the same. Flipping her onto her back, he levered himself above her. It was his turn to anoint her body, starting at the curve of her jawline and working downward. He lingered at her breasts, then skated to the curve of her belly before dipping lower, carefully avoiding her tattooed butterfly. He worshiped her with his mouth, finding and exploring the most sensitive spots on her body. By the time he'd finished, her body wept with a want more powerful than anything she'd ever experienced before.

She tried to say something, to plead. To beg for what she so urgently needed. He seemed to know already. Parting her legs, he slipped between them, then hesitated.

"I'll try not to hurt you."

Did he know? Had he picked up on her inexperience? He must have, for he eased his passage into her body and breached her innocence with exquisite care. Tears escaped from the corners of her eyes, dampening the hair at her temples. They weren't tears of pain, but tears of elation. If all she had was this one night with Brandt, she'd find a way for it to be enough. She whispered his name, her voice filled with wonder and joy.

He shuddered above her, shaking his head in disbelief. "It shouldn't be like this. I shouldn't feel like this." His throat worked. "But I do."

And then the ride turned wild, and they rode that wildness together in mindless ecstasy, burning painfully bright in the darkest part of the night. When the shattering came it went beyond all imagining, shaking Miri to the core. For endless minutes they clung to each other, lost to everything but the sensations that continued to shudder through them.

At long last, he rolled to one side and pulled her close, wrapping himself around her as though staking a claim. "I didn't think that was possible," he told her. "This changes everything. You know that, don't you?"

"Yes." She doubted she'd ever be the same again.

"Sleep," he urged. "We'll talk in the morning."

She didn't dare sleep. At some point, she needed to slip away. To leave and never look back. Snuggling deeper into his embrace she clung to each minute before it escaped her grasp, imprinted every second on her memory. The sound of his breathing and the gentle huskiness of his voice. The scent of his skin, as well as the perfume of their lovemaking. The final glow of moonlight as it kissed them farewell. The taste of his kisses that lingered on her lips.

Finally, she felt him relax into a deep sleep and cautiously untangled herself from his embrace. The worst moment came when she left the warmth of his bed. Tiptoeing across the room, she hesitated at the threshold connecting his suite with Alyssa's. Unable to resist, she glanced back.

As though aware of her regard, he stirred, groping for her. And then he said the one thing guaranteed to wound her more profoundly than anything else could have.

"Alyssa."

Five

Principality of Verdon, Verdonia
Ten weeks later...present time

"We're going to get in trouble," Miri warned her two sisters-in-law. "As soon as my brothers realize we've given our security people the slip, they're going to hit the roof. I've seen it happen before and you don't want to be anywhere in the vicinity when they blow."

Lander's new bride, Juliana, gave her dark wig a final tug over deep red curls. "No worries. We won't be anywhere in the vicinity when they blow. We'll be at the mall."

She settled a pair of plain-lens eyeglasses on the tip of her nose, the amethysts on her wedding rings flashing like purple fire. As always, they drew Miri's gaze, particularly the new stone Lander had unearthed and named the Juliana Rose, an amethyst that was neither purple nor blue nor pink, but rather a unique combination of all three. It reminded her of something, something from her childhood. Though it had teased her for weeks now, she'd never quite been able to put her finger on what it was about the ring that troubled her.

"Just one hour without an entourage or bodyguards or strangers watching my every move," Juliana was saying. Satisfied with her disguise, she turned to pose for the other two. "That's all I'm asking. Once Lander is elected king, I'll have a snowflake's chance in hell of ever being able to pull off something like this again."

"Lander will see to that." Miri could guarantee it. He'd proven himself intensely protective of Juliana, to the point of proposing to her just to salvage her reputation when the press had discovered they were lovers. And then he'd fallen in love with her. It had been a fairy tale come true. "You two have a lot to learn about my brothers if you think they won't have something to say about this little escapade."

"Stop being so pessimistic, Miri. I'm sure Merrick will understand." Alyssa made the statement with the blithe confidence of a brand-new bride blissfully in love with her husband and blind as a bat when it came to his flaws. Who'd have thought when Merrick had abducted her that they'd end up so happy together in such a short time? "We're all disguised. If anyone catches on or the press finds us, we'll leave. Where's the harm in that?"

"What if Br— Prince Brandt tries something again?" Miri fought back a blush at having stumbled over his name. "I'm familiar with the man's tactics. He doesn't give up easily. Look at what happened when he captured you and Merrick, Alyssa. There I was hiding on Mazoné, while you and Merrick were on the run, dodging Brandt's men. Then when you infiltrated his castle to rescue your mother, he sprung his trap. He was certain he'd married you. And when he realized he hadn't—"

"By kissing me!" Alyssa inserted indignantly.

"He then tricked you into revealing the true identity of his bride. Me." Miri broke off with a shrug. "As I said. Once Brandt is set on a path, he doesn't give up easily. If he's determined to win the throne, he'll find a way to get it."

Alyssa and Juliana exchanged worried glances, but it was clear they weren't concerned about Brandt's next move to gain the throne, so much as Miri's feelings for him. Obviously, they knew what had happened between the two after she'd taken Alyssa's place at the altar. She'd hoped she'd been successful at hiding her feelings for Brandt. Judging by their expressions, she'd failed miserably.

"He won't hurt you again," Alyssa reassured gently. "Merrick will make certain of it."

Tears welled into Miri's eyes, an all too common occurrence these days. "He didn't hurt me. Not the way you mean. I went to him, not the other way around."

Alyssa appeared shocked by Miri's confession, probably because Brandt terrified her. But Juliana's expression spoke of perfect understanding. These women had become so dear to Miri—the sisters she'd always longed for and never had.

"It's like that sometimes," Juliana stated with a knowledgeable nod. "If you'd asked me just a few months ago if I'd surrender common sense in order to be with a man, I'd have called you six different kinds of fool. Then I met Lander and the next thing I knew I'd lost every brain cell I possessed. Is that how it is with Brandt?"

"That's how it used to be." Miri shot to her feet, nearly unseating the light brown wig she'd been talked into donning. "The only feeling I have for him anymore is utter contempt. When he failed to steal the throne by marrying Alyssa, he reported Lander to the Temporary Governing Council and accused him of financial malfeasance. I'll never forgive Brandt for that."

"Maybe he believed your brother really was guilty." Alyssa's blue eyes widened as though astonished to find herself defending Brandt. She turned to Juliana for support. "Didn't you say that awful woman made it look like the Montgomerys were responsible for embezzling from Verdonia's amethyst mines?"

"Lauren DeVida." Juliana practically spat the name. "King Stefan's Chief Executive Accountant. More like his Chief Executive Thief, if you ask me. I hope they track that woman down and throw her in the deepest, darkest pit they can find."

A bit bloodthirsty, but considering Juliana had been the one to uncover the financial scam—a desperate and nearly impossible task that had taken every ounce of the financial wizard's mathematical skill and accounting genius—Miri could understand why she wanted to see Lauren DeVida suffer. And since it was Juliana's frantic efforts to gather the necessary proof that had ultimately saved Lander, Miri could sympathize with her sister-in-law's desire for revenge.

"If we're going to go, we should get moving," Alyssa recommended. "Are you certain no one will notice the car's missing?"

Juliana shook her head. "Lander has a fleet of non-descript vehicles he uses whenever he wants to escape public scrutiny. I managed to get hold of one, but only until three o'clock."

"Four hours?" Alyssa released a sigh of delight. "I'll take it."

Instead of a wig, she'd opted for oversized sunglasses and a scarf to hide her distinctive blond hair, pairing them with faded jeans and a plain white blouse. If Miri hadn't known who Alyssa was, she'd never have suspected the truth. For the first time in weeks she felt a return of her old spirit. Why in the world had she tried to talk the other two out of this escapade when not so long ago she'd have been the main instigator?

"Okay, girls," she said, determined to shake the old Miri awake. "Disguises in place?"

Alyssa and Juliana both mugged in front of the mirror. "Set," they chorused.

"Keys?"

Juliana nodded. "I have it on excellent authority that they're under the floor mat in the car."

"Cell phones in case we get separated?"

"Check and double check."

Miri grinned. "And most important of all…credit cards?"

That led to a mad scramble to make sure they had adequate resources for their shopping trip. Once satisfied, they made their way from their rooms in the palace to where Juliana had arranged to pick up the car. They nearly gave themselves away any number of times as they made good their escape. It didn't help that after each close call, one of them would give a snort of laughter and the others would break down giggling.

When they finally reached the simple white sedan, they got into a brief disagreement over who would drive. Miri settled the issue by snatching up the keys. "I know the fastest way there and I'm used to Verdonian traffic. Now, do you want to spend what time we have at the mall, or arguing?" That simple question put an end to any further dispute and had them all piling into the car and on their way.

The next few hours proved a true pleasure. Miri loved spending time with her new "sisters," bonding over cosmetics, shoes and lattes. They lingered in the stores as long as they dared, delighted when their disguises proved a total success. It was Juliana who reluctantly brought the outing to an end.

"Okay, girls," she announced, snagging each by an arm. "I just got a call that Lander and Merrick have returned to the palace. We need to shake a leg before they realize we've gone missing."

Gathering up their packages, they made a beeline for the lowest level of the parking garage where they'd left the car. They were only a few spaces from it when a pair of SUVs shot toward them from different directions. Brakes squealed, reverberating through the cement structure. The two vehicles screeched to a stop so close that the three women crowded back against the rear door of a dusty minivan, completely boxed in.

"Merrick," Alyssa said with a groan. "This is what comes from marrying the head of Verdonia's Royal Security Force. Apparently his people out-covert your people, Juliana."

Before Miri could correct Alyssa's error, men erupted from the SUVs. But it was the one who took his time exiting that held her full attention and caused the breath to bottleneck in her throat. Anticipation vied with animosity, tying her stomach in knots. "It's Brandt."

He approached as though he had all the time in the world, sweeping them a courtly bow. "Your Highnesses." Apparently, their disguises didn't fool him for one little minute. After a single, all-encompassing look, his gaze settled on Miri. "It's time to come home, my dear. If you'll say goodbye to your in-laws, we can be on our way."

"Home?" Miri shook her head, incensed by his cavalier use of the word. After choosing another woman for his bride, after two and a half months of silence, he dared call Avernos her home? "No, thanks. My home is here."

"It *was* here," he corrected mildly. "You changed all that when you married me."

Was he kidding? "We're not married. That ceremony can't possibly be legal."

He lifted a shoulder in a careless shrug. "That's for the courts to determine. Until they say otherwise, you are my wife. And I intend to have my wife in my arms when I go to bed at night." He signaled to his men. "Ladies, if you'd please hand over your cell phones and car keys, I'd appreciate it."

Though phrased as a request, demand underscored every word. In response, Juliana's brown eyes glittered with fury while Alyssa appeared close to tears. Miri could have gone either way. Or managed both at the same time. So many emotions overwhelmed her she could barely think straight. Outrage and bitterness over how his decisions had destroyed their relationship vied with a stunned disbelief that he'd come for her after all this time. Worst of all a whisper of hope fluttered to life, small and fragile, like the wings of a butterfly.

After a momentary hesitation, her sisters-in-law complied with Brandt's directive. Juliana slapped her phone into the hand of the nearest man. "You won't get away with this," she told Brandt. "And don't think I won't find a way to make you pay for making me sound like I'm a B-rated movie actress in some schlock melodrama."

Alyssa tossed her cell phone toward Brandt before turning to give Miri a tight hug. "Don't be afraid," she whispered. "Merrick will find a way to rescue you. He's getting good at that sort of thing."

"You're mistaken, Princess," Brandt informed Alyssa. Based on his smile he'd overheard her comment and found it amusing. "My wife neither needs nor wants to be rescued. In fact, I suspect she's been waiting for me to show up."

"If you really believe that, you're delusional," Miri retorted.

Brandt's gaze grew painfully direct. "Not only do I believe it, so do you, whether you're willing to admit it in front of your sisters-in-law, or not. You're just hurt because I took so long coming after you. For that, I apologize."

She wanted to deny it, and yet, a small foolishly romantic part of her did feel a betraying bubble of elation. Or it did until her more pragmatic nature reacted with a healthy dose of suspicion. *Why* had he come? What new, more devious plan had he devised to thwart Lander and how did it involve her?

"You have a hell of a lot more to apologize for than this," she told him.

"No doubt you'll give me a detailed list. Now, as much as I'd like to discuss it further, we should be leaving. We're on a tight schedule. But first..." He snagged her wig and tugged it loose, watching in approval as her hair tumbled free. "Ah. Much better. And back to its natural color, I'm relieved to see."

She shook the heavy curtain from her face and debated her next move. Maybe if she could delay him a bit longer, Merrick really would come for them. "Since you brought it up, why have you waited so long to come after me?"

"I would have been here weeks ago, but you've been too well guarded until today."

Understanding dawned and she inhaled sharply. "Who's been reporting to you? Who told you about our plans today?"

"That's not important." He turned to address two of his men. "We'll need half an hour to get to the landing

site and take off. You will protect Princess Juliana and
Princess Alyssa with your lives. In precisely thirty
minutes, return the cell phones and have them call for
assistance. You'll be notified when it's safe to leave
them unattended. Do you have your exit plans in place?"

The two gave swift confirmations and took up a
stance on either side of Juliana and Alyssa.

Brandt held out his hand to Miri. "Shall we go?"

He wasn't going to allow her to delay any longer.
Ignoring his hand, she stalked toward the waiting SUV.
She paused before climbing in and addressed her
brothers' wives. "Tell Lander and Merrick not to do
anything foolish, especially Merrick. I'll be in touch."
She glared at Brandt. "You will allow me to call my
family and reassure them that I'm safe and unharmed?"

He returned her cell phone to her. "Once we're in
Avernos, feel free to call them anytime you want. You're
not a prisoner. Not exactly." He turned his attention to
Alyssa. "Do thank Merrick for me, Your Highness. If he
hadn't given me the idea, I'd never have thought to try
this. But since abduction worked so well for him, I
decided to follow his example. And he was right. It's an
excellent plan."

"Right up until they arrest you and toss you into that
pit my brothers have waiting for you," Miri shot back.

Brandt inclined his head with one of the slow smiles
she adored—used to adore, she hastened to correct
herself. "Yes," he concurred. "Right up until then."

Finally. Finally his wife was in Avernos where she
belonged. Brandt leaned back in his chair and swirled

his single malt, inhaling the peaty aroma. Miri may not want to stay, but he'd change her mind, no matter what it took. He swallowed deeply and dropped the glass to the wooden tabletop. He'd let her escape once. He wouldn't allow that to happen again.

The door opened and he stood, his gaze intent. Miri walked into his study, hell, stalked in, anger reverberating with every step. He silently scrutinized her, gauging her emotions. Furious, no doubt about that. But he could also see the hurt that underscored all else.

She wore a silk suit in blistering red. It was one of the outfits he'd personally selected in anticipation of her return, knowing she wouldn't have anything of her own with her. The tailored lines revealed the weight she'd lost, making her appear even more delicate than usual. She'd pulled her hair back from her face, inky dark once again, the heavy length gathered into a sleek knot at the nape of her neck. The style emphasized the fine-boned curves of her face and drew attention to her eyes, eyes the deep green of a stormy sea.

"It's good to have you here, Miri."

"I wish I could say the same. I've been in touch with my family. Needless to say, they're not happy with you."

That had to be an understatement to end all understatements. "I'll deal with your family."

She approached, tossing her purse onto a side table before gesturing toward the chair in front of his desk. "Do you mind?"

He shook his head, amused. How could he have thought he'd ever be able to make a successful match with Alyssa? He wanted impulsive. Bold. Vibrant. A woman who brought color into his world. He wanted Miri. "Please, have a seat. I'm sorry I couldn't join you for dinner. Would you care for a drink?"

She shook her head. If he didn't know her so well, he'd think she were perfectly at ease. But he did know better. Her nervousness showed in the defiant slant of her chin and the tight grip she maintained on the padded arms of the chair. Even the curve of her mouth warned of emotional turmoil.

"Thank you for returning to Avernos," he began.

"Thank you for—" She stared in disbelief. "Have you lost your mind? You make it sound like I chose to return. In case you've overlooked a few dots, let me connect them for you. You gave me no other choice. I had to come back with you or you'd have—"

"I'd have…what?" he cut in.

She froze, like a deer scenting the approach of a predator. "Your men. You. You had all of us surrounded. I had to go with you."

"Do you think I'd have harmed you, or any of the Montgomery women for that matter?" He bit off each word, offended that she'd believe him capable of such a thing.

"Not harm, no," she conceded.

"You think I'd have forced you to come with me?"

Her head jerked up. "Yes." No equivocation this time, just that single fierce word.

He gave it a moment's consideration before lifting a shoulder. She might be right. He sure as hell wouldn't have left without her, he knew that for a fact. "Perhaps I would have used force if there had been no other alternative. I don't know. But since you chose to come of your own free will, I didn't have to make that decision, did I?" He picked up his drink and drained it, before setting it aside. "Well? Shall we get down to it? Would you prefer to start, or shall I?"

"I'm not sure." She eyed his glass. "Are you sufficiently fortified?"

He couldn't help but smile. "There's no fortification sufficient enough when it comes to dealing with you."

She relaxed ever so slightly at the admission, but didn't respond to his smile. "You want to discuss our issues? Okay. I'll go first." She leaned forward in her chair, fixing him with an unforgiving stare. "The first thing we need to discuss is who betrayed me. I want to know who told you I'd be at the mall unescorted."

"Next question."

"Tell me who the traitor is," she insisted.

"I said, next question."

A silent battle of wills ensued, neither prepared to back down. He'd just begun to wonder if they were going to sit there all night when she released her breath in a frustrated sigh. "Fine. Don't tell me. Explain something else instead. What possible excuse can you have for what you've done? For the lengths you've gone to, to try and gain the throne?"

He wouldn't prevaricate over that question. She wanted the truth? He'd give it to her, no matter who got hurt. "I received evidence implicating the Montgomerys in the theft of Verdonia's amethysts."

Miri nodded impatiently. "Juliana discovered the person responsible. It was Lauren DeVida, my stepfather's Chief Executive Accountant. That's old news."

"It wasn't old when I received it."

She hesitated, frowning. "No, I guess it wouldn't have been. But now you know the truth. That she was the one behind the thefts. That it wasn't the Montgomerys." Her voice gained intensity and he could hear the anger underscoring her words. "If you'd had the charges investigated when they'd first been given to you, you'd have discovered that for yourself. But instead, you used those accusations to try and snatch the throne from Lander."

He tilted his head to one side. Was she kidding? "How was I supposed to investigate the charges?" he demanded. "I didn't have access to the necessary records. I still don't. And I never will unless I'm elected king."

"Are you telling me you forced Alyssa to the altar in order to get your hands on a bunch of financial records?" she scoffed. "That's the excuse you're trying to sell?"

He fought the irritation that swept through him. "Sell? No. I'm telling you the unvarnished truth. Viable information was sent to me implicating your stepfather and Lander, and I considered any number of options before settling on marriage to Alyssa as my best option for resolving a critical situation. I had to protect Verdonia."

She waved that aside. "Oh, please."

He thrust a hand through his hair. Didn't she understand? "Listen to me, Miri. According to the experts I hired, the documents I received weren't faked. Someone has been siphoning off amethysts and selling them on the black market. And they've been doing it for a very long time. King Stefan was implicated directly, as well as Lander and Merrick, more recently."

"But it wasn't any of them," she argued. "I've explained that already. It was this DeVida woman."

He waited a beat before asking softly, "And who else?"

She looked taken aback. "Excuse me?"

"Think about it, Miri." Standing, he circled to the front of his desk, edging one hip on the tabletop directly across from her. "The amethysts leave the mines here in Avernos and are shipped to Celestia for processing. Some remain in Celestia and are purchased by local artisans, the rest go to Verdon for international sales and distribution."

"So?" she asked uneasily. "Every schoolchild knows that."

"My point is…how did Lauren DeVida steal the amethysts she sold on the black market?"

Miri stared at him blankly. "How did—"

"Lauren couldn't have done that on her own. It's not like she walked into the vault and helped herself to handfuls of uncut gems. There are only two places the amethysts could have been culled and the records altered." He ticked off on his fingers. "When they were brought out of the mines. Or when they were cut and graded in preparation for sale and distribution."

Miri fell silent, puzzling it out. "Whoever stole them wouldn't want uncut gems," she reluctantly offered. "They couldn't make as much from them."

"I agree. That suggests the second of our two possibilities is most likely. Which leaves us with the question of who. There's no way DeVida could have pulled this off on her own. She had to have help from someone, someone in a powerful position. Someone who could have circumvented the checks and balances King Stefan put in place. I want to know who that someone was."

"It wasn't my father!" Miri retorted, stung. "Or my brothers. We're not thieves."

"How do I know that?"

Hurt warred with anger. "How can you ask such a thing?"

"How can I not?" he asked grimly. "Look at it from my position. I receive incontrovertible evidence of a long-term theft ring that's brought Verdonia to a financial crisis. King Stefan was in charge during the years this was going on."

"He didn't know anything about it," she protested. "You can't blame him for that."

Brandt's expression hardened. "Yes, Miri, I can. It was his job to know. It was his responsibility. His duty as our king and protector." He hated criticizing the man she considered her father, but he had to make her understand it from his perspective. "His own accountant brought our country to the brink of ruin. And Stefan didn't have a clue. Why would I trust Lander to do a better job? Why should Verdonia?"

He winced at her drawn expression. "So you forced Alyssa to the altar because you didn't trust Lander? Is that what you're telling me?"

"My goal was to prevent any further malfeasance and to ensure that something like this never happens again. It's my duty to protect the people of Verdonia. To safeguard their future. The only way I can do that is from the throne. You may not approve of my methods, but at the time I didn't see any other option. Looking back, I still don't."

She stiffened. "My God," she whispered in disbelief. "You'd do it again, wouldn't you?"

"Marry Alyssa in order to keep Lander off the throne?" He didn't even hesitate. "Yes, I would."

"Regardless of what happened between us on Mazoné? Regardless of what we had?"

"Damn it, Miri." He scrubbed his face with his hands. "Do you think that doesn't tear me up? That I wouldn't wish for a different life, if it were possible? But, it's not. I am who I am. I can only act the way I've been raised to behave. The way I'm ethically bound to respond. I can't change that."

"Ethically bound?" She jumped to her feet and shot away from him. Halfway across the room, she spun around again, a flame of red fire. "Alyssa didn't want to marry you, Brandt. She was terrified, both of you and the situation she found herself in. But that didn't matter to you, did it? You sacrificed her on the altar of your precious code of ethics. She was no more than a pawn to you. How can that be right? How can that be just?"

He didn't back away from the question, but faced it squarely. "Not a day goes by that I don't regret what I did to her and to Angela." Pain carved deep crevices in his face. "It came down to forcing her to marry me and saving Verdonia, or allowing the corruption to continue until the entire country was destroyed. What should I have done?"

"That's so obvious, even a child could answer." Scorn filled her voice. "You should have brought the matter before the Temporary Governing Council, as you ultimately did."

He conceded the point with a nod. "Perhaps. But I couldn't be certain how deep the corruption ran. At the time, I didn't feel I could take the risk. Only after my initial plan failed did I dare take that route."

"So marrying Alyssa seemed like the best option, despite what we'd shared in Mazoné." She didn't phrase it as a question.

"The only option," he confirmed.

"Then what am I doing here? You brought me back to Avernos." Her hands fisted at her sides. "Why?"

A muscle jerked in his jaw. "You're here because I can't let you go." The words held a raspy edge. "I won't."

"And I won't be a consolation prize. Nor will I be second choice." She marched across the room and snatched up her purse. "You don't have the right to keep me here any longer. I want to go home. And by home I mean Verdon. Do you take me, or do I place another call to my brothers?"

Surging to his feet, Brandt came for her. "There's only one place you're going and it sure as hell isn't Verdon." Before she had time to react, he scooped her up in his arms and carried her toward the door.

"Let me go!" She fought to free herself, not that it did any good. "What do you think you're doing?"

"Taking you to my bed," he answered promptly. "Maybe once I have you there again you'll remember why you stayed the last time."

Six

Miri struggled in Brandt's arms, not that it did a bit of good. He carried her easily. To her outrage, the guards and servants littering the hallways were quick to avert eyes and hide smiles. How could they find this amusing? He was abducting her, holding her against her will!

Shoving open the door to his suite of rooms, he dropped her to her feet. "I'm not staying here," she informed him, backing away.

"You can try to leave, but you won't get far." He pursued her, his face set in inexorable lines. "Not again. My people won't make the same mistake twice."

"Don't blame them. It wasn't their fault," fairness compelled her to say. She edged her way clear across the room. Bumping up against the chair by the fireplace, the back of her knees clipped the seat and she sat down hard. Her cheeks turned a shade darker than her suit, but she recovered with impressive speed. Acting as though she'd planned to sit all along, she crossed her legs and smoothed the narrow skirt of her suit over her thighs. "They were ordered to guard Alyssa Sutherland, not Miri Montgomery. I made it clear who I was when I left. Why would they stop me?"

He took up a position in front of the mantel, far too close for comfort. "And because of that, you waltzed right out the front door."

"More of a stumbling run than a waltz," she muttered. Stiffening her spine, she fought to regain her focus and deal with the panther she somehow found herself caged with. Years of practice handling awkward situations in the course of performing her royal duties came to her rescue. "Let's have it, Brandt. What am I doing here?"

He regarded her in thoughtful silence for a brief moment. She'd never seen eyes such a rich ebony, nor so piercing in their intensity. Thunder rumbled in the distance, a perfect punctuation to his stare. "There are any number of issues we need to address. But why don't we start with a certain wedding ceremony that took place a couple months ago."

"Oh. That." She managed to dismiss its importance with a blithe carelessness. And if she took pleasure in the fact that his mouth compressed in annoyance, well, who could blame her? "I don't suppose you have any idea whether or not we're really married?"

"No, I don't."

She grimaced. He'd managed to out-blithe her and with irritating ease, too. "You haven't checked?"

"I'm satisfied with the status quo."

That had her mouth falling open. "You must be joking."

"Not at all." He folded his arms across his chest. "As far as I'm concerned we're married."

She uncrossed her legs, her heels hitting the floor with a decisive thud. "You can't possibly believe our marriage is legal. It can't be." She ticked off on her fingers. "You married me thinking I was Alyssa Sutherland. Her name was the one used during the ceremony, and on all the paperwork. Any one of those facts must be grounds for an annulment."

"Quite possibly." He tilted his head to one side. "What do you suppose would happen if I claim I knew it was you all along?"

She shook her head, alarmed. "That's impossible. You didn't know. You couldn't have!"

"You're certain of that?"

He'd left her grappling for a response. "If you'd known, you'd have stopped the ceremony. You'd have ordered your men to find Alyssa, just as you did later that night."

"Actually, it was early the next morning, not that it matters. Now, pay attention, wife." He leaned forward, crowding her to the point that she inched back in the chair. Lightning flashed, followed by a sharp crack of thunder as the storm closed in. She swallowed convulsively, her pulse fluttering in the hollow of her throat. "Since you're responsible for me losing my bride, I've decided you can replace her. Maybe our wedding ceremony is legal. Maybe it's not. To be honest, I don't give a damn either way because I plan to fight the dissolution. So prepare yourself, my sweet. If you want out of this marriage, you have an uphill battle ahead of you."

She shot to her feet. It helped that she'd found a pair of sky-high heels among the clothes he'd purchased for her. The extra height gave her a feeling of parity, even if an artificial one. "You can't fool me a second time. I know why you're doing this."

"Interesting. And why is that?"

"You're hoping that marriage to me will give you some of the votes you may have lost when Alyssa married Merrick." Her accusation had him staring in patent disbelief. "Well, it won't work. I—"

He held up a hand to halt her tumble of words. "Let me get this straight. I'm using you for votes. You're saying that with a straight face?"

She gave a decisive nod. "Yes. And it won't work." She planted her hands on her hips. "Not only won't *I* vote for you, I'm going to actively campaign for Lander."

He began shaking his head before she'd even finished speaking. "Campaigning for your brother might prove difficult."

His voice had gone deadly quiet, a warning sign if she'd ever heard one. Not that she'd allow it to intimidate her. Her chin shot up and she steeled herself for the coming confrontation. "And why is that?"

He straightened from his lounging position against the mantel. "Pay attention, wife." He used the word deliberately as he took a step toward her. "You're here of your own choice. But it's my choice when you leave."

She fell back a pace. This time instead of falling into the chair, she circled behind it, desperate for the barrier it provided. Rain stung the windows and another flash of lightning bled the room of color. Gripping the upholstered chair back, she confronted him. "Choice? You didn't give me a choice about coming here and you darn well know it. And now you think you can keep me here? Against my will?"

"Yes and yes."

That took the wind out of her sails. "Has it occurred to you that holding women against their will is becoming a bad habit of yours?"

He pretended to consider. "You know, you could be right. I'll take your concerns under advisement."

His levity left her quivering with the need to hit out. "Fair warning, Your Highness. I'm not staying. I came with you today for one reason and one reason only. To—"

"Rub my nose in how you helped Merrick steal my bride?" he offered helpfully.

"Yes. No!" She thrust a hand through her hair, loosening the knot. "Okay, maybe."

A brief smile came and went. "Admit it, Miri." His voice took on a more serious tone. "You came with me because you're furious. And hurt. You want to share the pain."

"You think I'm that petty?" She glared at him for endless seconds before her face crumpled and she slammed her fist into the upholstered chair back. "Damn you! You're right. I am that petty. I want you to hurt as much as I've been hurt. I want you to suffer for what you did to our relationship. But most of all, I want you to know that I despise you for what you've done, for being such an unbelievable bastard."

He came for her, reaching for her even when she threw up her hands to ward him off. Pulling her into his arms, he simply held her. It didn't seem to matter how rigidly she stood, he wouldn't be put off. He smoothed back her hair and the loosened coil unraveled beneath his touch.

"How could I have ever thought this belonged to Alyssa?" he murmured, filling his hands with the weight of it. "Or that it wasn't you I held in my arms. Maybe I did know on some unconscious level, knew and ignored the signs because desire overrode common sense."

"You didn't know it was me." Could he hear the hurt? Did he even care? "You called me by her name."

"Of course I did. You were using her name." His eyes narrowed and her heart skittered in her chest at his sudden look of comprehension. Thunder crashed overhead and echoed off the surrounding mountains. "My God. Were you hoping I'd figure it out? Is that why you're so offended?"

Yes, yes and yes! How could he be so blind? "You should have realized who I was the moment you kissed me," she said, horrifying herself by the accusation. Pain ate through her at the memory and her hands fisted around the lapels of his suit jacket. "Is my kiss so common, so ordinary, that you couldn't tell it from another woman's?"

"Do you think if it had really been Alyssa I held in my arms that I would have reacted the way I did with you?" he countered. "Lost control the way I did? I may not have been consciously aware it was you I took to my bed, but on some level I knew."

"How can you say that? In your head, in your heart,

you made love to Alyssa, not to me." It took every particle of restraint to speak the words, instead of howl them every bit as fiercely as the storm lashing at the windows. "You never gave me a single thought."

"You're wrong." His face darkened, filled with all the passion she could have wished. His eyes burned with it. His voice hungered from it. She could practically inhale the scent of it, a blatant need that electrified the very air they breathed. "The woman in my arms, the woman in my bed, the woman who caused me to lose every vestige of control was you. No other. And no other woman could have had the affect on me that you did."

"I don't believe you. I won't." She struggled to free herself, but he simply held on, refusing to release her. "Let me go!"

"Easy, sweetheart. Take it easy," he soothed.

She'd already discovered how pointless it was to struggle against him. That didn't mean she'd yield. She could still fight, with words, if nothing else. "Don't you dare call me sweetheart," she bit out. "You have no business keeping me here. No business touching me. No business forcing me to stay with you. You lost that privilege when you decided to marry Alyssa."

"I disagree. When you took her place, you gave me the right to keep you." He swept his thumb across her mouth. "To touch you."

"I never—"

"You did, Miri." His voice held an implacability she couldn't miss. "And you'll stay with me for as long as it takes."

"As long as what takes?" she demanded unevenly.

He cupped her face, turning it up to his. "For me to convince you that you belong here," he stunned her by saying. Lightning flickered, throwing his face into a stark relief that underscored his resolve. "You made promises to me and I intend to hold you to them."

"You must be kidding!"

"Not even a little. I might not have figured out who you were during the ceremony. And I may not have fully sensed the truth afterward. But you were well aware of who you promised to love, honor and cherish."

"I had to make those promises," she protested. Did he catch the defensive edge in her voice? Probably. Brandt didn't miss much. "If I hadn't repeated the vows, you'd have known I wasn't Alyssa."

He shook his head. "Not good enough. I heard your voice. I heard the emotion that permeated every single word. At the time, I thought you were pretending for our guests. But that wasn't true, was it?"

"I played a part. I was an actress performing a role, no more," she instantly denied. Who was she trying to convince, herself or Brandt? "I did what I had to in order to give Merrick and Alyssa time to escape. I'd have done anything to stop you, to keep you from stealing the throne from Lander."

"If that's true, then why did you stay?"

Naturally, he'd found the one flaw in her argument and nailed her with it. He studied her with an all-too-familiar mask, an inscrutable one that in the past had always filled her with intense frustration. How did he manage to keep his emotions in such an iron grip, when hers leaked from her grasp like a handful of water?

He'd become a master at throwing up walls, walls she'd only managed to fully breach once before—on their wedding night.

"You had plenty of time to leave before night fell, yet you didn't," he continued when she remained silent. "Why?"

Her chin shot up. No way would she humiliate herself with the truth. "As I said, I stayed to give Merrick as much time as possible to get away." She offered the lie without a moment's compunction.

His eyes were jet-black and so direct it was everything she could do not to flinch. "You made love to me, sacrificed your virginity, for the sake of kin and country?" he demanded. "Is that what you're trying to sell me?"

She opened her mouth to agree, but the words died unuttered. "Okay, I didn't stay with you to save Verdonia," she said with a sigh.

To her surprise, he relaxed ever so slightly. "Good answer."

"Would you have believed me if I'd insisted that it was the real reason?" she asked, curious. "Would you have believed me capable of making love to you as part of Alyssa's abduction plan?"

"No." Swift and unequivocal and punctuated by a hard rumble of thunder. "There's only one reason you'd ever go to bed with a man."

She fixed her attention on the tie knotted at his throat. It was slightly askew and for some reason that tiny imperfection filled her with a painful longing. She wanted to reach up and straighten that tie, to be entitled to perform such a casual, wifely duty. But she wasn't.

He'd chosen to give another woman that right. "If you already know why I'd sleep with a man, then you don't need an answer from me."

"I want to hear you say it anyway." A quiet urgency reverberated through his statement. "I want to hear you say you'd only give yourself to a man because you loved him."

She shook her head, unwilling to hand him such a huge portion of her soul. "I didn't stay because I loved you. I just wanted to say goodbye." It took every scrap of poise she possessed to look him straight in the eye and make truth from fabrication. "I said everything I needed to that night. I've worked through any lingering feelings I might have had for you. Whatever was between us has died a painful death, and I have no interest whatsoever in trying to resurrect it."

"I don't believe you."

She ripped loose of his embrace and finally he let her go. No sooner did she gain her freedom, than she found herself longing to be back in his arms again. "Believe what you want, Brandt. It doesn't change anything. I came here to confront you over what you've done and to tell you how despicable I think you are."

"And that's the only reason?"

"No." She'd recovered a modicum of her composure. Tossing back a swathe of hair, she faced him with a determined expression. "I also came with you today in order to find out what you plan to do next."

"Next?"

"To steal the election from Lander. Fair warning, I won't let you try anything else that might harm him or my family."

Anger flashed like lightning. "How are you planning to stop me?"

"Any way I can."

Where before his smile warmed, this time it chilled. "Then I suggest you stay close and watch carefully."

"Trust me, I will."

"Fine. Let's start here and now."

Brandt stripped off his suit jacket, and then his tie, and tossed them in the direction of the chair. His shirt followed a moment later. He watched as Miri fought to keep her attention on his face. But she betrayed herself with fleeting looks that swept across his bared chest and arms. They were hungry little glances, filled with the memory of another time and another night. Glances that gave lie to her claims of indifference. Glances that burned as much as if she'd branded him with an actual touch.

"What do you think you're doing?" she asked faintly.

"I'm turning in for the night. Why?"

Her head jerked toward the bed and away again. A hint of color bloomed across her cheekbones while memories darkened her eyes to the green of a forest buried in shadow. "In that case, I'll turn in, too." She hovered in the center of the room, appearing momentarily helpless. "Where do I…"

He gestured toward the bed. "Right there. Next to me."

He fought to hide his amusement at the way her mouth opened and closed. And those amazing eyes of hers went so wide he could have drowned in them.

"You must be joking."

"I told you in the parking garage. I intend to have my wife in my arms when I go to bed." He crossed to her side and snagged the lapel of her suit, anchoring her in place. Not giving her time to react, he plucked open the first button of her jacket. "Starting now."

"Stop it, Brandt." The breath trembled from her lungs and she attempted to refasten the buttons as fast as he unfastened them. "This isn't funny."

"I agree." He won the battle of the buttons and slid the jacket off her shoulders, allowing it to drop to the floor at her feet. "There's nothing in the least amusing about our relationship to date."

She slapped at him as he tackled the zip of her skirt, not that it did any good. "I'm not sleeping with you," she wailed.

"Fair enough. Then you can lie awake in my arms while I sleep." His hands closed around her waist and he lifted her. Her skirt plummeted down her hips, catching momentarily on the toes of her mile-high heels before both shoes and skirt gave up the fight and dropped to the floor.

"You have no right," she protested as he set her down.

"I repeat. You gave me that right." He yanked her silk shell up and over her head.

"We can't. Our marriage isn't legal." The words were muffled, but he caught the gist.

"It is until we're told otherwise."

She emerged from beneath the shell, hair tousled, face stormy. "I don't want to go to bed with you."

"I got that message." Loud and clear. "Want or not, like or not, you will join me in that bed."

He spoke in a voice rare for him, but one that guaranteed instant obedience the few times he used it. She stood before him in scraps of lace and silk, rumpled and ruffled, and still defiance vibrated in every muscle of her body. Tears glistened, most likely from anger, though it could be distress, and he steeled himself to ignore their impact. He didn't dare show any weakness with her, not until matters were resolved between them.

He approached and she stumbled backward a step before locking her knees in place and holding her ground with clenched fists and a jutting jaw. So strong, so defiant, so painfully defenseless. Reaching past her, he flipped off the light.

"We're both tired and irritable and this isn't the best conversation to hold when we're not at our best," he spoke into the dark. "I suggest we table it until morning."

He heard her breath escape in a relieved rush. "I can live with that."

"Fine. Then I have something for you."

He crossed to his dresser, moving through the unlit room with complete assurance. Opening the top drawer, he grabbed one of the nightgowns he'd purchased with her in mind. He'd gone a little crazy, buying a full dozen, each softer and more filmy than the one before, some silk and some the finest cotton he could find, but all barely enough material to fill his palm.

"Here, put this on." He tossed her the first one that came to hand. Even in the dark, the light color of the gown made it visible. It billowed as it floated in her direction, and she snatched it out of midair before retreating deeper into shadow.

He could hear the rustle of clothing as she stripped and struggled not to think about what she was doing or how she looked doing it. That path led to trouble. If he were going to get through the endless hours ahead with his sanity intact, he'd better keep his thoughts on something other than Miri undressing, Miri naked, or Miri undressing and naked.

He'd almost succeeded when a flash of lightning lit the room for a split second, spotlighting his wife and forever burning a picture of her nudity into his heart and mind. The sight sent a kick straight to the gut, robbing him of the ability to breathe.

She stood, tautly erect, arched slightly backward as she lifted the nightgown above her head. Her breasts were full and beautifully rounded, tipped in rose, while a river of ebony hair cascaded down her shoulders and back, just brushing the curves of a perfectly curved backside. Her legs were glorious, toned and shapely, and she'd turned just enough toward him to reveal the thatch of dark curls that stood out in stark relief beneath the unblemished ivory of her belly.

He saw it. He saw it all in that brief instant before the room was plunged into darkness once again. And seeing, he wanted. He wanted to snatch her from where she stood and rip the nightgown from her grasp. More, he wanted to carry her to the bed and brand every lush inch with his possession. Desire raged, the need that screamed through him so intense he thought he'd lose his mind from the overwhelming demand of it. Only one thing held him in place— the expression in her eyes, an expression of utter vulnerability.

"Please," she whispered into the night.

Her voice echoed that vulnerability with an apprehension so sharp, it cut like a knife. He'd already hurt
her, hurt her more than any man had a right to. He
wouldn't add to that pain.

"It's okay, Miri." His voice sounded like it was filled
with grit, but at least it held steady and gave a semblance
of calm. With luck, it wouldn't frighten her. He deliberately kept his distance, determined to ease her trepi-
dation. "Come to bed."

"I—I don't feel well."

He could read between those lines. "It's been one of
those days," he told her gently. "You'll feel better once
you've had some sleep."

"I'd rather sleep alone."

"I'm sure you would. And I wish I could let you." He
closed his eyes for an instant, his hands fisting at his
side. "But I'm not that altruistic."

Lightning cut through the room again, punctuated by
a rumble of thunder. She'd finished changing and the
staccato flash darted through the fine cotton of her
nightgown, showing him all he dared not touch. The
strobe of light also sent her flying across the room, but
not toward the bed. She slammed into the bathroom
and an instant later he heard her retching.

He came after her at a run. "Easy, sweetheart."
Sinking to his knees behind her, he held her hair back
from her face. "It's going to be okay. I've got you."

When she was done, she collapsed against the wall,
drawing her knees tight against her chest. Tears leaked
from behind her tightly closed eyes, tracking down
cheeks bleached bone-white. If he'd thought she'd

looked vulnerable before, it was nothing compared to how she looked now.

He settled down beside her and to his relief, she turned to him, huddling in his arms. And then she fell apart. He held her close and waited out the storm. When it had passed, he caught her hand in his and laced their fingers together. There was only one reasonable question to ask.

"You're pregnant, aren't you?"

Seven

Miri pulled back and stared at Brandt in horror. "No. No, that's not possible."

He swept her hair from her damp face. "It's quite possible. We made love two and a half months ago without protection." He lifted an eyebrow. "Were you on the pill at the time?"

Catching her bottom lip between her teeth, she shook her head. "No."

"And since we made love?" he pressed. "Has there been any indication you might *not* be pregnant?"

"I…I can't remember." What a liar she was. She knew full well she hadn't had a period since that amazing night. But that didn't mean she was pregnant. Desperation goaded her to debate the issue. "I've always been irregular. Stress can cause that sort of reaction. And so can the recent weight I've lost."

"As can pregnancy, or so the rumor goes."

"Oh, very funny." The tenderness with which he regarded her had tears flooding her eyes again. "I'm not pregnant. I can't be."

"It's a far more likely cause than either stress or weight loss." Leaving her side, he rose long enough to dampen a washcloth with warm water before joining her on the floor again. "Damn, Miri. Don't cry," he murmured as he rinsed her face. "It'll all work out."

"There's nothing to work out," she argued tearfully around the washcloth. "You have your life and I have mine. Problem solved."

He continued as if she hadn't spoken. "It's too late to do anything about this tonight. I'll call the doctor first thing in the morning and have him fit you in for an exam. I promise, he'll be discreet."

That dried her eyes. She pulled away from Brandt and stood, annoyed to find her legs weren't as steady as she'd have liked. "Don't interfere in this, Your Highness. I'll make my own doctor's appointment."

He gained his feet, as well. "As soon as possible, please."

Did he think her a complete idiot? "I wouldn't do anything to jeopardize the baby's health—assuming there is a baby." Her hand stole downward, splaying across her abdomen. Did a child rest there? A child Brandt had given her? His eyes narrowed at the telling gesture. "Of course, I'll see a doctor as soon as possible."

"Why haven't you before this?"

It was an excellent question. She opened her mouth to tell Brandt it was none of his business, but one look at his face convinced her of the wisdom of a candid reply. "I went back to Mazoné after…after Alyssa's abduction," she admitted reluctantly.

"Staying clear of the line of fire?"

"It seemed a smart choice," she muttered.

"A very smart choice." An odd expression glittered in his eyes, something hard and predatory that mingled with a lingering anger. "I'm not sure we'd have dealt well together those first few days after I found out the true identity of my bride."

Miri froze beneath that look. Brandt had always kept his emotions under tight control. Observing him now, she realized that control had evaporated when he'd learned of her identity. What would he have done if she'd been closer at hand? She shivered. Probably best she didn't know, and even better that she hadn't found out at the time.

"I stayed on Mazoné until right before Lander's wedding." They'd been long, hideous days of endless regret. But if the days had been bad, the nights had proven worse, plodding by, each interminable hour filled with a painful yearning. "To be honest, I lost track of time. I'd just begun to suspect something was out of kilter when I returned to Verdonia."

He nodded in perfect understanding. "I'm guessing it would have raised a few eyebrows if you'd run out to the corner druggist and picked up a pregnancy test."

"Something like that." More like it would have swept across Mt. Roche within the hour. And then all hell would have really broken loose.

He handed her a toothbrush loaded with toothpaste

and waited until her mouth was full of foam before continuing. "I know you don't want me interfering. But if you're pregnant, it's with my baby. Just so we're clear about this, I plan to involve myself in every aspect of the birth and rearing of our child."

She rinsed her mouth before turning to confront him. "You only suspected I was pregnant two minutes ago and you're already planning the delivery and parenting of our baby?" She lifted an eyebrow, struggling to present a strong front when all she wanted to do was pull the covers over her head and cry herself to sleep. "You can't even be certain it's yours."

He didn't hesitate. "If you're pregnant, it's mine."

Exhaustion stole the fight from her. "Fine. It's yours. Now, back off, Brandt. You're crowding me."

He ignored her, sweeping her into his arms. "I'll back off once I'm sure you're able to stand without help."

Unable to resist, she dropped her head to his shoulder. "I just need some sleep."

"I'll make sure you get it."

He lowered her to the bed and she turned her back on him, curling into a tight ball. Padding across the room, he opened the windows and an instant later a soft breeze swept through the room, carrying with it a rain-swept freshness. He returned to the bedside and she caught the rustle of his clothing as he stripped, before the mattress depressed beneath his weight. An instant later he wrapped her in the warmth of his arms.

"Close your eyes, love. We'll deal with all this tomorrow."

"I think I'd be more comfortable sleeping in my own bed," she whispered. "I can't do this. Here. With you."

"You don't have to do anything, sweetheart. Just sleep."

"You won't... You aren't—"

"I won't. I'm not. Not until you're ready."

"Thank you."

He didn't answer, just spooned her more tightly against his chest and she realized she'd been wrong. Horribly wrong. She wouldn't be more comfortable sleeping in her own bed. Having him with her, holding her again, was a pleasure just this side of heaven.

Sleep had just started to lay claim when she felt his hand shift, his fingers spreading wide and low across her belly. Her breath escaped in a trembling sigh. "I may not be pregnant," she murmured.

"But if you are..." His hand warmed her through the thin cotton of her nightgown. "Our baby sleeps here," he marveled. "A son or a daughter."

"Or twins. Fraternal twins run down my mother's side."

He laughed and she could feel the rumble reverberate down the length of her spine. "Heaven help us if they're as impulsive as you."

She could picture it, picture it as clearly as though her children stood before her. A daughter with her father's dark hair and eyes and serious nature, calm and logical and brilliant. And a son whose mischievous eyes were the same green as her own, who caused his parents fits with the trouble he seemed to generate as easily as breathing.

Her eyes squeezed closed. If she listened hard enough, she could almost hear them. Their laughter.

Their sweet voices calling to her. Their unique scent when she enfolded them in her arms. She wanted that. She wanted those babies more than she'd ever wanted anything in her life—with one exception.

Brandt. It wouldn't be the same without him. Her life would be full, but missing the most important ingredient if he weren't at her side. It didn't matter what had come before, did it? Not if they worked together to create a new life. They had a chance, right now, if they could only put the past behind them and move forward.

She slipped her hand on top of his, lacing their fingers together across their future. "What will we do if I am pregnant?"

"What we're doing now. We'll create a life for ourselves."

It was almost a mirror image of her own thoughts and she smiled. "And if our marriage is annulled?"

"If that happens, I plan to drag you in front of the nearest official and have us wed within the hour."

"And if I refuse?"

"You won't refuse. You wouldn't do that to our children." His hand tightened on hers. "You wouldn't do that to us."

"A baby isn't going to solve our differences. Nor will marriage."

"No. There's only one thing that will do that, and that's time for us to work things out." He feathered a kiss across the top of her head. "Sleep now, sweetheart. You need your rest. Everything else can wait until the morning."

Miri closed her eyes and allowed sleep to claim her.

And as she drifted off her last thought was one that put a smile on her mouth. Morning. When morning came she'd be where she most wanted—safe in Brandt's arms.

Brandt hung up the phone and swore beneath his breath. Shoving open the doors that led onto the private balcony off his study, he crossed to the balustrade and folded his arms across the top railing. He drew in a deep breath, struggling to regain his control. The mountains were alive with birdsong and a soft, cool wind swept down the hillside, filled with the scent of cedar and wild grass. Nature at its best and yet it did nothing to soothe his temper.

"Brandt?" Miri joined him on the balcony. "I've been looking everywhere for you." She broke off, instantly picking up on his fury. Crossing to his side, she gripped his arm. "What's wrong? What's happened?"

"I've just been informed that our marriage has been invalidated."

A slight frown touched her brow, but she shrugged it off. "We expected that."

"True." His mouth twisted to one side. "Just not so soon. I'd hoped to have more time. But apparently your family isn't interested in giving us that time."

"They're involved in the dissolution?" she asked, shocked.

"Lander called, personally. He's instructed me—" Brandt released a harsh laugh. "Hell, why be diplomatic? He ordered me. He's ordered me to return you within twenty-four hours or he'll make the abduction public knowledge. He'll also be—and I quote—

obligated to act. No doubt Merrick's security force is planning the takedown as we speak."

"I came to tell you my doctor's appointment is tomorrow. Once we announce I'm pregnant, they won't interfere if we choose to remarry." She hesitated, seeming to force out the words. "Unless…unless you'd rather end our relationship. If it's become a roadblock—"

A roadblock? Where the hell had that come from? Did she really believe they'd be better off apart? The mere thought of losing her left Brandt wild with possessive fury. He struggled to gather it in, to keep from exploding from the intensity of it. "No." Just that one word, pushed from between his teeth, but her reaction was instantaneous.

With an exclamation of relief, she threw her arms around his neck and kissed him with unstinting generosity. The last time she'd kissed him of her own accord—freely and openly, as herself—had been on Mazoné, and he didn't realize how desperately he missed her spontaneity, her initiating, not just responding. If he'd had their wedding night to live over, he'd never have been fooled into thinking he held Alyssa in his arms, that it was her mouth slanted beneath his. Miri put everything into her kisses and he realized she always had. She'd never been one for half measures.

He threaded his fingers into her hair, wanting a slow, thorough kiss. She gave him hot and greedy. He tried for gentle and sedate. With one teasing nip, she tumbled him into fierce and rapacious. She moaned into his mouth, the sound slamming through him, piercing straight to his heart.

When he finally lifted his head, he found her gazing up at him as though he'd just finished hanging the sun. His kiss had bee-stung her lips into plump, ripe berries, damp and parted and begging for more. He couldn't resist. He took her mouth again, only to be thrown off kilter when she gave him what he'd tried for originally. Very slow, and very thorough.

After endless minutes, she pulled back with a reluctant sigh. "Do you realize that by this time tomorrow we'll know if I'm pregnant?" Her eyes widened, filling with joyous tears. "Oh, my gosh. I might be a mother."

His arms tightened around her. "And I," he added with intense satisfaction, "will be a father."

Best of all, when her pregnancy had been confirmed, he'd be in a position to deal with the Montgomerys, once and for all. And then he'd make Miri his legally wedded bride, no matter what it took or who he had to go through in order to make it happen.

"I am sorry, Your Highness."

"So am I," Miri replied. She attempted a smile, but failed miserably. "I was so certain... Brandt and I, we both were."

The doctor touched her shoulder. "You're young. There's plenty of time to start a family. I should warn you, though. With your history of irregularity, it may take a little longer than the average couple. Just be patient. Watch your diet. Your body needs a little more weight than it's currently carrying if you want a healthy pregnancy. And try to eliminate stress from your life."

She nodded. "No more fake marriages and abductions. Got it."

The doctor's eyebrows shot skyward. "I beg your pardon?"

"Sorry. A poor attempt at a joke." She held out her hand. "Thank you for seeing me."

"With luck, you'll be back again in a few months and I'll have better news." He showed her to the door. "And my congratulations and best wishes to you and Prince Brandt. I hadn't heard that you were married."

"No, not many people have," she agreed absently. "It was a bit of surprise to everyone. Even to him."

"I see." She could tell from his confused expression that he didn't see at all, which was just as well. "Once again, Your Highness, I am sorry. I wish I had better news for you."

"So do I."

Miri left the doctor's office and crossed the parking lot to where Brandt's right-hand man, Tolken, waited with the car. Nerves skittered up and down her spine. "Thank you," she murmured as he opened the door.

She climbed into the car, fighting back tears. She'd been in a state of shock while with the doctor, but the hard, cold facts of the situation were rapidly setting in. She pressed a hand to her abdomen, feeling an emptiness there that reverberated straight to her heart. It wasn't as though she'd lost her child, she tried to reassure herself. There'd never been one to begin with. But it felt like a loss.

How would Brandt react to the news? He'd been so pleased at the thought of a baby, so considerate and tender. What would happen once he learned she wasn't pregnant after all? Would he be disappointed, or secretly relieved? Maybe it was just as well they hadn't been sexually active since their wedding night. This way they could make decisions about their future without having to add a baby into the equation. But she couldn't help but wonder…once the truth came out, would he still want to marry her?

Or would he decide to end the relationship?

The thought leapt to her mind, unbidden. Yet the more she considered it, the more likely it seemed. It wasn't as though they were really married. Not any longer. Granted, he'd come after her that day in the parking garage, had wanted her without suspecting she might be pregnant. But what if the abduction had been out of anger? Maybe he'd wanted revenge for all she'd cost him, and it wasn't until he'd believed her pregnant that those plans had changed, that he'd considered making their marriage a real one.

She covered her face with her hands. She didn't know what to think anymore. There was only one way to find out what he intended. She'd tell him the truth. She'd tell him she wasn't pregnant and see how he reacted. And then she'd know whether she had a chance at a future with him.

"I'm sorry, Your Highness. I wish I had better news for you."

"So do I," Brandt replied with impressive calm.

"I have a full staff of accountants and lawyers ready to assist you. Say the word and we'll do everything we can to get this straightened out. How anyone could possibly believe you were working in collusion with Lauren DeVida to steal Verdonian amethysts and sell them on the black market is beyond my comprehension."

"I appreciate the support."

"Your Highness!" His man of affairs sounded shocked by the comment. "Of course we support you. We know you'd never be guilty of such an outrageous crime. It's just the timing. The timing is quite unfortunate."

Now there was an understatement if he'd ever heard one. Brandt suppressed a laugh, not that it would have held any amusement. "The timing isn't unfortunate. It's impeccable." Too impeccable. "If you're a Montgomery."

There was a moment of appalled silence. Then, "I see. I'll get someone on this right away."

"Thank you, Maitrim."

Brandt hung up the phone with a grimace. He suspected that any number of "someones" could be put on the problem and it still wouldn't be resolved. Not until after the election. And maybe not even then.

He poured himself a drink while he considered his options. But instead of sipping the single malt, he stared into the amber liquid as though it held the answers to his questions. If it weren't for Miri's pregnancy, his decision would be a simple one. Honor. Duty. Responsibility. Sacrifice. It was his duty to protect the baby he'd created, equally his duty to protect Miri. Unfortunately, the two had just become mutually exclusive.

In order to protect his child, he had to marry the mother. In order to protect Miri, he had to send her away. So, who held the greatest claim to duty and responsibility? He swirled the whiskey in his glass. He knew what his grandfather would say. The baby was his top priority because it was the most helpless and innocent. If it weren't for the child… He downed his drink in a single swallow. Thank God for the pregnancy, because it narrowed his choices to one. If it weren't for the baby, he'd be honor-bound to protect Miri from the coming storm.

It would be his duty to sacrifice what he desired most.

Eight

As soon as Brandt set eyes on Miri he realized that something had gone terribly wrong. Had she found out about the charges being leveled against him? Or was it even worse than that? He shot to his feet. The baby! Please, God, don't let anything be wrong with their baby. After all that had transpired in the past twenty-four hours, their child had been the one good thing he could hold on to.

"What is it, sweetheart?" He circled the desk and wrapped his arms around her. "Is it the pregnancy? Has something happened to the baby?" he questioned urgently.

She shook her head, her eyes huge and dark and filling with tears. "I'm sorry, Brandt." Her chin quivered and a tear fell, sliding down her pale cheek. "I was wrong. I'm not pregnant."

"Shh." He tucked her close and held her while she

cried it out. "I'm sorry. I know how inadequate that sounds. But I am so sorry. I'd hoped—"

And so had she. Clearly, she'd wanted the baby as much as he had and he couldn't help but celebrate that fact, even as he mourned the loss of the child he'd spent the past two days imagining. He'd wanted to have a baby with Miri, had looked forward to its advent in his life. And now he realized that not only was that an impossibility, it would never happen in the future. He'd make sure of that. In one brief second he'd gone from having it all, to losing everything.

Brandt steeled himself for what would have to come next. Now that he knew for a fact that Miri wasn't pregnant, his choices had changed. He had a responsibility toward her. Honor and duty required him to protect her. And to protect her meant sending her home. There was no way he could do that without hurting her. But maybe it was just as well. If he hurt her, she'd be willing to leave. She'd *want* to leave.

He cleared his throat. "This seems to be the day for news, both good and bad."

She lifted her head from his shoulder. "Which is the baby?" she whispered, her undisguised pain threatening to rip his heart from his chest. "Good or bad?"

"Do you have to ask?" He smoothed the hair from her face and knuckled a tear from cheek. "I'm sorry there's no baby. I'd already made our child a part of my life. A part of our future."

Her breath caught in a sob. "So had I."

"There's something I need to tell you, Miri."

"The good?"

"Yes, the good." It cost him to keep his expression encouraging, to act pleased with his news. "Now that our marriage has been annulled and there's no baby, you're free to return home."

Her brows drew together. "How is that good news?"

Excellent question. "It's good because I won't be holding you here against your will any longer. I'm sure your family will be relieved about that. They feel, as do I, that it's inappropriate for you to remain here, given the circumstances."

She stared at him in disbelief. "You said Avernos was my home. You said we would remarry if the annulment went through."

"That's when we thought you were pregnant."

"The baby?" She tore free of his arms and took a stumbling step backward. "The baby was the only reason for us to marry? Is that what you're telling me?"

He hardened himself against the disbelief in her face. "I brought you here against your will, as you've told me on more than one occasion. Now I'm letting you go. It's the right thing."

"Please, Brandt. Don't do this. I don't know what's going on, but I…" Defiance radiated from her. "I won't go. Not until you tell me the real reason you're sending me away. Is it my family? Are they threatening you?"

He had one final card to play, one he'd hoped to avoid using. His hands balled into fists. One guaranteed to work. "I repeat. I brought you here believing we were still married. It's inappropriate for you to be here now that we're not. It's not just your reputation at stake. There's still the election to consider."

It only took a minute for that to sink in. The instant it did, the breath exploded from her lungs. "This is about winning the election? You're sending me away because...because what? Having me in your bed when we're not married might cost you some votes? You want to be king so badly that you'd sacrifice our life together to get it?"

He shoved out his response between gritted teeth. "Yes."

She stood there for an endless moment, as though waiting for him to take it back. Bit by bit her hope died a slow death, while he died inch by inch watching it. Finally her chin shot up. "Fine. If that's what's most important, you can choke on your damned crown. I'll go pack."

He retreated behind a regal facade. "Thank you. I'll arrange for your flight home. Tolken will inform you when the helicopter is ready to depart."

Miri turned on her heel and walked from the room, her head held high, despite feeling as though her life had just ended. It wasn't until she'd reached the hallway that she lost control. Helpless tears streamed down her cheeks. She ignored them, forcing her feet to keep moving, step after step, until she'd gained the privacy of their bedroom.

For endless minutes she stood in the middle of the room, looking around in bewilderment. She'd told Brandt she'd go and pack but she didn't have anything *to* pack. None of the clothes littering the closet belonged to her, though she'd bet her last dollar that Brandt wouldn't agree. Gifts, he'd call them. Well, she refused to take anything he'd purchased for her. She'd leave as she arrived.

The thought gave her direction, sending her flying to the closet. It didn't take long to find the clothes she'd worn when she, Juliana and Alyssa had donned disguises and snuck out of the palace for their shopping trip to the mall. Was it only two short days earlier? It seemed decades ago.

After washing her face, she changed into the slacks and tee she'd been wearing that day, and braided her hair in preparation for the trip home. She was just gathering up her purse when her cell phone rang. She checked the incoming number and almost burst into tears again when she saw her mother's name displayed.

"Mom?"

"I've just heard," Rachel said without preamble. "Are you all right?"

Miri sank onto the edge of the mattress. "I don't understand. How did you find out so fast? Who told you? Did Brandt call?"

"No, no. It was Lander. He got it from the Temporary Governing Council. Oh, honey. He's very worried. He's offering to help in any way he can."

What? Miri lifted a hand to her throbbing temple. That didn't make sense. How could the TGC know about her pregnancy? "I don't understand. What's Lander got to do with—" Something didn't add up. "Let's start over. Why are you calling?"

"I heard about the allegations against Brandt, of course."

"What allegations?"

"Don't you know?" Rachel made an impatient sound.

"Unbelievable. He probably thinks he's protecting you. That's his grandfather's influence, no doubt. Typical Verdonian man."

Miri's grip tightened on the phone. "Mom, for heaven's sake! What are you talking about?"

"I'm talking about the charges that are being leveled against Prince Brandt," came the crisp response. "They're claiming he was working in collusion with Lauren DeVida to steal the amethysts and sell them on the black market. Ridiculous, of course."

Miri shot to her feet. "That's outrageous. Who's claiming Brandt's involved? Who's made these allegations?"

"The Temporary Governing Council. New evidence has come to their attention."

"What evidence? Where? From whom?"

"I don't know. Lander's trying to find out."

"Well, I'm telling you it's impossible." Realizing she was shouting into the phone, Miri attempted to modulate her voice. "Brandt would never steal from anyone, certainly not the country he's sworn to protect. Not ever. Honor and duty are as much a part of him as blood and bone."

There was a long pause, and then Rachel said, "You love him, don't you?"

The gentleness in her mother's voice almost proved Miri's undoing. "Yes. I love him." It took her a moment before she could continue, to gather her self-control sufficiently to think straight. "He's sending me away, Mom. Our marriage has been annulled and since I'm not pregnant—"

"Pregnant!"

"Are you listening to me? I said *not* pregnant."

"Yes, I hear you." Rachel sighed. "As I said before, honey, it's clear that he's trying to protect you by sending you away. Obviously, he doesn't want your reputation tarnished by all this nastiness."

Was it possible? Miri sank back onto the edge of the bed. It was more than possible. Probable, bordering on definite. "Well, I'm not leaving him. Not now."

"He's not an easy man to thwart," Rachel pointed out. "And he can be very persuasive when he chooses."

Something in her mother's tone caught Miri's attention. "Just out of curiosity, how would you know all that?"

There was an awkward pause before Rachel replied. "Oh, all right. If you must know, Brandt convinced me to tell him when you would be away from the palace so he could contact you. He said he wanted to try and resolve your differences," she admitted reluctantly. "A fat lot of good that did. First he abducts you, and now he's sending you back again as if you were an article of clothing that didn't fit right. The nerve of that man!"

Miri keyed in on the most vital part of her mother's diatribe. "*You* told him where to find me?" She could scarcely believe it.

Rachel cleared her throat. "You were so upset," she attempted to explain. "In so much pain. Even if things didn't work out between you, at least you'd have made the effort. Darn it, Miri. I meant well."

"I know you did, Mom. To be honest, I'm sitting here debating whether or not to thank you."

"You say thank you, and I'll say you're welcome, and

we'll consider the subject closed. Now, how are you planning to fix this mess?"

Good question. "Give me a minute. I'm thinking." Miri rubbed her forehead. "The first thing I need is for Juliana to take a look at whatever evidence the TGC has and see if she can figure out what's going on. She found the discrepancy with Lander and cleared his name, maybe she can do the same for Brandt. Do you think she'd be willing to help?"

"She'll help. I guarantee it."

"Perfect. In the meantime, I intend to take a page out of Merrick's book."

"Oh, Lord. I'm almost afraid to ask."

"I'm going to abduct my ex-husband." Miri smiled grimly. "All things considered, it only seems fair, don't you think?"

Brandt tossed down his pen. "What do you mean she won't leave?"

Tolken shrugged. "Her Highness says she won't leave unless you accompany her."

"We'll see about that." Brandt thrust the papers he'd been working on into a folder and stood. Snagging his suit jacket from the back of his chair, he shrugged into it. "Let's go."

He found his wife—no, not his wife, he reminded himself—waiting on the lawn near the helo pad. She stood quietly off to one side, wearing a simple pair of bronze-colored slacks and a matching tee. She'd swept her hair back from her face and restrained it in a simple braid down her back. For some reason seeing her standing there, so small against the backdrop of the helicopter, with a single suitcase at her feet, made her appear delicate and helpless and lost. It took everything he possessed not to gather her up and return her to their bedroom and to say to hell with honor and duty and responsibility.

He fought to remind himself that Miri was anything but delicate, helpless, or lost. But that didn't curb his urge to head for the bedroom with her. He crossed to her side. "What's going on?" he questioned briskly. "What's wrong?"

"Nothing's wrong. I just informed Tolken I wouldn't leave unless you escorted me." She lifted an eyebrow in a regal manner. "All things considered, I think it's the least you can do. Don't you?"

He briefly considered arguing the point. But if agreeing to accompany her meant her prompt return to Verdon, without further debate or discussion, he'd go along with it. "Fine. I'll escort you home." He snagged her suitcase and gestured toward the helicopter. "Shall we?"

He'd half expected her to refuse to take any of the clothes he'd purchased for her, and it relieved his mind to see her being reasonable about it. Even though barely a quarter of the clothes filling her closet could have fit in her suitcase, at least a few of the items wouldn't go to waste. Tolken had them both on board in short order and as soon as he'd made certain everyone was strapped in, he joined the pilot and they went airborne.

Miri sat decorously at his side, hands folded in her lap, gaze focused straight ahead, and Brandt eyed her with deep suspicion. This was too easy. She had to be up to something. Before he had time to consider the endless possibilities for someone so impulsive, Tolken spoke to him through the headphones.

"There's a problem, Your Highness. The pilot believes something's wrong with the fuel line. He's looking for a place to set down while he checks it out."

"There's a clearing not far from here." Brandt shot Miri a concerned glance. His plan had been to get her out of harm's way, not put her in it. "Have him watch for a lake slightly north of our position. There's a cabin and boathouse at one end. There should be room to land there."

The helicopter gave a slight stutter, than banked sharply in the direction he'd indicated. Within minutes the lake came into view. With smooth precision, the pilot landed not far from the cabin, recommending as he did so that they exit the craft and stretch their legs while he ran through his inspection. Brandt unfastened his seat belt, and Miri and Tolken followed suit.

"How long will it take to diagnose the problem?" Brandt asked, once they'd moved clear of the churning blades.

Tolken frowned. "I'm not certain, Your Highness. I'll check with the pilot and give you a full report as soon as possible. If it's going to take too long, I'll call for a car. Would it be possible to borrow your cell phone? Mine doesn't seem to be working."

Brandt nodded, handing it over. "Yes, of course." He was so relieved that Miri was safe, he didn't care how long it took them to fix the blasted thing. If need be, he'd drive her all the way to Verdon.

"I'll return as soon as possible," Tolken said and trotted back to the helicopter.

Miri touched Brandt's arm and gestured toward the cabin. "This seems familiar. Have I been here before?"

Turning his back on the helicopter, he gave her an odd look. "Don't you remember?"

She shook her head. "No, actually I don't." She started across the knee-high grass in the direction of the cabin and he fell in step beside her. "When was I here? It must have been ages ago."

"Fifteen years, maybe a few more. I'm surprised you don't recall. This is where I rescued—"

Before he could finish, a loud escalating whine sounded behind them. Spinning around he watched in disbelief as the helicopter rose skyward. It hovered for a brief moment directly overhead, then banked to the south and vanished behind the tree line. All that remained in its place was Miri's suitcase. It sat in the middle of a circle of flattened grass, an incongruous monument to his massive stupidity.

Cold anger bit deep and he turned it on Miri. "What the hell is going on?"

"We needed to talk in private, where you couldn't either walk out on me or send me away." She shrugged. "Tolken was kind enough to assist."

"Tolken is fired."

To his fury, she didn't appear the least concerned. "Merrick will be happy to pick him up. He's been trying to lure Tolken away from you for years."

"This is ridiculous." He searched his pockets for his cell phone, swearing beneath his breath when he remembered what he'd done with it. "There's nothing left to be said between us. You're returning home now that there's no reason for us to remain together, and that's the end of it."

She planted her hands on her hips. "Honor. Duty. Responsibility. How does sending me away jive with those?" Her eyes narrowed. "Or does it jive with another of those lessons you learned at your grandfather's knee? Maybe this has to do with sacrifice."

"This has to do with the fact that you're not pregnant and we're not married and—" Damn it to hell! What was the other thing? She had him so worked up he couldn't think straight anymore. Oh, right. "And it has to do with my plans to steal the bloody throne from your bloody brother!"

She actually had the nerve to approach and poke a finger into his chest. "I don't believe you. All that talk about the baby and a future together was just that? Talk?"

His mouth compressed. "I'm sorry. I know we discussed a future. But this is a better option."

She shook her head in disgust. "It's clear I have my work cut out for me." Tramping across the grass, she snagged her suitcase and then headed for the cabin.

"I don't have a key," he called after her.

"I do."

He bit off a word that would have gotten his face slapped if Miri had heard. He could practically feel the frustration leaking out of his ears as she continued on her merry way, impervious to his wrath. Unlocking the cabin, she had to shove at the door to get it open and he made a mental note to have it sanded at the first opportunity.

After a minute's hesitation, he followed. "I'm going to ask you again, Miri. What are you doing?"

She moved through the main room of the cabin, throwing open windows to air the place out. A light breeze poured in through the screens, causing the light-weight curtains to flutter like flags of surrender. "What I'm doing is waiting for an explanation."

What was it about her? No other woman, hell, no other person he came into contact with on a daily basis, had the nerve to confront and push and demand the way Miri did. Didn't she understand? He spoke; she obeyed. That's how it worked. That's how it had always worked. It was that simple. He'd told her to leave, told her in the most brutal fashion possible. Why was she still here, torturing him? He needed her safe so he could deal with the charges against him, so he could focus on what was to come.

"This is pointless, Miri," he informed her harshly. "There is nothing left for us to say to each other."

"Really?" She paused in her examination of the cabin and confronted him, folding her arms across her chest. "What about the allegations against you? Theft of the amethysts, or some such? That should give us plenty to talk about."

He clamped his teeth together, literally seeing red. "How did you find out?" he ground out.

"Your spy is a turncoat. But then, that's what happens when you use my mother. She's susceptible to being flipped." Miri swept a hand in the air. "Past loyalties and all that."

He forked his fingers through his hair, fighting a losing battle to recover his self-control. "What do you want from me?"

She hesitated in front of him, her impudence fading,

replaced by a sincerity that just about killed him. "I'd like the opportunity to stand by you, if you'll let me."

He had no idea how he managed to shake his head, let alone speak past the emotions clogging his throat. But he did it. "That's not going to happen."

"We'll see." She marched into the kitchen and started poking and prodding through the cupboards. "I have three days to change your mind."

If he could have gotten his hands on Tolken in that minute, he'd have done serious damage. "Three days? I don't have three days, I have charges pending against me in case you've forgotten."

"There's nothing more you can do that isn't already being done on your behalf by people determined to prove your innocence. If anything critical happens, Tolken will come and get us." She moved from the cupboards to the pantry, checking the status of their supplies. "He said the cabin is well stocked, as is the lake. We won't starve, that's for sure." She smiled, as though she didn't have a care in the world. "I'm hungry. Why don't I see what there is to eat. I don't suppose there's a freezer around here?"

Brandt shook his head. "No electricity."

She actually brightened at that. "Are you serious? How romantic."

Romantic? Oh, no. Not romantic. Not if he could help it. He'd make sure of that, no matter what it took. Rage continued to burn within, desperate for an outlet, but he fought to restrain it. There'd be ample time to confront Miri over forcing him into this situation. But not now. Not with fury hovering on the bare edge of control. Stripping off his suit coat, he flung it over the nearest chair before rolling up his shirt sleeves. "If we're going to stay here tonight, we're going to need kerosene lamps. And flashlights. I'll take care of that, if you'll throw something together to eat. I'll also set up the bedrooms."

He started down the hallway, but her question stopped him in his tracks. "Just to clarify. Did you say bedrooms, plural?"

Oh, yeah. "Very plural."

"Okay, but fair warning. Plural is pointless, unless you're planning to lock your bedroom door."

"I'll nail it shut if that's what it takes." He kept his back to her. It seemed safer that way. "You're not pregnant, Miri. When we leave here you'll still not be pregnant."

"If that's the way you want it."

It wasn't. "It is."

"Okay. You take care of the bedrooms, plural. I'll see what I can put together for dinner. Then we can finish fighting."

She was as good as her word. The moment their dinner dishes were cleared away, she started in on him again. "All this quiet and solitude will give us plenty of opportunity to straighten out our differences." A gentle lob for a first sally.

"Differences?" Was the woman insane? "We don't have any differences. What we have here is a blatant disregard for the obvious." Darkness was fast descending and he lined up a trio of kerosene lamps. After trimming the wicks, he lit them, adjusting the brightness to a non-romantic level. "Let me make this simple. We can stay here three hours, three days, or three years, and it's not going to change anything. You're going home where you'll be out of the line of fire."

She picked up one of the lamps and carried it to a small end table centered between the two windows in the main section of the cabin. "I thought I was going home because you wanted the bloody throne. Or are you finally willing to admit the real reason?"

"Feel free to pick any reason you want, if it means you'll return to Verdon."

She crossed the room to stand in front of him. The nonromantic lamp light gave her skin a pearly sheen and lost itself in the soft green of her eyes. It even made her mouth seem fuller, rosier, and her hair richer, darker. "Please, Brandt." She rested a hand on his arm. "All I want is the truth."

Maybe if she hadn't touched him, he'd have been able to resist. But that one simple caress had him giving her what she wanted. "Fine. The truth is that I won't let you stay in Avernos, Miri. I won't let you run the risk of being tarnished by the accusations against me. Nor will I have a child of ours born under a cloud of suspicion."

She frowned. "I don't understand. You were willing to marry me if I'd been pregnant."

He conceded the point with a nod. "Our baby needed the protection of my name, more than you needed the protection of distance from me. Now that a baby is no longer an issue, you've become my top priority. I won't allow suspicion to fall on you. And I won't have you married to a man who could spend the rest of his days in prison. You'd have the responsibility for all of

Avernos. You'd have to give up your life to take over my duties. I won't tie you to that. It's too much."

"That's my choice."

"You're wrong. It's mine."

A hint of irritation gleamed in her eyes. "Lander tried this very same thing with Juliana. He didn't want her touched by the scandal that erupted when you took your accusations against him before the TGC. He tried to keep her in Texas while he faced the charges. He wouldn't let anyone tell her what had happened."

Brandt winced. "I didn't know."

"She didn't tolerate it and neither will I."

"It's not your choice. Lander and Juliana were married." He braced himself to hurt her. "We're not."

Her mouth formed a stubborn line. "Fine. Be that way. Not that it matters. None of this will be a problem much longer."

"You can't know that."

"Actually, I can," she retorted. "I have Juliana looking into the accusations as we speak. By the time Tolken returns I expect to have all this resolved."

He froze. "What did you say?"

She must have picked up on something in his reaction because her eyes widened and for the first time that day she seemed wary of his temper. "I said Juliana is looking into the charges. Like she did with Lander."

"You brought your family into this?" he asked in a soft voice.

"You're…you're my husband. Legally or not." She fell back a pace, as though scenting danger. "Of course, I brought my family into it."

He stalked closer. "First, I'm not your husband. Chances are excellent I never will be. Second, you had no business involving the Montgomerys in this. Considering their culpability in the financial crisis Verdonia is facing, I don't want them anywhere near me or my problems. Is that clear?"

Color ebbed from her face. "Crystal. One question."

"Ask."

"When you say 'Montgomery' like that, as though you despise the very name, does that include me?"

"Of course not. I don't—"

"Good. Because in case you've forgotten, I'm a Montgomery, too. Or perhaps I don't count because I'm not one by birth." She lifted her chin. "Is that why you tolerate me? Because I'm not a real Montgomery?"

"I don't tolerate you. I mean—"

"*That* has become painfully obvious." Snatching up one of the kerosene lamps, she stalked to her bedroom and slammed the door behind her.

Damn it! That wasn't what he meant and she knew it. This was her infuriating way of putting an end to an argument when she was clearly in the wrong. Involving her family. Claiming she wasn't a real Montgomery. Come morning he'd have a thing or two to say on those subjects. And with another couple days of blissful togetherness, he'd make sure she heard, loud and clear, even if he had to blissful her backside. Grabbing up the mate to her kerosene lamp, Brandt headed for his own bedroom, reasonably confident that he wouldn't need locks or nails to keep her out of his bed. And if his door shut just shy of a slam, she could blame it on the wind.

Out in the main room of the cabin, the wind did blow. The lightweight curtains caught each gust, swirling in their own private dance. They danced well into the night, danced like moths drawn to the bright flame that came from the kerosene lamp that sat on the table between them.

They danced until their wings were singed and they finally caught fire.

Nine

Miri never knew what woke her. Perhaps it was the sound, a continuous and intense snap and pop that disturbed her sleep because it was so out of place. Perhaps it was the odor, the insidious permeation of smoke where no smoke should exist. Or perhaps intuition had her bolting upright in bed, going from unconsciousness to wide-eyed wakefulness in the span of a few disorienting seconds. Whatever the reason, the instant she came to, it was with the gut-level certainty that something had gone seriously wrong.

Scurrying from the bed, she ran to the door, remembering just in time to check the knob for heat before opening it. The metal blistered her fingertips and she jerked her hand back, retreating across the room. For endless seconds she stood there, the sound of her breath jackhammering in and out of her lungs so loud she couldn't think straight.

Stay calm! she ordered herself. She couldn't afford to panic. She needed to get a grip and figure out the best way to deal with the emergency. "Brandt," she whispered.

Why wasn't he here? He had to still be asleep or he'd have beaten down the door to get to her. Oh, God! Could his inaction be due to something more serious? Could the smoke have already reached his room? Was he unconscious? Suffocating, while she stood here in a daze? She had to move. Now.

Spinning around, she darted to the window. Endless seconds were wasted as she struggled to unlock it and then pry it open. Age, humidity and a recent paint job made it a struggle, which was why she hadn't opened it earlier. The crackle from the outer room of the cabin grew louder, nearly a roar, and she threw a swift, fearful glance over her shoulder.

To her horror, wisps of smoke slipped beneath the door. She finally managed to raise the window as far as it would go, but a screen blocked her egress and she shoved at it with all her strength. It bowed outward, then popped free of the frame. With more speed than grace, she tumbled through the opening onto the porch that surrounded the cabin. Leaping to her feet, she ran to the window adjacent to her own, pounding frantically on it. The screen deadened the noise.

"Brandt!" she shouted. "Brandt, the cabin's on fire. Wake up!"

No response. There could only be one reason. He'd passed out from smoke inhalation. Fleeing the porch, she searched in the dark for a rock or stick large enough to break the window. She managed to find a decent-sized stone by stubbing her toe on it. Limping back to the porch, she heaved the rock at the window with all her might. It ripped through the screen and shattered the glass beyond.

Smoke poured from the opening, and with a sudden, ferocious explosion of heat and light, flames flashed through the room with a deafening howl, consuming everything in their path. The intensity of it drove Miri back. Sobbing, screaming herself hoarse, she circled the burning cabin, hoping against hope that Brandt would come stumbling from the building in the nick of time. But with each passing minute, hope faded, and likelihood became impossibility.

Flames shot skyward, erupting from every window now and eating through the roof. There wasn't a part of the cabin that wasn't fully on fire, no safe place for a person to escape from. Tripping over the dragging hem of her nightgown, Miri fell heavily to the ground.

No. No, Brandt couldn't be dead. She couldn't go on if she lost him. She loved him, loved him more than she thought it possible to love another human being. He couldn't be gone. Life wouldn't do that to them. Not now. Not when they'd come here to work out their differences. She began to shake. Not when *she'd* forced them to come here.

But staring at the raging inferno, she knew that no one could still be inside that and survive. Hopelessness consumed her. Brandt was dead, probably gone from smoke inhalation before she'd even awoken. She was a fool to pretend otherwise. This was her fault, all her fault for thinking she could force him to love her. That she could force him to acknowledge feelings that weren't there and never would be. Dragging herself away from the heat and rain of hot ash, she huddled beneath a nearby tree, curling into a tight ball of utter desolation.

And then she wept, deep, helpless sobs that came from the very heart and soul of her.

Brandt pointed the beam of the flashlight along the path in front of him, hoping a lap around the lake would exhaust him enough that he could sleep instead of picturing Miri alone in her bed without him. He was a fool. A fool to have abducted her. A fool to have kept her. And even more of a fool for sending her away again.

He glanced toward the lake to check his position. Almost exactly halfway around and nowhere near exhausted enough for sleep. Maybe he'd need a second lap around. Or a third. He caught a flash out of the corner of his eyes, a flicker of light that didn't belong, and paused for a closer look. Clicking off his flashlight, he peered through the darkness.

It only took a minute to comprehend what he was seeing. On the far side of the lake a deep orange glow erupted through the trees. There was only one thing that could cause that. A fire.

"Miri." He swore violently. "Please, God, no. Not Miri."

Flicking on the flashlight, he ran, flat out. Brambles and branches overgrowing the path reached out to snare him, ripping at his clothes and tripping him. He didn't slow. Roots. Rocks. Logs. He flew over every obstacle, keeping his eyes focused on the path ahead as he pounded the endless distance back. Every step of the way he could see the flames from the periphery of his vision, and could tell the fire was building in intensity. And he knew, no matter how hard he tried to deny it, that he wouldn't make it back in time. He'd be too late to save her.

She was dying as he ran. And it was all his fault. If he'd stayed. If they hadn't fought. If he'd been willing to take her to his bed and give her one last night of love, she'd be alive. But he hadn't done any of those things. Hell, no. He'd been determined to face the accusations on his own, to protect her from the public outcry. God, what irony. Instead of protecting her, he'd killed her.

He dashed sweat from his eyes and raced on. Maybe she woke in time. Maybe she got out. Maybe she escaped unscathed. She had to be alive. She had to. He couldn't survive without her. The litany ran in a desperate loop, ran in pace with the driving thud of his footfalls. And all the while the cabin burned, a ferocious testament to his failure.

He could barely pull air into his lungs by the time he reached the clearing where the cabin stood—or rather, the conflagration that had once been a cabin. He desperately scanned the area, searching for some sign of life, some sign of Miri. There was nothing. He shouted her name but got no answer. No one burst joyously from the darkness. No one raced to throw herself into his arms. There was only the roar of a hungry fire.

Brandt needed to get away from here, clear his head and lungs of smoke. But he couldn't leave. Not yet. Not without Miri. He straightened and began another circuit, slower this time. Heavier.

Up ahead something white flickered beneath the trees and he stared at it dully. An animal crouched near the flames. No, that didn't make sense. Animals ran from fire. Only humans were foolish enough to embrace it.

The crumpled heap of white stirred. "Brandt?" His name escaped in a disbelieving quaver. "Is it really you?"

Joy burned hotter than the fire, shooting through him like quicksilver. "Miri? Oh, God. Miri!" He raced across the singed grass. Scooping her up in his arms, he sagged to his knees, his hands sweeping over her face and shoulders, her torso and legs. "Are you hurt? Are you burned? Talk to me, sweetheart. Are you okay?"

"No, yes. I'm fine. I'm fine." She cupped his face with shaking hands, her words barely coherent. "Where were you? I called and called and you never answered. I thought you were—" Her voice broke and she wept helplessly, tears tracking sooty lines down her face. "I thought I'd lost you."

"I went for a walk. I was clear across the lake when I saw the flames." He rained kisses down on her face. "You have no idea how I felt when I saw the fire. When I realized I'd never get to you in time."

"Don't leave me. Don't let go."

"Never. Never again."

He wrapped her up in his arms, holding her so close he could feel her heart pounding in rhythm with his own. Beyond them the cabin continued to burn, the snap and pop of the wood mingled with an occasional ping of exploding nails. Heat radiated from the blaze. And yet, they remained crouched in the grass, clinging to each other. It wasn't until the wind shifted, blowing soot and ash in their direction that he felt compelled to move.

Helping Miri to her feet, Brandt urged her in the direction of the lake. "Come on. Let's get cleaned up."

"We don't have anything to change into." She glanced over her shoulder, shuddering. "All our clothes are burned."

"There are towels in the boathouse. We can rinse the soot out of what we're wearing and wrap up in towels while our clothes dry."

He heard her take a deep breath and could literally see her gathering up her self-control. It showed in the stiffening of her spine and her proud carriage, the squaring of her jaw and the way she planted her hands on her hips. He could only shake his head as he watched, amazed at the undaunted perseverance that was such a natural part of her.

She scanned the area. "Is there a stream that feeds the lake?"

"A quarter of the way around," he confirmed.

She nodded. "We can get fresh water from there. And I'll bet if you have towels stashed in the boathouse, there'll be fishing poles, too. We may have to rough it until help arrives, but we won't starve or die of thirst."

He smiled at the proof that her spirit had returned. It was one of the qualities he'd always admired about her. Nothing kept Miri down for long. They picked their way across the wild grass to the boathouse, only to discover a large padlock barring their entry.

"Forgot about this," he said. "Hang on."

He circled the structure until he found a decent-sized stone he could use to hammer off the lock. It only took a half dozen whacks before the clasp broke. Tossing the pieces aside, he opened the door. It was pitch-black inside.

"I don't suppose there's a light switch?" she asked.

"No. And I seem to have lost the flashlight I had earlier. But I vaguely remember keeping extras on a shelf just inside the door. Ah, here they are. Now if the batteries are still good." The first was dead. The second emitted a weak beam that lasted long enough for them to collect a stack of towels and a tarp. "Come on. Let's get rinsed off. Then we'll set up a bed for the night."

He led the way to a narrow beach adjacent to the boathouse, a sweeping sickle of imported white sand far softer than the rock-strewn ground closer to the cabin. He spread the tarp and padded it with towels.

Miri had wandered to the lake's edge where the water lapped her bare feet. Overhead the moon sent a halo of silver spilling over her. A light wind stirred, wafting her soot-stained nightgown against her legs, outlining their shapely length, and lifting her hair in a rippling ebony flag. A flag of triumph, of survival. She glanced over her shoulder and tossed him a teasing grin. Then facing the lake, she waded in, looking like some sort of mythical sea nymph returning to her watery home.

She gave a small gasp as she sank to her waist, no doubt reacting to the chilly temperature. Then with a light splash that echoed across the lake, she vanished beneath the surface. He didn't wait any longer to join her. Toeing off his shoes, he crossed the sand at a dead run and dove toward where he'd seen her go under.

They surfaced side by side, almost on top of each other. "Refreshing," he said, pulling her into his arms.

Her nightgown swirled around them, then clung, anchoring them together. "More like freezing." She scooped water into her hands and washed the grime from his face and neck, scrubbing at a spot just beneath his jaw. Her fingers slowed. Lingered. Traced the harsh planes and angles of his face as though they were the most beautiful sight in the world. "There. Much better."

He pointed to the corner of his mouth. "You missed a spot."

"So I did." Using his shoulders for leverage, she surged upward long enough to kiss the place he'd indicated. "I think I got it."

Not even close. But she would soon enough. "Your turn," he informed her.

Settling his feet on the lake bottom, he started with her face, skimming deftly across her forehead, then down her nose and finally across her arching cheekbones. He paused at her lips, replaced his hands with his mouth, and kissed her. Inhaled her. Lost himself in the honeyed flavor of her.

"I don't know what I'd have done if I'd lost you," he said, the words rough with emotion.

She buried her face against the crook of his shoulder. "Watching the cabin burn, believing you were trapped inside…" He could hear the traces of horror lingering in her voice. "I've never been more frightened in my life."

He gathered the wet nightgown tangled around her

and in one smooth motion, pulled it over her head and tossed it to the lakeshore. Now that they'd rinsed their clothes, they didn't need them anymore. He let go of her just long enough to strip off his slacks and shirt before sending them chasing after her nightgown.

"Shouldn't we hang those—" she began.

"No, we shouldn't. There are more important things for us to do tonight than hang laundry."

Catching her hand in his, he drew her back into his embrace. Their bodies collided, wet and slippery. Everything about her was soft. Her mouth, full and moist and hungry. Her breasts, the water breaking across the generous slopes. Her abdomen. He grazed that feminine curve, remembering what it had felt like when he'd believed his child lay there, tucked safely within her womb.

Her legs scissored at the unexpected contact, sending her bobbing upward. "I can't touch the bottom."

"You don't need to." He hooked his hands behind the backs of her upper thighs and parted her legs, sliding between them. "Hold on to me, love."

She shuddered in his grasp, her muscles spasming at the tantalizing brush of flesh against flesh. Masculine against feminine. "Please," she moaned, her eyes fluttering closed. "Say my name, Brandt. Make love to *me* this time."

"Look at me, Miri." He fisted his hands in her hair, waiting until she complied. "That's right, sweetheart. Look at me, just like I'm looking at you. I know who I'm holding. And whether you believe it or not, some part of me knew who it was on our wedding night."

Her chin wobbled. "It wasn't our wedding night. It was yours and Alyssa's."

"You're wrong." How could he make her understand? "I thought I could forget about you. That I could marry Alyssa and put you out of my life. But it wouldn't have worked. The minute I would have tried to make love to her—the real Alyssa—it would have turned to ashes." He spun her around to face the fire. "Look at it. You and I, we're that blaze. That's what happens when we touch. Alyssa and I would have been the cold ash we'll find over there come morning."

"You called me by her name." She treaded water, allowing a chilly gap to form between them. Moon-beams caught in her eyes and highlighted her pain. "That was the last word you spoke to me."

"I'm sorry. It was never my intention to hurt you."

"You did."

So simple. So direct. He'd broken something he wasn't sure he could repair. "Listen to me, sweetheart. It wasn't Alyssa in that bed with me on our wedding night, anymore than it was Alyssa standing beside me at the altar when we spoke our vows."

"The church has annulled our marriage," she inter-rupted. "Those vows are meaningless."

"They're not meaningless. Not to us." The words, loud and vehement, echoed across the lake, silencing the nighttime chatter coming from the surrounding woods. He caught hold of her hand and towed her closer. "The church may not recognize our union, but I recognize it. And so do you."

Slowly, the evening songs resumed. High-pitched

insect strumming and trilling birdcall, the bass accompaniment of nearby amphibians, as well as the light clatter of branches, called to life by an insistent breeze. He kissed her to the sound of that music, a kiss as tender and sacred as if they were standing once again in front of an altar.

"Admit it, Miri. In your heart, you're married to me. That's why you refuse to give up on us. That's why you have Juliana working to clear my name. We're joined, in every way it's possible for a man and woman to be joined."

He sealed the words with another kiss, this one more ardent. He could feel the longing in her, taste her yearning. What he wanted, though, was her passion. And then it came, bursting from her, hot and demanding and unconditional. That one kiss nearly devastated his self-control. He fought to hold on, determined to make this the most special night of her life. He owed her that much at least.

He drifted toward shore with her, his caresses following the shallowing waterline. He kissed the moisture from the taut sweep of her neck, then the slope of her shoulders. He followed the length of her arms, all the way to her fingertips, before cupping her breasts and lavishing teeth and tongue on each pebbled tip. He skated lower still as they reached the shore, catching the beads of moisture that slid down her belly.

Sinking to his knees, he held her upright while he traced a line from the womanly flare of her right hip across her soft belly to her left. He could just make out the jeweled butterfly that fluttered there. It took on a whole new meaning—a testament to their time on

Mazoné. Where before he'd avoided it, this time he gave it his full attention. Satisfied, he steadied her before sinking lower, finding the very heart of her.

Her entire body reverberated, burning like an inferno as intense as the fire still roaring behind them. She arched backward until her hair swirled in the water, the strands wrapping around them, binding them together. She went bowstring taut, her throat working in a silent shriek. He pushed her higher. Harder. With a breathless cry, she tipped over the edge, the breath gusting from her lungs. And then she folded, collapsing in his arms, trembling in reaction.

Turning, he beached them and gathered her close. The storm raging through her abated, but only for the moment. Not giving her time to do more than catch her breath, he drove her upward again.

"I know who I'm holding in my arms. It's you, Miri. Only you."

Possessiveness burned in her gaze, filling him with an urgent desire to touch every part of her, to take his time feasting on every inch. He reared upward, baring her to his gaze. The moonlight tracked across her damp body, a glistening swathe of silver. She lay open to him, her eyes dark with want. The air shuddered from her lungs, preventing speech. Instead, she reached for him, impatience implicit in every movement as she tugged him into her waiting embrace.

"Easy, love," he murmured.

"I don't want easy." She sealed his mouth with a hard, greedy kiss. "I want out of control. I want you to show me that I'm the only woman who can make you feel like this."

"Don't you know?" He smiled tenderly. "No other woman exists for me, but you. When I hold you like this—" his hand swept over her "—touch you like this, I'm blind and deaf to everyone but you."

He took her then, filled her, drove her back into the storm. She followed the rhythm he set, dancing to the primitive song, moving in perfect counterpoint. The storm built, sliding into their veins and thundering through them. He rode the wild center of it, struggling for a control that escaped his grasp. What was happening between them defied control, defied anything and everything but absolute surrender.

It had been like that last time, too, so different from every other sexual experience that it had made an indelible impact on him. How could he have ever thought he'd made love to Alyssa all those weeks ago, when every touch, every sound, every movement and scent whispered Miri's name? No, not whispered. Shouted. Screamed. She'd branded him with her essence, made herself a permanent part of him. And he wanted to mark her the same way.

He surged into her, driving them together again and again in a frenzy of need. He threw back his head, wanting to howl at the moon, mindless with desire. It was no different for her. Her expression glowed in the silver light, more beautiful and wildly iridescent than he'd ever seen it.

And then the storm reached its height, broke over them, giving them up to ecstasy. They went over the edge together, united in heart, body and soul. She cried afterward, from joy, she tearfully insisted. Murmuring ridiculous words of reassurance, he lifted her in his arms and carried her back into the lake. There he gently washed the sand from her body. When he was through he took her to their improvised bed. Towels became blankets, cocooning them from the cool night breeze.

As sleep claimed them, he tucked her close and gave her his heart.

Ten

Early morning sunlight woke them. Miri stirred, so comfortable she didn't want to move, much less get up. She lay on her side, wrapped partially in towels and partially in Brandt, her head cushioned against his shoulder.

His gruff voice rumbled above her. "I'm thinking we should have hung up our clothes."

She laughed softly. "If it came down to a choice between that and what we did instead, I'll take option number two."

"I think I will, too."

"You think?" She poked him in the ribs, drawing a husky chuckle. "You better know, Your Highness."

"Oh, I know, all right."

Her amusement faded. "How do you suppose the fire started? Was it something I did?"

"Funny you should ask. I'd just been wondering if it was something I'd done wrong." His brows drew together. "I'm pretty sure we left one of the lamps burning in the main room. I was so angry when we went to bed, I didn't give it a thought. I'm guessing the wind must have blown the lamp over. Or maybe something flammable blew up against it."

"Frightening." She curled closer, lifting her head so she could watch his expression. "Brandt—"

"Uh-oh."

"We need to finish our discussion from last night." A wry note crept into her voice. "Though I wouldn't mind if we did it without losing our temper or starting any more fires."

He released his breath in a gusty sigh. "No promises, but we can give it a shot."

"Do you still insist we go our separate ways?" Determination filled her. "Fair warning, marriage or not, I plan to stand by you regardless of what happens with the allegations."

He tucked an arm behind his head and stared out at the lake. The fact that he avoided her gaze didn't bode well. "Once the allegations against me have been disproved so they can't adversely affect your reputation, you can do anything you want."

A tentative hope sparked to life. "Are you saying that after your name is cleared we can be together again?"

"That's just it, Miri. Nothing may happen." His expression turned brooding. "There may never be clarity. I may remain under suspicion forever, living beneath a shadow I can't escape."

She stared in disbelief. "Is that an admission of guilt? Because if it is, I'm not buying it. I know you, Brandt. You'd never steal from your own country."

"Someone wants it to look like I have," he argued doggedly. "The charges—"

"Will be cleared up, just like they were with Lander," Miri stated firmly. "Juliana's agreed to examine the records again. And don't you dare rant and rave at me about involving her. When it comes to finances and accounting there's no one better. You're lucky she's willing to help. Juliana will figure it out."

"And if she doesn't?" He turned to look at her then. At some point in the last day deep crevices had carved a path on either side of his mouth. A tightness gathered around his eyes—eyes flat with exhaustion. "It's not like she has a lot of incentive to clear me. As things stand now, your brother will win the election by a landslide. Why would she do anything to change that?"

"You're not the only honorable person in Verdonia, Brandt." Miri put a sting in the words. "You're not the only one who puts duty and responsibility ahead of personal desire or self-interest, or who has Verdonia's best interests at heart. Juliana is an honorable person. So are Lander and Merrick and Alyssa. The problem is you don't trust the Montgomerys. I'm not sure you even trust me."

He jackknifed upward, spilling towels in every direction. "What the hell are you talking about? Of course, I trust you."

"You don't trust me enough to let me in." She sat up, as well, fumbling to retrieve some of their covers. "I don't need your protection, Brandt. I don't need you to take care of me. I'm quite able to handle that job all on my own. What I want is a partner. A lover. A confidante. Isn't that what you want, too?"

A muscle jerked in his cheek. "Yes."

"But you still won't offer that, will you?"

"No."

She'd asked for frankness, and she'd certainly gotten it. She struggled to change tactics. In the little time they'd had together, she'd discovered that logic worked best with him. Granted, it wasn't her strong suit, but she'd give it a stab if it meant getting through to him. "You wouldn't be asking me to leave if our marriage hadn't been annulled," she pointed out. "Or if I'd actually been pregnant."

"I explained my reasoning on that."

"I remember. You would have been honor-bound to protect the baby. To give it your name." Curling her legs beneath her, she gathered up one of his hands and laced her fingers with his. "While you're so busy considering honor and duty, maybe you should consider one more important detail."

"Which is?"

"You abducted me and brought me back to Avernos. You announced to the world that I was your wife. You insisted I sleep in your bed. Basically, you compromised me. What effect do you suppose that will have on my reputation, and the manner in which people regard me? Whether or not I'm pregnant, your honor won't allow you to do anything other than marry me. And I can guarantee, my mother and brothers won't accept anything less, either."

"You...I—"

"*We,*" she emphasized. "Not 'you' and not 'I,' but we. That's how it's supposed to be and how it's going to be from now on. You don't have to let me in, if you don't want. It's your choice. But every time you leave your home, you're going to find me camped on your doorstep. I'm hoping you'll eventually get tired of stepping over me and let me in."

"Damn it, Miri. I won't be stepping over anyone if I'm in prison."

"Brandt—"

"No more." He sat up, tossing aside towels, baring them. "Come on, Princess. Let's see if there's anything useful left out there."

She let the topic die. For now. It would give her time to regroup and come up with a new slew of arguments. "What about our clothes?" she asked, looking around for where they'd ended up. "I doubt they're dry."

"Then you'll have a choice. You can either wear wet, sticky clothes, or leave them off. Personally, I think you'll be more comfortable without them, though I'm not sure I'll be more comfortable watching you run around nude." He pretended to consider, a wicked gleam sparking to life in his black gaze. "I will, however, enjoy it more."

She scrambled up, wishing she was as relaxed and unabashed in her own skin as Brandt seemed to be. She considered his suggestion, to saying the hell with everything and embracing her wild side. The idea lasted an entire two seconds before she found herself scooping up one of the clean towels with a studied indifference and wrapping it around herself. It earned her a slow grin before Brandt followed suit.

While he headed toward the remains of the cabin, Miri tracked down their clothes. Sure enough, they were still wet and she spread them in the grass to dry, shaking her head over their condition.

Her nightgown was a disaster. Aside from several small rents in the skirt and in the seams, it also had numerous burn holes from the hot ash, and the soot-stained hem was ripped loose. Brandt's clothes had fared little better, probably as a result of his race through the woods to reach her. Both shirt and trousers were torn, some showing bloodstains where branches or vines had snagged more than cloth. He'd also collected his fair share of burn holes and soot marks, as well.

Realizing she couldn't do anything more about their clothes, she joined Brandt. She found him waiting for her not far from the cabin. The fire had finally died, all that remained a pile of glowing embers. She shivered at the grim sight. Luck had been with them last night, tragedy barely averted. As though picking up on her distress, he slung an arm around her shoulders and held her close.

"Come on. This is pointless," he said. "Let's check out the boathouse and see what we can find there."

"Fishing poles would be nice." Her stomach grumbled. "A fresh trout breakfast would be even better."

"I'll see what I can do."

They did have their trout breakfast, though it took a few more hours than Miri would have liked. Even so, it was well worth the wait. By the time they'd eaten, their clothes were dry enough to wear, though she felt ridiculous running around in a nightgown. Still, it was better than a towel. Barely.

Standing by the boathouse while they returned the fishing poles to their proper places, Miri stared out across the lake and frowned. "Why does this place seem so familiar to me?" she muttered. Brandt had started to tell her yesterday when the helicopter's departure had interrupted them. She swung around to ask again. "Tell me about the time I was last here."

He regarded her in surprise. "You really don't remember? I thought that was just a ploy to distract me."

"Well, yes." She fought back a blush. "But it was a sincere question. I really have been here before?"

"You and your family came to the palace to celebrate my grandfather's seventy-fifth birthday. The next morning we all drove out here to spend the day at the lake."

She shook her head. "I don't remember."

"You should. It was the first time I rescued you."

"That was here?" She stared at the lake and surrounding woods with new eyes, trying to equate memory with reality. "I guess it was such a traumatic experience, I put it out of my head. I remember begging my brothers to play hide-and-seek. And then…" Her brow crinkled in a frown. "I got lost and you found me. Is that what happened?" she asked uncertainly.

"You found a small cavern and squeezed inside. Then you couldn't get out again. It took hours to find you."

"You were the one who got me out." Wonder lit her eyes. "How could I have forgotten? You sat there and talked to me for the longest time until I'd calmed down. That's when I first fell in love with you. You told me to feel around for a pebble and hold it in my hand because it was magical and could shrink me small enough to squeeze back out. And it worked. Or at least, I believed it did at the time. I still have it in my jewelry box. It's the prettiest stone—" She broke off with a gasp.

"What is it? What's wrong?" His head jerked skyward. "Got it. I hear it, too. The helicopter's returning."

"No, that's not what I meant. Brandt—"

He caught her hand. "Come on. Rescue party's here."

"Wait. Brandt, wait! You have to listen to me."

The helicopter dipped low, making a curving sweep along the lakeshore, the noise from its propellers drowning out her voice. It landed in the exact same spot as yesterday. Within seconds of touching down, Tolken emerged from the still churning copter, appearing distinctly white-faced.

He sketched a deep, humble bow. "I apologize, Your Highness, for my part in yesterday's events, as well as for not getting here sooner. Less than an hour ago we received reports from a pair of hikers of a possible fire. Are you and Princess Miri hurt? Do you require medical attention?"

"That won't be necessary. We could use a change of clothes, but we're fine otherwise."

Tolken's gaze flickered in Miri's direction and then swiftly away. "I have a spare jumpsuit stashed in the helicopter. It'll be a trifle large for Her Highness, but might be preferable to the alternative."

"Since the alternative is my nightgown, I'm forced to agree," Miri inserted dryly. "If you'll get it for me, I'll change in the boathouse."

"Yes, Your Highness."

The instant he returned to the helicopter, Miri grabbed Brandt's arm. "Before we go, I need to speak to you in private. It's important."

He shook his head. "Enough, Miri. There's nothing left to be said. We both have our own opinions about honor and duty, and I don't see either of us changing our mind anytime soon."

"It's not about that. It's—"

Tolken hustled back, a bright orange pair of coveralls in his hands. Left with no choice, Miri snatched it up and headed for the boathouse to change. The outfit was huge, leaving her swimming in an ocean of orange. Acres of excess material dangled off her wrists and ankles, tripping her every time she tried to take a step. Opening the door, she called for Brandt.

"Hey, I need help in here."

He broke off his conversation with Tolken. Not that it was much of a conversation. It looked more like he was giving the poor man hell. With a final hard comment, he left a visibly shaken Tolken and approached, his stride long and lethal, reminding her more than ever of a stalking panther. Heaven help her, His Highness was back in charge and didn't appear to be in the best of tempers. So much for last night. So much for the gentle man who'd held her through the night. Comforted her. Made love to her.

He entered the boathouse and pushed the door to behind him. "What's the problem, Miri? We need to leave."

"And you need to listen." Before he could interrupt again, she flipped her dangling cuff at him. "First, help me with this stupid thing. It's dragging every which way."

"Then we leave. No more talking."

Together they rolled up the material at her wrists and ankles. She looked down at herself with a sigh. "I look ridiculous, don't I?"

He nodded. "Just a bit."

"Gee, thanks," she grumbled. "You're supposed to say I look adorable."

"Your nightgown looked adorable. This…not so much."

"That bad?" She grabbed a pair of rubber sandals from off one of the storage racks and slipped them on. "Bad enough to keep you from ravishing me?"

He waited a beat. "Never that bad."

"Okay, then. I feel better now." When he would have opened the door again, she caught hold of his hand. "Listen, Brandt. That cavern. The one where you found me all those years ago? Do you think you can find it again?"

"I'm not sure. Maybe." He frowned impatiently. "You don't mean today?"

"Yes, today," she insisted. "As in, right now, this minute."

He shook his head before she'd even finished speaking. "That's impossible. According to Tolken, there's a situation brewing back at the palace. I'm needed there."

She waved that aside, nearly unraveling her sleeve again. "Forget the palace. This can't wait." She didn't want to tell him of her suspicions, not if it meant raising his hopes, only to dash then again. Not when it promised to cement his determination to get rid of her. But she could see he was going to refuse her request and desperation had her speaking without consideration. "I'll make you a deal. If you'll do as I ask, I'll agree to return to my family without a fight." Oh, God, what was she saying? "I'll…I'll do whatever you want about our future, no matter how thickheaded and foolish I consider it."

Okay, maybe that last part could have been phrased better, considering she hoped to win his cooperation. But really. He was being thickheaded and foolish by refusing to allow her to stand at his side while he faced the charges being leveled against him.

She could tell her impulsive offer had given him pause and he studied her in the dim light seeping into the boathouse. "You? A walking, talking argument? You'll do whatever I want?" His eyes narrowed. "What's going on, Miri?"

If she'd been a child, she'd have been jumping up and down and pleading incoherently by now. "I'll explain if you find the cavern. I might be wrong and I'd rather not say anything until I know for certain."

He shook his head. "It's been a long time and I'm not sure I remember exactly where it was."

"Please, Brandt. You have to try."

"And if I agree? Do we have a deal?" He spoke with his grandfather's voice, serious and regal. The voice of a man who ruled a principality, and one day, maybe, a country. "You'll return to your family as soon as we get back to the palace?"

She flinched from the ultimatum, but she'd made a promise and she'd stick to it. "Yes. We have a deal." She closed her eyes in despair. So, this was what sacrifice tasted like. She couldn't say she cared much for the flavor of it. The dish held far too bitter a bite. "I'll return to my family as soon as we get back to the palace."

He jerked his head toward the door. "Come on, then. Let's go."

"Wait."

He thrust a hand through his hair. "What now, Miri?"

"Before we go…" She moistened her lips. "I want you to kiss me one last time."

He stilled. "Is this some sort of trick?"

She laughed, hoping against hope he couldn't hear the underlying tears. "No trick. Just a goodbye kiss, that's all I'm asking."

He didn't argue further. Hooking his index finger into the plunging neckline of her coveralls, he propelled her into his arms. And then he kissed her, driving every thought from her mind but the need to lose herself in his embrace. He took her mouth with exquisite tenderness and she moaned softly, opening to him. His tongue mated with hers, teasing her toward the raw, primal urges she'd experienced both times he'd made love to her. It only took that one kiss for her to want again, to be filled with a fierce longing to have him take her the way he had last night. One touch, and she lost all rational thought.

His reaction was no different. Sunlight streamed through the narrow gap in the door and fell directly on his face. Harsh color slashed across his cheekbones, the wildfire burning in his eyes glittering with deadly intent. He was a man reduced to his most primitive, his desire raw and blatant. She stared up at him. Breath and heart-beat quickened. If the time and place had been any different, he'd have taken their embrace to its ultimate conclusion.

But it wasn't another time or place, and she'd made a deal. Snatching a final kiss, whispering a silent farewell, she released him and stepped back. "Thank you, Your Highness," she managed to say. Crossing to the door, she flung it open and stepped into the painfully bright sunshine. If she blinked hard, it was only because her eyes were slow to adjust to the light. Nothing more, most certainly not tears.

Turning to Brandt, she gestured toward the surrounding wood. "Which way?"

The search proved hot and exhausting. More than once Miri was on the verge of giving up. But there was too much at stake to quit. "Try again," she urged when they hit another false trail.

"I know you couldn't have gotten too far from the lake. The brush has probably grown up around the cavern," Brandt said, wiping the sweat from his brow. He paused to study the surrounding terrain. "It should be on a hillside."

She pointed farther out. "We haven't checked there."

He hesitated, before nodding. "I would have thought that's too far, but it took a while to find you when you originally went missing. So, let's give it a try."

As soon as they approached the area, he picked up his pace. "This is it. I'm sure it's over here."

And there it was, a narrow slash in the earth. Miri could only stare at it, shaking her head. How in the world had she managed to fit in there, even at the tender age of eleven? She approached the cavern and dropped to her knees, grateful for the bulky coveralls. Carefully, she slid her arm into the opening and groped along the floor, gathering up a handful of the pebbles. Sending up a silent prayer, she pulled her arm from the opening and slowly opened her hand. Sunlight struck the stones she held.

"Are these what I think they are?" she asked Brandt unevenly.

Crouching beside her, he expelled his breath in a long sigh. "Only if you think they're Juliana Rose amethysts."

Eleven

"How did you know?" Brandt asked, shaking his head in amazement.

She examined the stones with a practiced eye. "It was Juliana's wedding ring that tipped me off. That new colored amethyst looked so familiar for some reason. I couldn't think why until you reminded me about getting trapped in the cavern when I was eleven. Then it clicked. I remembered the pebble I'd kept from that day and the odd color and—" She threw herself into his arms. "Oh, Brandt. I can't believe we found more of them. Wait until everyone finds out that those few in her ring aren't the only Juliana Roses in existence."

He gathered her into a tight embrace, resting his cheek against the top of her head. How many more times would he be able to hold her like this before he'd be forced to let her go? "Honey, we need to keep this a secret until we're certain about what we have here."

"Yes, of course. I won't say a word." A small frown touched her brow. "How soon can you get a geologist to the site?"

"I'll have a crew out here before the end of the day."

"That soon?" She beamed in delight. "And how long before they know how large the deposit is? Tomorrow? The end of the week?"

"Slow down, Miri," he cautioned. "It could be a while. Accuracy is more important than speed."

"But if it's a large deposit?" The hope filling her eyes was painful to watch. "Will it be enough?"

"It could save Verdonia." He held up a hand to stem her excited exclamation. "Let's not get too worked up. We have to wait for the initial report to come in. And then for the final one. A lot can happen between now and then."

"In the meantime, maybe Juliana has discovered something about the accusations against you." It was her turn to cut him off. "Don't tell me not to get my hopes up. I'm not all doom and gloom like you. I want to believe that everything will work out. I've already decided that my darling sister-in-law will clear you and our find is going to be the tip of a huge mine full of Juliana Rose amethysts. Don't bother trying to talk me out of it. That's what's going to happen. My mind is made up."

He couldn't help but smile. Miri's green eyes glowed with excitement, her cheeks as bright a pink as her lips. Dirt smudged the side of her nose and her hair remained in a hopeless tangle down her back. But he'd never seen her look more beautiful. Unable to resist, he snatched a kiss. The color in both cheek and lip deepened.

Reluctantly letting her go, he hunkered down in front of the slash and scooped up another handful of stones, dropping them into his pocket. From what little he could tell without the appropriate equipment, they showed serious promise for depth of color, size and clarity. He'd be very interested to hear what his master cutter had to say about them.

Looking around for a suitable rock, he gestured to Miri. "Unroll one of your sleeves. I want to mark this spot." He used the sharp edge from a piece of quartz to jab a hole in the material. Ripping it, he tore free a strip of orange and tied it to a nearby bush. "Okay, let's go. We've done everything we can here. I need to take care of whatever crisis is going down at the palace."

She threw the cavern a final excited glance before falling in beside him on their return trek through the woods. Tolken and the pilot were waiting patiently by the helicopter, ready to lift off at a moment's notice. The ride back to the palace took no time, and no sooner did they step from the craft than one of his guards came for them at a dead run.

He sketched a hasty bow. "Please, Your Highness. All hell's breaking loose in there—" He gulped when he realized what he'd said, and stared at Miri in horror. "Begging your pardon, ma'am."

She waved aside the apology. "What's going on? What's happening?"

"I think they've come to arrest Prince Brandt. They're

all in there arguing." He turned back to Brandt. "If you would, Your Highness. You need to come."

"Go tell them I'm on my way."

He would have followed the guard if Miri hadn't thrown herself in front of him. "No. No, you're not going."

"Sweetheart—"

"Don't sweetheart me." She gripped his shirt and one of the seams gave way. "You listen to me. I don't want to hear another word about duty, or honor or responsibility. And so help me, if the word sacrifice ever leaves your mouth again, I swear, I won't be held accountable for my actions."

"I am who I am," he stated simply.

Her chin wobbled. "And I love who you are, Brandt. Even those truly annoying parts."

He offered a slow smile. "Thanks."

"If you go in there, I'm going with you. And I'm going as your wife."

He shook his head. "You aren't my wife."

"I will be," she said fiercely. "I don't care if I have to tie you up and drag you in front of the nearest church official, we will be married. You will allow me to stand by your side while you face these charges."

His smile faded. "You made a bargain with me, or have you forgotten?" From the way her face went stark white, he realized she had. "You promised to return to your family and I intend to hold you to your word."

"Don't. Please don't make me leave you."

She was killing him, slicing off pieces of his soul. "When my name is cleared—"

"No! Not when it's cleared. Right now, when it

counts most. I want to declare my love openly. I want the entire world to know how I feel about you." Tears choked her. "Please, Brandt. I know you can't say the words back. Honor won't allow you to. But I want you to hear them from me. Here. Now."

Her hands crept to his face, smoothing each harsh line with a tender caress. He'd never seen such blatant adoration on a person's face before. The fact that it was for him was humbling.

"I love you," she said. "I love you more than I ever thought possible. I'll love you until the day I die. And then somehow, someway, I'll love you for all of eternity. When we go in there and face whatever there is to face, if you'll let me, I intend to shout my feelings to the entire world. But for right now, in this instant of time, my feelings are private and for you alone."

He enfolded her in his arms, knowing it was the last time he'd ever hold her. Cupping her face, he brushed away her tears. "If I were a free man, if I were any man but the one I am, I would tell you I love you, too. But I can't as long as I'm under suspicion. I can't tell you that I adore you, that you are my life. I can't tell you that you're more precious to me than all the amethysts in Verdonia. I can't tell you that more than anything I want our night together to have borne fruit, to watch you ripen with my child. I can't tell you how much I long to spend the rest of my life making you happy." He kissed her, a lingering kiss of farewell. "If it weren't wrong, I'd tell you that I'll love you today, tomorrow and every tomorrow until the end of time."

The guard had reappeared, almost dancing with impatience, and Brandt reluctantly released her. "I have to go, sweetheart."

"At least let me stand by you through this much," she pleaded.

"Your Highness?" the guard interrupted. "I thought I should let you know that Princess Miri's family is in the study with everyone else. They've requested her presence, as well."

Her surprise gave way to sheer delight. "Perfect. You were going to send me back to my family. Now we both get what we want." She glanced down at herself and gave a small gasp of horror. "We are not facing them like this. I'm sure everyone can wait five minutes while we clean up."

By the time they'd showered and changed, it was closer to thirty minutes than five. They headed for his study hand in hand. Miri wore her red power suit and mile-high heels, no doubt for courage, and she'd coiled her hair in a sophisticated knot that made her appear every inch the princess.

"Did you have to wear black?" she asked him in a disapproving undertone. "It makes you look like you're going to your funeral."

"Entirely possible." He paused outside his study, stopping her heated response with a shake of his head. "I don't know what we're going to find when we go in there, but no matter how it goes down, I don't want you to interfere."

Her mouth compressed at the order, but she nodded, worry deepening the color of her eyes. "I'll try not to say anything."

Honest, if not quite what he'd asked. Still, it would have to do. Strident voices came from behind the heavy wooden door. Many voices, both male and female. Turning the knob, he pushed open the door. Inside, he found sheer pandemonium.

At first, all he could see were Montgomerys, every last one of the royals, as far as he could tell. Even Joc Arnaud, Juliana's brother, was present, lending weight to the proceedings. They surrounded the chair in front of his desk where a small cringing man sat, clutching a briefcase to his chest as though it were a lifeline. The chief executive councilman of the TGC, if he didn't miss his guess. And they were all shouting at him, even Miri's mother, Rachel. Off to one side hovered Alyssa's mother, Angela. And holding her in an embrace that looked as intimate as it did comforting stood Erik Sutherland.

"Interesting. I thought Erik was Angela's stepson," he said sotto voce. "That hug doesn't look terribly maternal."

Miri gave a soft laugh. "Boy, are you out of date. I was just a baby at the time, but maybe you have a vague memory of Erik's father divorcing Angela?"

"A very vague memory. Alyssa was…what? A year, maybe two at the time? That would have put Erik in his early twenties."

"That's about right. Well, the reason for Angela's divorce from Prince Frederick is hugging her as we speak."

"So, Alyssa…"

"Is Erik's daughter, not Prince Frederick's." Miri's eyes narrowed in speculation. "What I'd like to know is why the two of them are here. What do they have to do with all this?"

"I'm almost afraid to ask. But I can't help wondering if it has something to do with Erik abdicating to Alyssa. If he hadn't, she wouldn't be ruling Celestia right now."

"And you wouldn't have tried to marry her in order to win the election."

He winced at the tart edge to Miri's tongue. "Bygones, love. Water definitely under the bridge." He scrutinized the group around the councilman. "Hell. I'm not sure I want to wade into the middle of that mess."

As though his comment caught everyone's attention, all focus honed in on them. They were instantly enveloped in Montgomerys, every last one of them talking at once. Brandt folded his arms across his chest and waited it out. As soon as it became clear they weren't planning to stop anytime soon, he held up a hand. To his surprise, they actually fell silent.

"What the hell is going on?" he asked mildly.

The councilman hastened to his feet and offered a small, awkward bow that left him juggling with his briefcase. "I apologize, Your Highness. But I've come to inform you a warrant has been sworn out for your arrest."

Lander turned to confront the man. "And we're telling you, you're not arresting him. My wife has evidence—"

"That the documents you have are forgeries," Juliana broke in, waving a sheathe of papers. "And I can prove it."

The councilman bobbed his head. "Yes, Your Highness. I understand your position. But we've voted and—"

"You're going to have to take another vote," Merrick spoke up. "Because my security force has no intention of allowing you to arrest von Folke and that's the end of it."

"Please, Your Highness. Your Highnesses," the councilman pleaded. "You can't do this. The TGC has proof of these improprieties. Now, I understand you have conflicting evidence, but until this is straightened out, I have no choice. I have my orders. Lauren DeVida had help stealing the amethysts and getting them out of the country. All the evidence points to Prince Brandt. He has control of the mines and is in charge of transporting the gemstones from those mines to Celestia. He must be stopped before we lose any more amethysts. The discrepancies we've uncovered point to his being responsible for some very serious…er…accounting errors."

"Accounting errors or thefts?" Brandt asked in a deadly voice.

"Thefts," the councilman squeaked.

"Erik," Angela urged. "You have to tell them the truth. Explain about Lauren and why you abdicated."

Erik nodded, squaring his shoulders. "Lauren DeVida did have help. But it was my father, Prince Frederick, who helped her. After his death, I found documents implicating him. I…I chose to abdicate because of it." His voice faltered. "It seemed the only honorable course of action. To try and make amends, I did my best to track the woman down and have her brought to justice."

"Did you find her?" Brandt asked, genuinely curious.

"Two days ago. She's in custody and being extradited to Verdonia. She's agreed to cooperate fully with the investigation. We won't recover all the money, but we'll get a large portion of it back."

Everyone started talking at once. Brandt bowed his

head, struggling to take it all in. "They supported you," Miri said in a soft voice. "They defended you. All of them."

"I…I didn't expect that." Unable to resist, he pulled her close. "You were right about them, sweetheart. They are honorable. All of them."

"Do you finally believe your name—*our* name—will be cleared now?"

He laughed, the sound a tad rusty, but still a laugh. "I believe."

"Then do I have your permission to say something now?" The demure question was contradicted by the mischievous gleam in her eyes.

He swept her an elegant bow. "Now that my name is cleared, I release you from your bargain. You're free to say anything you wish."

"In that case…" She raised her voice. "Will you marry me?"

That silenced the entire room. Brandt released his breath in an exaggerated sigh. "Considering how badly you've compromised me, I don't see that I have any choice. Yes, I'll marry you. For real, this time."

And then pandemonium broke loose again.

The sun broke across the mountains on Miri's wedding day, pouring its warmth and light across Avernos like a loving balm. The palace overflowed with guests from every corner of Verdonia, all of whom found cause to dart into Miri's room for a quick visit before the ceremony. Not that she minded. As far as she was concerned, sharing her happiness added to her enjoyment of the festivities.

Finally, it came time to dress and everyone left except her mother, and Juliana and Alyssa, who helped Miri get ready. The wedding gown she'd ultimately chosen was as different from that first ceremony as she could have wished. Dainty, elegant, romantic, it was the sort of gown she'd always hoped to wear when she married. In celebration of the discovery of the largest supply of Juliana Rose and Royal amethysts in Verdonia's history, the bodice was liberally studded with both gemstones, as was her veil. They were a statement, each glittering flash a promise to Verdonia of future harmony and prosperity.

A few hours later, standing in the vestibule of the chapel moments before the wedding was scheduled to begin, she couldn't help but compare the two ceremonies she'd experienced here. Only there was no comparison. One had been darkness and despair. This was light and joy. One had been the result of bitterness and the need for vengeance. This was a marriage of love, the bonding of heart, mind and soul.

There was no thunderous processional to escort her up the aisle this time, only the soft strains of a string quartet. Instead of walking the endless length on her own, she clung to Lander's arm. He'd honored the occasion by dressing in full military uniform, right down to white gloves and a saber strapped to his side. When they reached the altar, Lander joined her hand with Brandt's. Then he crossed to the front pew where the entire Montgomery family stood in beaming approval and joined his wife, Juliana, and her brother, financial wizard, Joc Arnaud.

Through the layers of lace and tulle, she saw Brandt

give her a slow, teasing smile. Snagging the hem of her
veil he lifted it and peeked beneath. "Just checking," he
explained to their guests.

Laughter rippled through the chapel. Where before
the ceremony had been torturous, cold and deliberate,
this time a warmth and lightness permeated. Most
poignant of all were the vows, spoken with such love
and sincerity, there was no doubting that the wedding
was a love match.

Once again they were pronounced husband and wife,
and this time Brandt not only lifted her veil, but swept
it completely off her head, releasing her hair from its
elegant coil. It streamed down her shoulders and back
and he thrust his fingers deep into the loosened strands.
"I love you," he told his wife. "You are more important
than anything else in my life."

And then he kissed her, a kiss of promise. Of honor
and duty and responsibility. There was only one thing
missing in the kiss he gave her. Sacrifice. Instead of sacrifice, they found healing. When he finally released her
there wasn't a dry eye in the chapel.

Turning, they started to make their way back down the
aisle, when Lander stepped from his pew, directly into
their path. For a long minute the two men faced each
other, two men who would be king. The tension grew,
stretching nerves to the limit. Then Lander did something
that shocked Miri to the core. In a smooth, practiced move,
he unsheathed his saber from its scabbard and offered it
to Brandt. Utter silence descended on the chapel.

Brandt hesitated. "Are you certain?" he asked in a
voice only the three of them could hear.

"It's time for a change. Verdonia needs you."

"It needs you and Merrick, as well." There was no doubting Brandt's sincerity. "I would appreciate your help."

"You'll have it."

With a nod of agreement, Brandt accepted the sword. He signaled to the musicians, who immediately resumed playing the recessional. Then he and Miri continued their trip down the aisle. Instead of waiting in the vestibule to greet their guests, he ushered her outside. Brilliant sunshine greeted them. Urging her onward, they cut through the courtyard and into the garden. Crossing to the far end, he set the saber on a bench adjacent to the woods.

Miri stared at it. "When Lander gave you his sword…did that mean what I think it did?"

"It was a gesture of fealty," Brandt confirmed. "By tomorrow the news will be all over Verdonia." He shook his head in disbelief. "He just handed me the election."

Tears filled her eyes. "I told you he was an honorable man."

"With all that's happened, Verdonia needs him more than ever. As do I. He won't regret what he's done today."

It was then that she recognized the significance of where they were standing. "Do you realize that this is where it all started?" She gestured toward the bench. "That's where I took Alyssa's place."

Brandt folded his arms across his chest. "We've come full circle."

"The perfect 'happily ever after' moment?" she asked in an odd voice.

He smiled, that slow, sweet smile of his. "Can you think of a better one?"

"Just one." She returned to his arms. "Remember our night at the cabin? The night of the fire?"

His breath escaped in a laugh. "How could I forget? It's indelibly printed on my memory for so many reasons. But mainly..." He took her mouth in a leisurely kiss, one of barely restrained passion. One that hinted of what they'd share when the day was through. "Mainly I remember because of what came after the fire."

"Something else came of that night. Something very special and unexpected." She caught his hand in hers and cupped it low on her abdomen. "There's someone here, my love. Someone who wants to say hello to you."

* * * * *

Don't miss Joc's story –
The Billionaire's Baby Negotiation –
Day Leclaire's passionate new romance coming this June from Desire™.

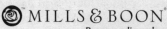

Celebrate 100 years of pure reading pleasure with Mills & Boon®

To mark our centenary, each month we're publishing a special 100th Birthday Edition. These celebratory editions are packed with extra features and include a FREE bonus story.

Plus, starting in February you'll have the chance to enter a fabulous monthly prize draw. See 100th Birthday Edition books for details.

Now that's worth celebrating!

15th February 2008

Raintree: Inferno by Linda Howard
Includes FREE bonus story Loving Evangeline
A double dose of Linda Howard's heady mix of passion and adventure

4th April 2008

The Guardian's Forbidden Mistress by Miranda Lee
Includes FREE bonus story The Magnate's Mistress
Two glamorous and sensual reads from favourite author Miranda Lee!

2nd May 2008

The Last Rake in London by Nicola Cornick
Includes FREE bonus story The Notorious Lord
Lose yourself in two tales of high society and rakish seduction!

Look for Mills & Boon 100th Birthday Editions at your favourite bookseller or visit
www.millsandboon.co.uk

0108/CENTENARY_2-IN-1

2 FREE

BOOKS AND A SURPRISE GIFT!

We would like to take this opportunity to thank you for reading this Mills & Boon® book by offering you the chance to take TWO more specially selected titles from the Desire™ series absolutely FREE! We're also making this offer to introduce you to the benefits of the Mills & Boon® Reader Service™—

- ★ **FREE home delivery**
- ★ **FREE gifts and competitions**
- ★ **FREE monthly Newsletter**
- ★ **Exclusive Reader Service offers**
- ★ **Books available before they're in the shops**

Accepting these FREE books and gift places you under no obligation to buy, you may cancel at any time, even after receiving your free shipment. Simply complete your details below and return the entire page to the address below. You don't even need a stamp!

YES! Please send me 2 free Desire volumes and a surprise gift. I understand that unless you hear from me, I will receive 3 superb new titles every month for just £4.99 each, postage and packing free. I am under no obligation to purchase any books and may cancel my subscription at any time. The free books and gift will be mine to keep in any case.

D8ZED

Ms/Mrs/Miss/Mr .... Initials ....

BLOCK CAPITALS PLEASE

Surname ....

Address ....

....

.... Postcode ....

Send this whole page to:
UK: FREEPOST CN81, Croydon, CR9 3WZ